D1528165

# THE
# STRANGE CASE OF
# MISS ANNIE SPRAGG

BY
## LOUIS BROMFIELD

AUTHOR OF
**THE GREEN BAY TREE,
EARLY AUTUMN,
POSSESSION, ETC.**

## GROSSET & DUNLAP
**PUBLISHERS        NEW YORK**

*Printed in the United States of America*

"He did not tell Mrs. Winnery that in attempting to solve one mystery, he had simply found himself face to face with another and more terrifying one which neither saints nor prophets nor scientists had ever solved in all the centuries of the world's recorded existence. It made Mr. Winnery seem to himself small and impertinent, and being a vain man, he did not care to have his wife share this discovery."

# NOTE

The author does not hold himself responsible for opinions expressed by his characters. Therefore if any reader feels moved to write an abusive letter, he is asked to address it to Father d'Astier, the Principessa d'Orobelli, Mrs. Weatherby, Mr. Winnery, Bessie Cudlip or even poor Miss Annie Spragg herself. By this time she knows more about God than any of us who are left on the earth.

# CONTENTS

|  | PAGE |
|---|---|
| THE THING FOUND IN THE CESSPOOL | 1 |
| THE MAN WHO BECAME GOD | 46 |
| TWENTY YEARS OF DEVOTION | 66 |
| A PRAIRIE IDYLL | 92 |
| A SENTIMENTAL PASSAGE | 113 |
| THE CRIME OF MEEKER'S GULCH | 132 |
| FATHER D'ASTIER'S STORY | 147 |
| STAY ME WITH FLAGONS | 165 |
| THE END OF AUNT BESSIE | 180 |
| SISTER ANNUNZIATA | 223 |
| CODA | 243 |
| THE JANITRESS' TALE | 270 |
| THE ROMANCE OF MR. WINNERY | 279 |
| MR. WINNERY'S PRIVATE MIRACLE | 301 |

# THE STRANGE CASE OF
# MISS ANNIE SPRAGG

# THE THING FOUND IN THE CESSPOOL

I

IT WAS a broiling afternoon of mid-August in Brinoë and everybody who was anybody had long ago quit its burning pavements and chilly palaces for the mountains or the sea. Left behind there were only stray bands of sweating tourists and a few such remnants of the permanent colony as Mrs. Weatherby and the mysterious companion whom no one had ever met; old Mrs. Whitehead, Mr. Binnop, the curate of the English church, the usual Marchesas and Contessas, thick as flies, and Mr. Augustus John Winnery. Except Mrs. Weatherby all these stayed in baking Brinoë for the same reason. (The old Contessa Salverini put up her shutters and lived in the back of her house, giving out word that she had gone to Montecatini for the cure, and receiving all her letters by arrangement with the *poste restante* of Montecatini.) None of them would have given you the real reason. They stayed because they could not leave their beloved Brinoë or because they were engaged in some work of an archæological or literary nature which forced them to remain. The real reason was that they were all too poor to leave.

In the case of Mr. Winnery, he could not leave

because he was engaged upon a colossal work which already had taken up the greater part of his life. It was called "Miracles and Other Natural Phenomena." In speaking of this work he always placed a profound emphasis on the word *natural* lest you should think that he was taken in by such nonsense as miracles. He was a small, bald man of fifty-two and a quarter of a century earlier he had written parodies and light verse which had appeared now and then in the *Yellow Book*. But a kind of blight had fallen early on his literary career and for years now he had been devoting his none too great energies to demolishing the idea of miracles in general and the legends clustered about the saints in particular.

His work kept him in Brinoë. It had kept him there for twenty-nine previous and consecutive summers, and it was not yet completed. (Indeed, only Mr. Winnery knew that it was still in a chaotic stage, consisting almost entirely of huge accumulations of notes and copyings from various little-known books on the saints.) Still, it served its purpose, and year after year it continued to give him a faint echo of that fleeting glory which he had known as a young literary radical. Old Mrs. Whitehead and those Anglo-Saxon Marchesas and Contessas who had not become more Catholic than the Blackest Black still spoke of Mr. Winnery's work with a kind of awe. Mr. Binnop, the curate, who prided himself on being broadminded, did not mention the work at all, but he did not, on the other hand, allow it to interfere with his friendship with Mr. Winnery.

And now in the scalding heat of the August mid-afternoon Mr. Winnery was driving in a decrepit fiacre up the long winding road that led to the heights of Monte Salvatore. He cursed the heat and himself and Mrs. Weatherby, Miss Annie Spragg, the coachman and Brinoë itself—sacred, beautiful, romantic Brinoë, surrounded by blue hills covered with clouds of blue violets and fragrant narcissus. Of course, thought Mr. Winnery bitterly, the poetic temperament always chose to write about Brinoë in May and never in August. Now if a scientist, a realist, had written of Brinoë, it would have been another story. He hated Brinoë, not because it actually lacked all the miraculous qualities attributed to it by Browning, Longfellow and the advertisements of the tourist agencies, but because he *had* to live there. Poverty and inertia had chained him to Brinoë for twenty-nine years and now at fifty-two he saw no prospect of escaping from it even in death. In the end he would be laid to rest, after a service read by Mr. Binnop (who read the service so badly) in the Protestant cemetery. It would have to be the Protestant cemetery because there was no special cemetery for agnostics. He would rest in death among all the poets, spinsters, retired colonels, widows, decayed clergymen and adulteresses who since the eighteenth century had lived and died among the exaggerated beauties of Brinoë. Probably he would be laid to rest beside old Mrs. Whitehead. Perhaps even in her grave she would rattle her false teeth over her dish of tea. Doubtless she would be buried with a collected edition of "Ouida" placed at the head of her coffin.

The fiacre moved in a cloud of yellow dust. Yellow dust covered the black cypresses and the grey olive trees and the blue-black ilex that wilted against walls turned a bilious yellow by the unrelenting sun. "Ah," thought Mr. Winnery bitterly, "the beautiful blue cloudless sky of Italy. Italy, land of laughter and sunshine. Ha! Ha!" But it was worse than that, for added to the baking sun there was a hot wind from Africa. It had been blowing steadily for two days, having sprung up on the night of Miss Annie Spragg's death. It bore on its restless bosom clouds of dust and heat from the Sahara all the way across the blue Mediterranean to the foothills of the Alps. You wakened in the morning to see the trees on the hills above Brinoë swaying in what appeared to be a cool fresh breeze and then you thrust your shutters open to find that it was a wind charged with the heat of all Inferno. And quickly you clapped the shutters tight again, feeling slightly insane.

The driver of the fiacre smelled of sweat and garlic and beat his bony horses from time to time with the butt of his whip across their already scarred and blistered rumps. "Ah," thought Mr. Winnery bitterly, "these gay, kindly, carefree Italians. Children of Nature." (So read the tourist circulars.) He fell to cursing Ruskin and Browning. "Where you rest, there decorate," wrote Mr. Ruskin. (He was not sure that he had the quotation correctly, but that was the idea.) The Italians never stopped decorating. It was their passion for decoration that had induced them to cover the seat of the fiacre with great excrescences of soiled imitation filet lace.

The seat was at least black. You would not have noticed the dirt. Or if they must decorate, why did they not wash the decorations from time to time?

Mr. Winnery was a bachelor and wore yellow gloves to keep microbes from his plump pink hands.

Fifty-two years of bachelordom had induced a certain inflexible routine into his manner of living. For at least twenty years he had lived in the same rooms, eaten the same food, risen and gone to bed at the same hours, always found his cigarettes in the same spot and his books where he had last put them down. He had sent off his querulous book reviews and his fashionable correspondence to the *Ladies' Own World* at exactly the same day by exactly the same post. On Thursdays he went to the Principessa Bologna's, on Mondays to Mrs. Whitehead's, and on Wednesdays to the Marchesa Barducci's.

Today he had shattered the routine for the first time in order to torture himself with the long drive to Mrs. Weatherby's villa. When he had gone more than half-way he told himself that he had simply gone insane with heat and boredom; but having already suffered a really colossal discomfort it did not seem worth while to turn back. In the cool of the evening the journey would be an easier one. At least it could not be more uncomfortable.

The only concrete reason he could discover for the temporary outburst of insanity was a desire to know something of Miss Annie Spragg, and Mrs. Weatherby appeared to be the only person in all

Italy, or all the world, for that matter, who knew anything of her. Mr. Winnery was out in the sun in the interests of science.

## II

For twenty-nine years he had been writing his colossal work and now for the first time a miracle had occurred, as one might have said, just beneath his nose. It was the miracle of the stigmata. In death an eccentric old maid, who lived in one room of the ruined old rookery known as the Palazzo Gonfarini, had received the marks of the Crucifixion. It was the miracle of Saint Francis of Assisi and Saint Catherine of Siena. Three persons had witnessed it, besides all the mob that broke in afterward to carry off as relics all the furniture and even the clothes of Miss Annie Spragg; these witnesses were a nun known as Sister Annunziata, a priest called Father Baldessare and the janitress of the tenement, a bawdy, irreligious, anti-clerical Socialist shrew, who called herself Signora Bardelli.

Here, Mr. Winnery told himself, was a perfect laboratory specimen of a miracle. He might investigate and pull it apart to his heart's content. It was not, Mr. Winnery told himself, a very rare miracle. It was always happening somewhere. There were more than a hundred such cases on record. Only last month there had been a sausage-maker's daughter in Bavaria. . . . And there were only two cases which had been recognized as authentic and one of these at least—that of Saint Catherine of Siena— he looked upon as dubious. No one but Saint Cath-

erine herself had witnessed the scars because she had
prayed that they be made invisible to others.  And
then, as he pointed out in his work, she had also a
great motive in the rivalry between the Franciscans,
who claimed the miracle for the founder of their
order, and the Dominicans, of which she was in
reality, if not in name, the head.  Pope Sixtus IV
had issued a decree at that time giving a monopoly
of the miracle to Saint Francis and making it a censurable offense to mention Saint Catherine's experience as authentic.  Saint Catherine, Mr. Winnery
thought, was a powerful but not a very original
woman.

But Miss Annie Spragg was neither Dominican
nor Franciscan.  Indeed, no one seemed to know
whether she was anything at all.

For at least fifteen years Miss Annie Spragg had
been one of the sights of Brinoë, like the Etruscan
excavations, and so Winnery had seen her countless
times.  But it was not until she was dead that he,
in common with the rest of the world, learned her
name.  Today it was a name printed in newspapers
all over the world. . . . In Paris, New York, Milan, Bombay, Copenhagen. . . . Tired journalists
had arrived in Brinoë from Rome and Paris and
Milan to report upon the mysterious happening.

For at least fifteen years Miss Annie Spragg had
wandered the streets regardless of heat or cold,
storm or sunshine—an eccentric old maid whom the
Italians looked upon merely as one of the phenomena of a generous Nature, and whom the foreign colony resented as something a little shameful.
She seemed never to have had but one costume.

This consisted of a bedraggled but miraculously
serviceable suit of tweed with a skirt which trailed
the ground alike in dust and mud, and a large
flowered picture hat on which the roses, from the
constant assault of the brilliant Italian sunlight, had
long since lost the glory of their original aniline
mauves and magentas. Over this hat she wore a
thick black veil and always on her hands she wore
white cotton gloves.

So little was known of her that in death there
seemed no one who was certain even of her national-
ity. One of the two Brinoë newspapers (bitter
rivals of each other) described her as "Miss Annie
Spragg, born at Newcastle-on-Tino (sic), England,"
—a quite natural mistake due to the conviction of
all Italians that anyone eccentric must be English. It
was the mysterious Mrs. Weatherby who stepped
forward and corrected that impression. In bad
Italian she tactlessly addressed a letter to the rival
paper pointing out with some nationalistic feeling
that Miss Annie Spragg was certainly not English,
but American, and that she had once been a resident
of Winnebago Falls, Iowa, a city of which Mrs.
Weatherby was herself a native. Mrs. Weatherby
wrote that she had recognized the old maid soon
after coming to Brinoë when she encountered her
one day in the Piazza San Giovanni. The letter
was signed Henrietta Weatherby (Mrs. Alonzo
Weatherby), Villa Leonardo, Monte Salvatore.

Mrs. Weatherby was herself, Mr. Winnery believed, something of an eccentric. In winter and in the
spring she was to be seen driving about the town in
a fiacre, clad all in white, with a flowing white veil.

In season she frequently carried a bouquet of tube-roses. She was a middle-aged woman of powerful build and in the circles frequented by Mr. Winnery it was said that she was a seeress and contemplated founding a new and what she chose to call an "eclectic" religion. In May it was her habit to retire to the Villa Leonardo in a lonely valley some miles beyond Monte Salvatore for the sake, it was said, "of meditation and soul growth." Old Mrs. Whitehead, who sought out every newcomer at least once, reported an encounter with Mrs. Weatherby which left her confused and baffled, owing, she said, to the spiritual cast which Mrs. Weatherby insisted upon giving to their brief conversation.

She was always accompanied by a plump and youngish woman dressed in black who appeared to be a sort of companion-secretary. No one had ever heard the name of this lady and she had had speech with no one. It was rumored that she was a deaf-mute.

III

As the fiacre reached the crest of Monte Salvatore Mr. Winnery's nerves became worn to a fine edge. He began even to think gloomily of suicide. His whole life, he told himself, had been a failure. He had attained the age of fifty-two without anything having happened to him. He had known neither love nor love's twin sister passion, and of late the thought of the experiences which he had overlooked troubled him profoundly. It was becoming a kind of neurasthenia. On its philosophic side he found the thought terrifying. It meant that he had missed the most important of human experiences.  Perhaps, he told himself, that was what the world found lacking in his work; a touch of passion might have made him popular if not distinguished. On the physical side of the question it had occurred to him lately that the attainment of such experience had not yet become an impossibility.

He was, he supposed, at that period which people called in capital letters the Dangerous Age in Men. And lately he had noticed a certain physical change in himself, as though some gland too long inactive had begun at last to perform its functions.  He who had always been a thin, fragile little man began to grow heavier and feel stronger.  Even his liver seemed to trouble him less.  He had begun to ex-perience the growth of a new force and vitality which at times shook him like a fever.  He sup-posed it was that new force which had driven him out today in the burning heat.  On the intellectual side he had begun to have a curiosity about life which was altogether new and quite disturbing.  It made him feel uneasy and restless, but although he slept less well, the lack of sleep did not appear in his new-found vigor to trouble him.  Until the age of fifty-two he had been a literary and classical writer who wrote of love only in its more refined aspects.

The carriage reached the square of Monte Salva-tore (that romantic Monte Salvatore of which he had dreamed in his Victorian youth and which now looked a bilious yellow and smelled badly).  It passed through the baking streets and began to slip down the opposite side of the hill into another pocket-like valley filled to the brim with dust and heat. Why, Mr. Winnery asked himself, should anyone exchange the heat of this valley for that of the other in the belief that it was cooler here or that the air was any better. No one but a fool like this Mrs. Weatherby. . . .

As the fiacre descended into the second valley Winnery was forced to admit to himself that it did seem cooler here. The trees appeared thicker and less jaded and the dust less overwhelming, though that may have been only because the road was rarely used. They ascended for a time and then began a descent so sharp that the fiacre pressed close against the buttocks of the bony horses, and presently on turning a corner the driver turned and in a wave of garlic exclaimed with an operatic gesture, "Behold the Villa Leonardo."

There was no villa to be seen, but only an island of dark thick trees clinging to the side of the mountain and leading up to it a long avenue of venerable oaks. As they drew near, it became evident that the narrow road ended at the villa itself and had no other reason for existence. The clump of trees was like a patch of black sewn upon the side of the grey and yellow hill. There was no other building of any sort near it. Indeed, thought Winnery, it must be impossible to see from there any human habitation. (He was a gentleman given to rather pompous language, who had known his great flowering in the day of the *mot juste*.) It did seem cooler here, though it may have been only the sense of isolation that enveloped the ancient villa.

On either side of the long straight drive leading

up to the house stood pillars of reddish stone, each
surmounted by a panther and a goat with a serpent
at their feet. The panther and the goat held between them a shield upon which no arms had ever
been cut. So damaged were the figures by time and
weather that a less antiquarian eye than Mr. Winnery's would not have known them for what they
were. Straight ahead the avenue lost itself in the
shadows of gnarled and ancient trees which hung
closely over the road.

After they had gone a little way, the villa itself
came into view—a commonplace yellowish villa set
among cypresses and olive trees with a flat façade
ornamented in the fashion of Spanish rather than
Italian baroque. It had an unkempt look with its
shutters all closed against the heat and the shrubbery all scraggly and unpruned. At the door, just
beside a large clump of sword-like yuccas, stood a
smart motor painted black with a delicate red stripe
running about the top. It was an eccentric, Latin
and expensive car, shining with too much polished
metal and too many elegant appurtenances, of the
kind known as *une voiture de grand sport*. The
sight of it tended to raise the spirits of Mr. Winnery. It meant that he would not be compelled to
encounter the formidable Mrs. Weatherby alone.

As he came nearer still, he saw that a part of the
villa on the side next to the valley had been built
upon a sort of terrace foundation of a much older
period. This, Mr. Winnery saw, was of Roman
construction. It might be that underneath it lay
an even more ancient foundation of Etruscan origin.

"Extremely interesting," he murmured, so loudly

that the driver turned as if in expectation of an order and then saw at once that his fare was thinking of other things.

The house was placed so that it commanded a superb view of the lonely valley, a view indeed which one would never have suspected from the approach. Perhaps, he thought, it had been chosen in the beginning by some Roman for its sense of space, a thing so rare in the crowded valleys about Brinoë. At the very bottom of the valley there was a yellow line tracing the course of a freshet, now completely dry in the heat of mid-August. And suddenly he felt suffocated once more and choking with dust.

The carriage stopped before the door and Mr. Winnery, after putting on his yellow gloves and endeavoring vainly to brush the thick dust from his clothing, went up the steps and pulled a copper bell-handle made in the form of a ram's head and covered by a patine of verdigris. There was an answering tinkle of a bell, but no other evidence of life. He rang again and then again with no more success, and suddenly he was aware that the driver was looking at him with an expression of malice as if he said, "You forced me to come all the way out here in the heat for nothing." It was a perfectly blank expression, but touched with insinuation. It made Mr. Winnery suddenly angry and embarrassed. It reminded him how he detested Italians as a race. He pulled violently and the bell answered again with a mocking violence. Then he turned and saying, "Wait for me here," came down the steps

and took a grass-grown path that led through a
tangle of ivy and cypress hedge toward the back
of the house.

## IV

For more than a hundred feet Winnery made his
way through a sort of tunnel of foliage, so thick
that even at this season the earth beneath his feet
seemed damp and moist, and then all at once he
came upon the most extraordinary and beautiful
garden. It was large and square in size and so
placed upon the artificially raised terrace that it
seemed to hang in space above the valley. The garden was entirely of greenery, a sort of vast chamber
of which roof and walls were made of foliage.
There was no flower of any sort. The villa itself
made one wall and the other three sides were entirely closed by the thick walls of ancient cypresses
of a size Winnery had never seen save at Tivoli.
Near the ground where the cypresses had no foliage,
light, reflected from the grey and yellow valley below, filtered in between the ancient grey trunks.
Over the whole garden there was a living roof made
by the branches of countless plane trees planted to
form colonnades and so trimmed and trained that
their yellowing leaves shut out all heat and light.
Within this area the sun never penetrated and there
was no grass but only a carpet of red clay flecked
here and there by patches of moss which in the extraordinary light had turned an unreal and poison-
ous shade of green. It was as if in the entire
parched and desolate valley, life, green and exuber-
ant, flourished only within this enclosure.

At first he had thought the garden empty, too, and silent like the house, but after a moment, when his eyes had grown accustomed to the fierce blaze of hot light from the valley below, he discovered a group of figures at the far end. There appeared to be several servants and working men, and four women, of whom one, a vision of fluttering white, was unmistakably the seeress, Mrs. Weatherby. There was also a tall gentleman dressed all in black, with silver hair. They stood gathered about a hole which appeared to be the termination of a long trench freshly cut from the direction of the villa itself. The damp red clay lay heaped about their feet. And then as he approached he discovered the object of their scrutiny—something which appeared to be the size and shape of a man and which was flecked and discolored by the clay.

"Ah," thought Mr. Winnery. "They have been digging a cesspool."

It was the smallish plump woman in black who first noticed him and spoke to Mrs. Weatherby. The seeress turned and came toward him. She did not walk; she floated in an artificial and gracious manner which made him know at once that she had practiced this walk for many years. She was a heavy woman not without a certain handsomeness due to her size and her majestic carriage. As she drew near she held out her hand and, exposing an array of flashing, healthy teeth in a practiced smile, said, "Mr. Winnery, I presume."

And Winnery, fixing his face determinedly into a smile, murmured, "It was good of you to let me come, Mrs. Weatherby."

Together they turned toward the others.

"I am afraid there was no one to answer the bell. We had all come out here, even the servants. We have just made a remarkable discovery. While digging a new cesspool, the workmen unearthed a statue. We have been unable to identify it. It seems to me a very strange statue."

In the back of his mind Winnery kept thinking, "I loathe this woman because she is *refined* and because she is so healthy and therefore so entirely out of place here." Because he had a liver, healthy people full of vitality had long been abhorrent to him, like people who whistle and sing in their morning tubs.

He was then introduced, first to a tall, handsome but rather battered woman of fifty, dressed smartly and much too youthfully in clothes which by their simplicity and cut bore the mark of the most expensive of Paris dressmakers. The woman had for him a faint air of familiarity. It was a face he had seen somewhere, the face of a woman of fifty which has been much worked over. She wore a great many bracelets and a string of real pearls.

"Principessa d'Orobelli," murmured Mrs. Weatherby, with a quiver of satisfaction. And then Mr. Winnery *knew*. She was one of those brilliant birds of passage whose photographs taken at the Lido surrounded by naked young men, whose names were of no importance, appeared from time to time in the illustrated weeklies. Although he had never seen her before, he had written many paragraphs for the *Ladies' Own World* concerning her movements hither and yon across the face of Italy. She was the smart, the almost notorious, d'Orobelli.

"And Father d'Astier," murmured Mrs. Weatherby with a pleased and gracious nod in the direction of the silver-haired gentleman. Father d'Astier bowed, a tall, handsome man with intense black eyes, a fine nose and a splendid rather sensual mouth, a figure at sixty possessed of great vigor and distinction. Winnery knew of him, too, a priest without any parish save all of God's world, who lunched and dined "everywhere." He had a simple mission in life: it was to convert the rich who married impoverished titles and to help on their way to grace any others of considerable wealth who felt a leaning toward Rome. He was a confessor to many fashionable and scandalous ladies, to great bankers and members of decayed royal families. Old stories of Father d'Astier and "the d'Orobelli" (as Winnery thought of her), heard at second-hand through years, rolled through the back of his mind. For an instant it gave him a pleasant, warm sense of moving in the great world.

"And Miss Fosdick," concluded Mrs. Weatherby with a slight and careless gesture as if she were tossing a piece of dirt over her shoulder. The gesture indicated the plump, shy little woman dressed in black who stood in the background with a touching air of timidity. This, of course, was Mrs. Weatherby's companion, the deaf-mute. Out of the corner of his eye, Winnery saw how she hovered in the background, almost tremulously, obscured by that figure all in white which seemed at once so vaporous and so solid. Miss Fosdick was like shadow. She was shy too and frightened like a bird. Mr. Winnery felt a sudden wave of pity for her.

"What an awful life!" he thought.

While they had been talking a workman appeared coming down one of the long light-flecked corridors of the garden, carrying in each hand a pail of water. In his wide belt of black elastic was thrust a scrubbing-brush. He was a young man, dark and black-eyed, who wore blue trousers stained with the red clay and a checkered shirt open to expose his dark sunburned chest. Winnery, who through years of boredom had come to amuse himself at desperate moments by watching the sly, half-concealed actions of people, saw Princess d'Orobelli's eye rove over the masculine young figure. Herodias, he thought. The workman knelt down and with the scrubbing-brush began to remove the patches of red clay from the freshly disinterred statue.

They stood about watching while the statue, slightly pitted here and there by the action of acids hidden in the sour ground of the dark garden, emerged in all the beauty of its time-worn creamy white marble. Princess d'Orobelli whispered something to Father d'Astier. One of the maidservants giggled and was silenced at once by a glance of venom from Mrs. Weatherby, who had clearly determined to regard this as a sacred moment.

Priapus himself had risen from the mouldering soil of the ancient garden.

Whatever hand carved the figure had moved with understanding and passion. The statue carried in every line a kind of quivering voluptuousness. The

very curves of the muscles and the line of the back
and hips quivered between the realms of ecstasy and
that disgust which follows quickly upon satiety. It
was a glorification of sensuality. Indeed, the
sculptor had done his work so well that for a long
time the little group about the excavation stood
awed into silence, as if something had risen from
the red clay which roused disturbing memories in
those who were experienced and disturbing intima-
tions in those who had remained until that moment
virginal. No one could have remained entirely
chaste after looking upon the statue.

There were certain portions of the statue missing,
and Mrs. Weatherby, noting this, said, "I'll set
Giovanni to work tomorrow digging for the rest."

But Father d'Astier protested quickly, perhaps in
the interests of the church or perhaps because he
thought such a piece of marble better buried forever.

"I think it's no use, Mrs. Weatherby. You
might dig up the whole garden without discovering
anything. That is usually the case."

Giovanni suddenly turned the statue full upon its
back so that the face, amazingly preserved, looked
up at them. It was the face of an old man, but a full
vigorous face partly covered by a magnificent curling beard drawn back to expose the lips, in which
there was that same sensual beauty hovering between
ecstasy and disgust. Winnery, looking down at it,
thought, "It is a beautiful thing, but a dangerous
and disturbing one. Having it about, no one would
ever have peace. Perhaps it is safe with Mrs.
Weatherby. She is possibly insensitive to everything." And then he saw suddenly that Miss Fos-

dick was watching him and that she was blushing.
There was an odd flicker of sympathy between
them.    Neither was very young and both were
without experience.    Suddenly he thought her
appealing and young (though she must have been
at least thirty-five) beside the hardness of the notorious d'Orobelli, the cold worldliness of Father
d'Astier and the florid pretense of Mrs. Weatherby.

They set the statue against the wall of the garden above a soft mattress of green ilex and then,
with Mrs. Weatherby floating before them in a
cloud of white, they turned back toward the villa.
Winnery found himself walking beside Miss Fosdick, for he already detested his hostess and was
shy and frightened in the presence of such creatures
as the d'Orobelli and Father d'Astier.   A sense of
depression still haunted them all.   Once Winnery,
feeling embarrassed by this unnatural silence, murmured to Miss Fosdick, "It is a beautiful thing—
that statue."

To which the answer came quickly with blushes
and an unexpected passion.   "No, I think it's horrible."

He knew then that the story of her being a deaf-
mute was not true.

V

They had tea in a great room painted a faded
pink and decorated with a series of frescoes depict-
ing the amorous excursions of Jupiter to the earth.
These frescoes might well have been called The
Apotheosis of Anatomy, for they were done by

some painter with an admiration for Luca Signorelli and every muscle was thrown into high relief. The whole effect was one of a plump and writhing unrest. But the proportions of the room were noble and threw the frescoes into obscurity. Unfortunately, Mrs. Weatherby had added fresh horrors. The furniture was an odd mixture of periods and styles, all of them the frankest imitations. On the chairs she had placed indiscriminately pillows of satin in the most brilliant shades of Veronese green, Tyrian purple and mustard yellow, all trimmed with black and gold lace—pillows such as are born only of the Latin imagination. She explained that it was always the general effect at which she drove rather than the detail, and that therefore the authenticity of furniture was of very little importance to her. "The effect," she murmured, "on entering a room . . . the effect." She allowed the sentence to finish itself in a vague, fluttering gesture, also (thought Mr. Winnery) the result of much practice. A grey parrot squawked on a perch in one corner and two tiny Pomeranians ran out screeching and yapping as the party entered.

But when the shutters were thrown open the room became magnificent, for one discovered that the whole valley lay spread out beneath the windows. The same golden light that filtered through into the deep garden poured in through the great arched openings that made one side of the room. The sun had begun to slip down below the crests of the mountain at the head of the valley and all the African dust suspended in the hot air had caught and reflected its rays in a blaze of extravagant color.

In the bottom of the valley the lights were blue and purple and at the top these turned to green and yellow and a curious shade of red gold. It was exaggerated and, to Mr. Winnery's English eyes, a little overdone, like everything in Italy.

"What a marvelous place," murmured the Princess in a deep, throaty voice. "Why have I never seen it or heard of it?"

At that moment a servant brought tea, bad tea, of the kind bought in Italy in ancient tins, and biscuits, also out of tins, that were dry and hard.

"I have never placed much importance upon food," observed Mrs. Weatherby as she seated herself in an imitation Renaissance chair inlaid with mother-of-pearl. "I have lived for seventeen years on the spirit, ever since I lost Mr. Weatherby and discovered the consolations of religion." She turned suddenly and addressed her companion. "Will you pour, Gertrude?" And again to the Princess d'Orobelli, "Yes, it is a place rich in tradition and history, rich indeed." Again her words trailed off into space as if she found them poor, shabby things to express all the beauty of which she alone was conscious.

Winnery began to suspect that this transparent woman fancied herself as an enigma, a kind of Sibyl. Watching her, he began to suspect, too, that she was a very rich and a very mean woman, and that she sought to gloss over her meannesses by any motive at hand. She would have dragged in God Himself if necessary. He saw also that Father d'Astier and the Princess were profoundly bored and that upon both their faces had appeared that mechanical smile which is a strange mixture of condescension, absent-mindedness and a desire to be polite—a smile which is one of the marks of persons frequenting smart society. Thirty years of this practice had fixed hard lines on the face of the Princess. He asked himself suddenly why that strange pair had stayed to tea when they might easily have sped back to Brinoë in the black and red motor. Indeed, he could not see why they were there at all.

Mrs. Weatherby, who had now struck an attitude in the awkward Renaissance chair, continued her discussion of the history of the place. It went back, she said, to Roman times at least. The very statue they had just discovered proved as much. Then certainly it had once been occupied by Leonardo da Vinci, who, it was said, had used the cowshed for his famous experiments in flying, and after that it had been the property of the Spanish Ambassador at Brinoë, who used it as a summer residence and added the baroque façade with its agitated statues. Mrs. Weatherby ornamented the account with many minute and boring details, most of them completely inaccurate, since Mrs. Weatherby possessed but the sketchiest ideas of Italian history. Each inaccuracy caused Winnery to wince and struggle with a desire to set her right, for he was one who cared profoundly for detail. He would have spoken, but that instinct told him his effort was certain to make no impression and would only delay the story of Miss Annie Spragg. A woman accustomed to making over religions would not be awed by history. Besides, as in the case of the furniture, it was the effect she sought rather than the accuracy of detail.

During all this time Miss Fosdick sat quietly, her little pink hands resting in her lap, but it was clear that her thoughts had wandered far from the impressive account which she must already have heard a thousand times. She kept looking out into the magnificent valley, that valley which as night came nearer and nearer, began to approach in a miraculous fashion that ideal which Winnery had once had of the beauties of Italy. Here through these windows one beheld no beggars and no Fascisti, one was aware of no smells and no dirt, but only the magnificence of Nature itself undefiled by the touch of man. Winnery for a moment felt that its beauty compensated a little for the boredom of being compelled to live in Brinoë.

But presently he found himself more fascinated by Miss Fosdick than by the beauty of the view. He no longer heard Mrs. Weatherby. Her sonorous voice had become simply a dim annoyance, like the buzzing of a fly. Her rapturous bosom no longer heaved and fell within the line of his vision. He was touched by the look of hunger in the eyes of her poor companion. It was a look which showed itself in the eyes alone, for the rest of the face wore a fixed and practiced expression of sweetness and contentment as befitted the handmaiden of a great religious teacher. She even managed to look as if she were interested. Once more she seemed to him touchingly young and innocent, like a bird . . . (he groped for a moment for the proper literary image) . . . like a bird that is being tormented. She was aware, he thought, of a beauty which lay beyond the valley, a beauty, too, which had nothing to do with

the caltimine of the religions through which Mrs.
Weatherby must have dragged her by the hair of
her head.  And then suddenly he experienced excitement at the sight of her soft full throat and the
rather matronly curve of the bosom beneath the
shining black poplin.  He began to see her for the
first time—her fine hair and melancholy eyes, her
high color and all her Rubens curves.  The experience startled him for a second, as something new
in all his experience.  He could trace it vaguely
only to the strange obscene influence of the statue.
But it pleased and flattered him that the emotion
should have occurred at all.

Mrs. Weatherby had by now become launched
upon her period of religious experiment among the
numerous sects of Southern California, but the
Princess d'Orobelli arose and, taking the matter
firmly in hand, cut her short and at the same time
revealed the reason for her coming to the Villa
Leonardo.  She said, "Do tell us, Mrs. Weatherby,
what you know of this Spragg woman?  I am dining
with friends and must leave soon.  I should like to
know the story.  It will help make the dinner a success.  No one is talking of anything else but Miss
Annie Spragg."

So that was the reason why the Princess and
Father d'Astier had made the hot, dusty journey!
They had come to the apparent fount of all knowl-
edge upon the subject of Miss Annie Spragg.

Mrs. Weatherby, upset for a moment at being
interrupted in the process of making herself enig-
matic, recovered quickly and said, "Of course, I
never really *knew* her any more than I *knew* her

here in Brinoë. We lived in the same community
but, as you might say, in different worlds. Gertrude
knew her better than I. Isn't that true, Gertrude?"
She turned to wrest the attention of her companion
away from the unsafe extravagant beauty of the
valley and back into the room. From the irritation
in her voice it was clear that she had known all
along, despite even Miss Fosdick's perfected expression of deep interest, that her companion's thoughts
were wandering. It was clear also, thought Winnery, that later, when the guests were gone, Miss
Fosdick would pay for her inattention. She would
pay dearly.

"Yes, Aunt Henrietta?" replied Miss Fosdick
mildly.

*Aunt* Henrietta, thought Winnery. Then she
must be the niece of Mrs. Weatherby.

But Mrs. Weatherby displayed no intention of
allowing Miss Fosdick, however well she knew the
story, to tell it. She rolled into it in sonorous but
refined periods, embroidered by a great deal of explanation as to setting and background.

VI

Fifteen years earlier Mrs. Weatherby had been
the richest and the most important woman in
Winnebago Falls, since her husband, the late Mr.
Alonzo Weatherby, had been president of the
Farmers' Bank and also held a monopoly on the
new water works. Since then, Mrs. Weatherby indicated modestly, she had become vastly, incalculably
richer due to the fact that Mr. Weatherby before

dying had invested money in certain tracts of waste
land in Oklahoma which now poured forth gold in
the form of oil. He had been, one gathered from
her accounts, a shrewd but ineffectual little man
whom she had browbeaten into the status of a con-
sort. Winnery saw him perfectly—the husband of
Mrs. Weatherby, Mr. Henrietta Weatherby. He
had observed a great many Mr. and Mrs.
Weatherbys among the American tourists who
visited Brinoë. She spoke of him with condescension and even with a little contempt, as vaguely useless and perfectly insignificant.

"I think I can say honestly," she added, "that he
was always spiritually my inferior."

The town of Winnebago Falls, which she also described with a great amount of detail, rose up in a
kind of crude reality as a town old as towns went
in Iowa, of big houses built in the florid style of the
eighties and set back from streets lined with rows
of cottonwoods and elms—a town which was the
center of an agricultural community and so rather
sleepy and quiet and the last place in which to expect such stories as she had to tell of Miss Annie
Spragg.

"Winnebago Falls," she said proudly, "was not
one of those German settlements in Iowa. It was
founded by New Englanders. One of them was my
grandfather."

She made it clear that she was important, not
alone by wealth, but also by blood, and even more
than that by the faith into which she had been born.
"Miss Fosdick and myself were both Congregationalists, and in such a place the best people were

always Congregationalists. That is one of the
reasons why I never *really* knew Miss Annie
Spragg. She was a Primitive Methodist and kept
house for her brother, who was much older than
herself and a Primitive Methodist preacher. But
the Primitive Methodists were an insignificant lot
and mostly poor whites from the Kentucky mountains."

At this point Father d'Astier, speaking English
with all the elegance of one who knows a foreign
tongue perfectly, interrupted to ask exactly what
was a poor white. He listened with great interest
while she explained and when it was made clear she
said, "Of course, Miss Fosdick knew Miss Spragg
better than myself. There were reasons for that."

She made clear the reasons. Miss Fosdick's
mother had been a girl friend of Mrs. Weatherby.
They had gone to school together and been married
on the same day, but from that moment their courses
had diverged, for Mrs. Weatherby's husband had
gone up in the world and Mrs. Fosdick's had slipped
steadily down into poverty. With poverty social obscurity came to her old school friend and Mrs. Fosdick's daughter, who now sat plump and on the verge
of middle age in the Villa Leonardo, had been forced
to do the best she could. Thus she had come into
contact with individuals in Winnebago Falls whom
Mrs. Weatherby knew only distantly if at all.
Among these individuals was Miss Spragg.

"But I never forgot that Emma Fosdick had always been my friend," continued Mrs. Weatherby,
"and I did all I could for her daughter Gertrude."

She indicated her companion with the gesture of

one showing his good works to the Lord. The wretched Miss Fosdick turned quickly and gave an appreciative smile in the direction of her benefactor and then fell once more to staring out of the window into the purpling valley, looking confused and tortured and miserable.

To Winnery, watching her, the thought occurred again that she was like a plump pigeon used by the preposterous woman in white as an object upon which to practice some obscure and sadistic torment.

Mrs. Weatherby shifted her position a little, causing the imitation chair to creak beneath her weight. At the same moment the parrot burst with a terrifying suddenness into a series of shrill screams and squawks.

"He wants to go to bed," said Mrs. Weatherby, turning to Miss Fosdick. "Will you take him away, *dear*? He should have gone long ago."

Miss Fosdick rose with an awkward self-conscious gesture of brushing imaginary crumbs from her lap, and murmuring, "Yes, Aunt Henrietta," took the unpleasant bird from its perch and carried it, still screeching horribly, off into the shadows of the great echoing hall where the darkness appeared to quiet its nerves.

As she went out the door, Mrs. Weatherby murmured, "She is a good girl and a great comfort to me. She has lived with me now ever since she was eighteen, when Mr. Weatherby died and I went to California. She has never cared to marry. Indeed, I think she has never found a man worthy of her."

With the disappearance of Miss Fosdick, Mr.

Winnery felt a little pang of disappointment like
the first faint warnings of an approaching indiges-
tion. She seemed to him the only healthy, simple
creature in the room.

"But to get on with Miss Spragg," said Mrs.
Weatherby. "She always lived a very quiet life
and seldom went out except in the evenings. She
was always a little queer, but she grew queerer and
queerer as she grew middle-aged."

Miss Spragg had occupied, it seemed, with her
brother the clergyman, a small wooden house of
some six rooms set back from the street in a tangle
of lilacs, maple trees and vines in the poorest part
of town. Soon after she came there, either she or
her brother had a high wooden fence built to enclose
the back yard. What went on inside the fence no
one knew very clearly, but it became known grad-
ually that it concealed a weird collection of animals.
The old maid, people said, was very fond of them.
There were guinea-pigs, rabbits, cats, a pair of decrepit dogs, and at one period, Mrs. Weatherby
heard, even a skunk. The thick trees about the
house were alive with birds and they came from all
over the town to be fed within the enclosure.

"That," interrupted Father d'Astier, "would perhaps explain her having chosen Saint Francis of
Assisi for special adoration in her old age."

"It was Saint John the Shepherd," put in Mr.
Winnery; and then with a burst of Non-Conformist
emotion, "who in the Roman church is merely a sur-
vival of the pagan Dionysus."

Mrs. Weatherby ignored the comment, perhaps
because she had no idea of Saint Francis, of Saint

John the Shepherd, or Dionysus, and sweeping on, said, "I used to see her sometimes, but I never cared for her. She had a proud way of walking, like a cat, and she gave herself airs, as if she was better than other people. In the end that was what made other people hate her. The congregation of her brother's church took a great dislike to her because she would never join in church work and never went to call on any of them. I don't suppose there was anybody in the town who in all the years she lived in Winnebago Falls had a dozen words with her. Nobody ever knew anything about her. They just took her for granted after a time. It was the black goat that first began to make trouble."

From somewhere, perhaps from some Irish family living near the railroad in Winnebago Falls, the old maid acquired a black he-goat to add to her pets. There was no reason, said Mrs. Weatherby, why a goat should seem a pet more strange than a dog except that the human race has always had a curious feeling about goats, and in Winnebago Falls this feeling turned to comment and indignation at the sight of an old maid walking through the streets with a goat by her side. For she developed the habit of taking the goat at dusk each evening to the outskirts of the town to feed on the thick sweet clover that grew by the county road.

"It was a queer thing to do," observed Mrs. Weatherby. "And in small towns, of course, everything gets to be known and people aren't as tolerant as, well . . . we are in a place like Brinoë."

This remark she accompanied by a sweeping gesture in the direction of the distant city, as if she

would gather it up and enclose it within her over-
plump arms. It was *her* city, Brinoë—Winnery
suddenly had the feeling that she would make her
own anything which she thought might be of use to
her. She spoke as if her grandfather, instead of
being a Congregationalist, had been at least a Gon-
zaga or a Sforza.

"But the worst trouble," she said, "came about
when a man called Hasselman, who delivered milk
in Winnebago Falls, told the story that he saw her
coming home one morning just after daylight across
the fields from a place called Meeker's Gulch."
She paused for a moment and then added, "And the
goat was with her."

The last sentence she uttered slowly and with a
great ponderousness and then waited a moment.
The Princess, whose thoughts had clearly been wandering, was sitting upright now. She had stopped
glancing at her watch and was listening, and into
the eyes of Father d'Astier there had come a queer
look of pain.

"Nobody ever proved the story," said Mrs.
Weatherby, "and Hasselman was known to drink,
so a great many people thought he had been seeing
things. But the people in the town began to get
uneasy about Miss Annie Spragg and say that she
ought to be shut up. A committee from the church
was going to see her brother about having her sent
away the very day he was murdered."

Somewhere in one of the other rooms the parrot
began again to screech and Mrs. Weatherby, annoyed, suddenly rose and, floating across the room,
called out, "Gertrude, Gertrude, what are you do-

ing to Anubis?" There was an echo of cold savagery in her voice, as if the parrot were the only thing in the world she loved besides herself.

Miss Fosdick appeared again and in a tremulous voice murmured, "He doesn't seem to like being shut up now. That's why he's screeching."

"Well, take the curtain off his cage and then fetch a light."

It had grown quite dark and the only light in the room was the faint reflected glow of the dying sunset. Mrs. Weatherby seemed a little, thought Mr. Winnery, like a figure out of a nightmare which might suddenly turn out to be real. It was not true, he told himself. There wasn't any such person as Mrs. Weatherby.

The Princess was murmuring, "But the murder, my dear Mrs. Weatherby. . . . You left us in midair."

"It has never been explained," said Mrs. Weatherby. "He was found beaten to death in broad daylight by the side of the road on the edge of the town. It seems he used to compose his sermons while taking long walks and it happened to him then. They never found out who did it. People said that she must have had something to do with it and that she ought to have been shut up long before. I think they arrested her, but they couldn't prove that she was even out of the house that day. I never knew much about it. It happened a little while after I moved to California to begin my experimental work."

And then suddenly, as if the story had come to an end before she meant it to, she said weakly,

"And that's all there is. After the murder she left the town and nobody knew where she went until I saw her in the Piazza San Giovanni two years ago. I couldn't believe my eyes at first, and then I seized Miss Fosdick and said, 'That's that Spragg woman, isn't it, Gertrude?' and Miss Fosdick looked too, and said, 'Yes!' We didn't speak to her, because she seemed so queer and we didn't want to attract attention." She turned suddenly to Father d'Astier. "I suppose that was not humble of me or Christian or Catholic, but I hadn't then received the light."

There was something about this remark and its entire unexpectedness which made Winnery start and ask himself, "What is she up to now? What game is she playing with Father d'Astier?"

"I remember it was two years ago because it was at the Easter procession and it rained on Easter and she was kneeling in the rain and was wearing a big picture hat covered with faded flowers. And the colors were running in the rain."

### VII

At that moment Miss Fosdick appeared, carrying a huge wrought-iron candlestick almost as tall and almost as heavy as herself. In it, burning, there was one of those fat round candles which are to be seen everywhere in the churches in Italy. In place of a flame there was an electric bulb. She came in quietly, put down the candlestick and retired silently into the shadows.

The d'Orobelli rose abruptly and said, "What a very interesting story! But I am late. I must go."

She made it clear none the less by some skilful intonation of her voice or expression in her eyes that she had really found it a boring tale badly told and not worth the trip to the Villa Leonardo.

Mrs. Weatherby became a miracle of graciousness and, bidding them all good-by, murmured, "I must have a word with Father d'Astier."

Winnery would have gone into the hall with the Princess, but he remembered that Miss Fosdick, forgotten and ungraceful, was lingering in the shadows. He turned to speak to her and found that she was coming toward him in order to light them out. At the same moment he heard Mrs. Weatherby murmuring something to the priest. He was able to catch only two words—"prayer and meditation"— and began to think that he had gone mad.

"You will have to go out by the garden," Mrs. Weatherby was saying. "Margharita has stupidly lost the key to the main door and no locksmith will come from Brinoë until the end of the week."

They moved down the hallway between dark rooms, from one of which came the muffled indignant squawking of the parrot Anubis, King of Darkness. Winnery had taken the candlestick from the frightened Miss Fosdick and was heading the little procession. In the garden the light still filtered in between the black trunks of the gigantic cypresses, but it was a different light now, feeble and blue and diffused, the light from a hot waning moon that had risen above the mountains on the opposite side of the valley. Far away, at the end of one of the tunnels made by the plantain trees, the statue, scrubbed white now by the strong brown hands of Giovanni,

gleamed against the black ilex hedge. Mr. Winnery saw it again suddenly in his imagination. He
saw with a remarkable clearness all its beauty and
sensuality. It occurred to him that at some time in
the remote past there must have been other people
living here in this same ancient spot, living here and
perhaps worshipping the ancient figure of Priapus
—troops of harlots and courtesans and voluptuaries.
And their successors had been Mrs. Weatherby and
Miss Fosdick, bringing with them so much that was
the essence of a country that lay beyond Atlantis,
unknown and unimagined in the days when this Priapus was carved.

In order to reach the front of the villa it was
necessary to pass again through the tangled green
tunnel which was too low to allow the passage of
the great candlestick. Miss Fosdick solved the
problem by removing the candle itself and leading
the way. In order not to fall in the darkness they
took hands in chain fashion, first Miss Fosdick and
then Winnery, then the Princess and last of all
Father d'Astier. Miss Fosdick's hand was plump
and soft and placid, but the hand of the Princess
was thin and hard and feverish. Winnery thought
it was trembling violently.

And then as they approached the other side there
arose in the thick bushes very near at hand the faint
sound of a scuffle and a torrent of words uttered in
a soft masculine Italian and then the laugh, hot and
voluptuous and almost hysterical, of a woman. For
a second Mr. Winnery had the wild thought that he
had overheard the ghosts of that ancient garden,
and then the Princess, emerging from the hedge,

called out sharply, "Enrico! Enrico!" There was
a silence and she repeated the call and out of the
bushes came a chauffeur, dark and smartly dressed.
She loosed on him a torrent of nervous, impatient
abuse. She was in great haste, she said. She was
already late. Why had he kept her waiting while
he amused himself pinching servant girls?

It was the vulgar performance of a well-bred
woman whose nerves were frayed.

Then Father d'Astier proposed that they take
Mr. Winnery in the motor. Turning, he said, "If
you go back in the fiacre you'll have no dinner until
nearly midnight."

The driver of the fiacre grumbled at being deserted after darkness on a road so lonely, but Winnery, in an unbalanced moment of extravagance,
paid him for the whole journey and a little over and
he retired, still mumbling his indignation.

It was the Princess herself who drove. She had
Father d'Astier by her side and Mr. Winnery was
placed in the back with the sulking Enrico. They
bade Miss Fosdick good-night and the car suddenly
sprang forward with a wild roar, violating the silence of the remote valley. The sound echoed and
re-echoed through the hills, shattering the strange
mood that had settled on Winnery. He was alive,
after all. It was the twentieth century. This was a
*voiture de grand sport* in which he had clearly found
a perilous seat.

It shot through the green tunnel at a terrifying
speed, so that the leaves whisked by with a hissihg
sound. Looking back he saw the black figure of
Miss Fosdick, still bearing the electric candle, dis-

appear into the copse of myrtle and ivy and laburnum. At the end of the drive, when they had passed between the panthers and the fauns, he turned again and there on the terrace beyond the room where they had been sitting a little while before stood Mrs. Weatherby. In the thin moonlight she would have been invisible save for the whiteness of her gown. He thought she stood with her arms held outstretched toward the sky, but he could not make certain. The car suddenly shot ahead with a wild roar. The Princess drove as if she were a mad woman.

## VIII

The ride back to Brinoë was much quicker, but no less free from discomfort, than the ride out in the fiacre. It was only a different sort of discomfort. Winnery, who never rode in motors because he could not afford it, felt that he was being shot through Italy in a cannon-ball. There was no dust this time, for the dust was left far behind, and even the dust which remained on his clothes was blown away by the very speed at which the big car hurtled along the narrow roads. In Monte Salvatore and beyond, the Princess set the strident German horn to shrieking at each wall and turning. It was as if all the violence of a wild, undisciplined nature had been loosed. The big Grebel lights ate through dust and darkness alike and presently Brinoë lay below them huddled in the tight little valley and glowing faintly in the moonlight, covered by a thick canopy of heat and dust. The wind from Africa still blew.

Once inside the city the Princess was forced to

drive more slowly as the car, making rumbling
noises of impatience, turned and twisted through
the crooked streets. In the poor quarter they were
compelled suddenly to draw up altogether and stop
for a moment. In front of them, before the door
of an ancient palace, stood a crowd that filled the
street from side to side. It was the ancient Palazzo
Gonfarini where Miss Annie Spragg had died two
days before. The throng made way sullenly for
the big motor and as it passed the door of the palace
Winnery discerned in the dim light from a battered
jet of gas three figures—a stout Italian woman leaning on a broom made of twigs, a gigantic nun, and
a fat short little priest. These were no doubt the
janitress and Father Baldessare and Sister Annunziata, the witnesses of the miracle. Against the
grey wall just beneath the gaslight knelt the black
figures of two peasant women, praying.

Winnery shouted suddenly to the Princess, "I
will get down here. . . ." The car stopped abruptly
before the pastry-cake façade of St. Stefano and he
descended. Thanking them, he bade them good-
night. The car suddenly shot ahead, leaving him
on the sidewalk alone, knowing that he would never
see them again. They did not belong to his world.
They were not interested in him. They were gone
about their business and he felt a sudden wild pang
of literary curiosity. Where was the d'Orobelli
bound in such haste? What would they be doing
that night? Why was her hand so feverish? Why
did it tremble so violently? Where had they come
from? What tragedies, what delights, had touched
their lives? Why had they gone to the Villa

Leonardo? They were growing old, too, like himself, and the d'Orobelli was frightened.

Suddenly, as if awakening, he turned toward the old palace where he occupied two shabby rooms. Something odd had happened to him and he was aware of it all at once with a sudden quickening of the heart. He had gone up the hill feeling a bitter and disappointed man, old at fifty and lost forever, and now he felt suddenly no age at all. It was as if age did not exist. Even the boredom had vanished—that awful boredom in which nothing interested him, in which everything lost its value and slithered to a common level of monotony. There were two things he wanted passionately. One was to escape somehow from Brinoë and the other to live a little before he died. It was becoming an obsession with him. It seemed that until now he had existed in a kind of literary spell completely detached from reality, and now when he had begun to be old he was aware of life.

He felt a disturbing desire to wander off alone in search of adventure, moving in the constant romantic expectancy that something might happen to him. He had no idea what it was he expected nor what he would do with it when it arrived, but it seemed to him that he could not go back to his flat to unlock the door and find the same chairs, the same books, even the same food that he had known day after day in years of endless monotony. He halted and turned abruptly, setting out for the Piazza Garibaldi, where there were lights and music and gaiety.

He had a poor dinner and some vinegary wine,

neither of which seemed to matter greatly. He listened to the sugary Italian music played abominably by a band seated under the arcade. "The Italians," he thought bitterly, "are a musical people." He listened to fragments of talk and fanned himself because of the heat. Yet he enjoyed himself as he had not done in years. He felt life stirring about him. He fell again to speculating upon the mystery of such lives as Father d'Astier's and the d'Orobelli's, which seemed so obvious and were in reality so mysterious. He thought of that preposterous woman Mrs. Weatherby and found himself wondering what it would be like to love and be loved, to have a home and wife and perhaps children. He could not see why these things had never occurred to him before and he thought himself a little mad. Perhaps it was the heat and the hot wind, and perhaps it was the queer change which had come over him lately. Indeed, he even blushed a little in the darkness. He thought a great deal about Miss Fosdick.

At last when he had finished dinner he went for a walk in the moonlight along the river. The wind had died down and it occurred to him suddenly that in the moonlight Brinoë seemed as romantic as people supposed it to be. In the moonlight even the terrible equestrian statue of Victor Emmanuel seemed romantic.

As he walked, his own past began to concern him more and more as a sterile thing which had meant nothing to the world and very little to himself, a past filled with promise that had always seemed foredoomed to disappointment. At twenty-four he had been a brilliant and promising fellow. His parodies and his verse had appeared in the *Yellow Book* alongside the work of other men whose promise had been fulfilled. People had taken him up and asked him about—him, the son of humble parents, educated at Oxford by his uncle who made a fortune as a ship chandler. Critics wrote of him that "he struck a new note," et cetera, et cetera. He had been one of the literary radicals of his day. And then suddenly something had happened and people grew tired of him. No one wrote of him any longer. The fashions changed and his sort of thing was no longer wanted. The *Yellow Book* died. And now all the parodies and verse lay encased, forgotten and dusty, in copies of a periodical filed away in dusty museums. It was a curiosity. It all dated now. Nobody wanted that kind of thing. It dated. It was older than the writing of the Venerable Bede.

In all the symphony of literature he had been able only to harp on one string and long ago that string had grown flat and monotonous from too much use.

Now for fifteen years he had been writing items about the English who lived in Italy and about those fashionable and gaudy creatures like the d'Orobelli and Father d'Astier who passed through Florence on their way from Rome to Paris or Rome to Venice. He knew them not. He only wrote what filtered down from their world into the duller circles which he frequented. Sometimes he wrote querulous book reviews, mostly of travel books written about Italy, and these, too, appeared in the

*Ladies' Own World* between advertisements for
scents and flesh reducers. It was all sordid and unworthy, but it helped to eke out the income given
him by Uncle Horace. Well, sometime he would
finish his book on Miracles. . . . Some day if he
had any money and could escape from the boredom
of Brinoë.

And then again when he had been on the verge of
inheriting all that money from Uncle Horace the
old man chose in his dotage to marry a strumpet, a
cheap Cockney woman young enough to be his
granddaughter. Aunt Bessie! He thought of her
with disgust as he had seen her in the Temperance
Hotel in Bloomsbury on the day he went to buy her
off with promises of money after Uncle Horace
was dead. A yellow-haired slattern, fat and vulgar,
with a Cockney accent. But then Uncle Horace
had always been a common, vulgar old man. . . .
To leave all that income to her with the provision
that when she died it was to go on to him, her
nephew! And that woman—his Aunt Bessie—was
ten years younger than himself and had the consti-
tution of an ox! No, he had been haunted by bad
luck. Nothing ever came out right. And now he
was nearly fifty-three. His life meant nothing to
himself or to anyone else. He had been a failure
and it was too late now to accomplish anything.
Nothing that mattered had ever happened to him.

IX

At eleven o'clock when he turned again toward
his own flat he went by way of the Palazzo Gon-

farini, through crooked narrow streets, filled with rubbish and smells, where shadows seemed thicker than shadows should have been. The crowd before the battered doors of the old palace had thinned a little, but there were still people there, gossiping and looking up toward the window just beneath the eaves, and near the doorway there were three devout women kneeling in the dust beneath the room of the mysterious old maid who would be buried tomorrow.

All the way from the Gonfarini Palace to his own flat Mr. Winnery turned over in his mind the power of superstition, against which all the logic and the intelligence in the world appeared to make no progress. There were things which science could not yet explain, but some day it would explain all and then in a moment of triumph superstition, religions, churches, all would be swept away and man liberated to command his own destiny untrammeled by dark heritages of the past. Some day he would finish his book. For the moment he had at hand splendid material, a laboratory, as it were, a perfect specimen in the case of Miss Annie Spragg. He would go deeper and deeper into her story. Mrs. Weatherby had not told everything. Clearly she knew things she had chosen for some reason not to tell.

His own flat was dark and after he had turned on the light and turned down his bed, he discovered that the charwoman had thrust a telegram under the door. It might, he thought, have come from the editor of the *Ladies' Own World* asking for information of some special importance.  He had had such telegrams before.  He picked it up and opened it.

YOUR AUNT BESSIE DIED TODAY.
JOHN WILLIS

Who was John Willis?  For a moment he stood quite still with the telegram in his hand, uncomprehending.  Then for a second he felt suddenly ill. And slowly it began to make sense to him.

Aunt Bessie was dead and he was a rich man. His whole life was changed.  He need no longer live in Brinoë because he had no money.  He need no longer write grudging book reviews and bits of gossip about people he did not know.  Aunt Bessie was dead.  Aunt Bessie, who was younger than himself and whom he had never expected to die.  She could not have been more than forty-two and she had stood between him and his uncle's wealth for nearly twenty years.  Aunt Bessie with her Cockney accent and low manners who had kidnapped into marriage a rich old man three times her age.  All that money was his.  It was an act of God.

When he had recovered his senses a little, he sat down at the table and stuck the telegram in the letter-rack.  He was a careful man and he knew that when he wakened in the morning he would need to see it there in order to believe that he had not been dreaming.

Then his eye fell upon the pile of paper on which was written his weekly correspondence for the *Ladies' Own World*.  An hour later he would have

taken his pen and added, "Among those who paid
Brinoë fleeting visits during the month were Father
d'Astier, the well-known dignitary, and Princess
Faustino d'Orobelli.  She wore, etc., etc., etc."  At
this season, when there was no one in Brinoë every
item was precious.  Now he simply took up the papers and, tearing them twice across, threw them into
the waste-paper basket.  Then, feeling the need of
air, he pushed open the windows and as he stood
there looking down at the river, he found himself
thinking of Miss Fosdick.

"She is of a suitable age," he thought.  "Neither
too young nor too old.  She is not a widow, so she
will have had no experience.  She is innocent, more
innocent than myself.  I must find out more about
her."

As he turned away from the window it occurred
to him that all the evening he had been aware of
some vague thing disturbing himself and all the life
about him.  Perhaps it was only because the wind
from Africa had died down at last.

He was intensely lonely.


## THE MAN WHO BECAME GOD

### I

ONE crisp autumn morning in the year 1840 a
little after dawn there appeared out of the
mists covering the Illinois prairies a great covered
wagon drawn by four oxen and guided by a man of
great physical power and beauty who wore his hair
cropped at the line of his shoulders and a black curl-

ing vigorous beard that covered his whole breast.
In the wagon rode his wife and the four children
which she had borne him in five years.  Guiding the
oxen with a long pole, he walked beside the cart
much as Abraham in the glory of his strength
walked beside his flocks, erect and beautiful and
full of dignity.  In his eyes there was a burning
light and on his arm he carried a great Bible fastened and locked with brass clasps.

Beneath the ox-cart swung a crate filled with
shivering fowls and behind it walked a cow, a black
he-goat and two milking she-goats.  He had come
from the Mormon settlement where a little while
before he had been publicly cast out for immoral
practices.  Behind him in the colony he left two
wives and three other children.  The wife who slept
in the covered wagon with the nursing child in her
arms was his first wife, a woman called Maria
Trent, two years older than himself and the daughter of a fur trader of St. Louis.  The youngest child
was a male child who had already been baptized by
his father in the waters of the Mississippi with the
name of Uriah.

On the outskirts of a shabby village the wanderer
halted his wagon, unyoked the oxen and set about
building a fire, and in a little while a dozen early
morning risers wandering out from the village gathered about to stare at him.  Of these he took no
notice either by word or glance, but went on filling
an iron pot with water and oatmeal.  This he hung
over the fire.  Then he turned toward the wagon
and called out "Maria!" and a pale, sickly woman
with reddish hair opened the canvas and climbed

down carrying a baby in her arms. In turn the
stranger lifted down three small children, two boys
and a girl. When they had seated themselves on a
log beside the fire, the man turned his face toward
the sky and raising his mighty arms began to pray
in a voice of singular beauty.

For a moment the little crowd gathered about
the wagon became uneasy, as if looking upon something not meant for its eyes. One of the men
grinned with a self-consciousness rare in that crude
frontier world. And then slowly the voice and presence of the stranger began to work its effect upon
them. They were simple people and the words of
the stranger's prayer were commonplace and filled
with noble expressions of a grandeur long since worn
threadbare by the mouthings of countless bad and
insincere preachers. But the same worn phrases in
the voice of this preacher became different.

"O Lord of Hosts," he prayed in the beautiful
voice, "guide Thy poor children in their wanderings
through the wilderness. Look upon Thy poor
servant and humble him. Take him as Thy rod and
Thy staff to spread Thy truth like a morning sun
piercing the darkness. . . ."

He prayed for a long time and one by one the
three village women knelt on the frozen clay. One
of them threw off her shawl and flinging herself
down cried out, "Forgive us our sins, O Lord.
Hallelujah. Forgive us our sins." One of the men
began to pray and the others stood about in silence,
staring resentfully at the ground. The wife of Cyrus Spragg began to rock to and fro on the log.

silencing the baby Uriah, who had begun to cry with cold and hunger.

When the stranger had finished, he opened his eyes and looked round him with the empty stare of one who had come back from a great distance. Then the burning eyes rested in turn upon each of the kneeling women, and he murmured, "Arise, my children, and go your ways, telling publicans and sinners ye have found him on whom the Spirit of the Lord is descended. Blessed be he who fills the belly of the Prophet of God."

They went away in silence and in a little while the three women returned bringing with them two boys who carried bags of beans and potatoes, late melons and bread and a quarter of fresh mutton. These they laid beside the fire and then one of the women, a plump and handsome young thing, pulled her shawl more closely over her yellow hair and speaking in a low, timid voice said, "Will you come and preach for us, Reverend? It's been a long spell since we had a good preacher." There was a curious hot excitement in her voice.

When they had gone again the woman on the log looked up at her husband with the strangest expression. In her eyes there was the light of admiration, but the thin mouth curled as if in derision. She was the only woman in the world who *knew* this man, and she could not bring herself to leave him.

II

He stayed and preached. His wife played for the services on a melodion which they carried in the

covered wagon. Each night brought souls to God.
Each night brought singing and weeping. In that
little town all came to God save one old man whose
deafness shut him out from the sonorous beauty of
Cyrus Spragg's voice and whose blindness hung a
veil between him and fire in the preacher's eyes.
They came to him, each one, in secret to ask forgiveness from their sins. He was to them the
Prophet of God.

He left at last with his ox-cart and chickens and
goats, his wife and children, and he took with him
a store of food and a young heifer bred and due
to calve the following spring, and on the day he left
a little crowd followed the covered wagon for three
miles beyond the village, and in it were women weeping and crying out hysterically. When at last he
took leave of them at the ford in a muddy prairie
stream, he stood on the back of the wagon and
made a long prayer while they knelt on the frozen
turf. And when he had finished he said, "And God
came to His servant in a dream and said, 'Go ye into
the wilderness and when ye find a place where three
streams meet, there shall ye found a new kingdom
which shall be called the New Jerusalem. And it
shall flourish and flow with milk and honey, and to
all the faithful the founding of the kingdom will be
revealed by a sign, and the faithful shall sell all
and leave their homes and firesides, their wives and
husbands, nay even their children, and come at last
into the Kingdom of Heaven.' "

Then he blessed them all and taking up the long
wand by which he guided the oxen, set out through
the water to cross the ford. One woman, the plump

comely one who had spoken to him on the first morning, rushed into the cold water up to her knees, but
he turned her back saying, "Until the Lord send you
a sign, tend your hearth and your home."

Inside the wagon the wife lay with her face buried
in a new feather-bed, her fingers pressed against her
ears. She was sobbing and ill and pregnant with
another child of the Prophet.

And in the village early in the following summer,
the plump blonde woman gave birth to a child which
she said was not her husband's child, but the child
of God and that she must take it to the Prophet.
Some thought her mad and some whispered about
her, and her husband hired a woman to keep watch
over her while he worked in the fields, but one day
when he had gone to Chicago she escaped, and with
the child joined a wagon-train bound westward and
they never heard of her again.

### III

The tale of Cyrus Spragg is a legend of the flat
country, of those prairies of the Middle West
where one can travel for days discovering only
monotony, and the origin of Cyrus Spragg is as mysterious as his end. No one ever knew whence he
came and none knows when he died. There is no
record of his grave. Some said that he was a
gypsy, but he was far too massive in build for one
of the Romany race. Others said that he was the
son of a French-Canadian father and a New England mother, and others that he was of German
origin, the son of immigrants from the Palatinate,

and still others that he was the son of a white man
and an Indian woman. It is known only that he
came out of the wilderness somewhere on the borders of Canada. It is likely that he had Indian
blood and that it was the blood of the Five Nations.
But there is little chance that the truth will ever be
known, for the Spraggites ceased to exist half a
century ago. The sect died when it no longer had
a God and those remaining alive who saw him in
life never knew anything of his origin.

The first existing record of his physical appearance is to be found in the works of Miss Amelia
Bossert, a lady of a highly emotional nature who
became the poetess and historian of the Spraggite
sect as well as the mother of three children by the
Prophet. After she had passed middle age and was
no longer attractive she quarrelled with the sect and
was publicly expelled from the colony. But her
impressions had been written as a girl and having
been already printed and distributed she found it
impossible to collect and destroy them. She was
seventeen at the time when Cyrus Spragg first entered her life. She saw him on the morning he
entered Valencia, Illinois, driving a wagon-train
laden with food and household furniture sent West
into the frontier country by an enterprising Phila-
delphia merchant. She must even then have been a
woman of an hysterical nature easily susceptible to
a faith which rested upon outbursts of wild religious
ecstasy. There was a great deal in her account that
was significant.

She wrote: "He was a handsomely made man of
about six feet two inches with a remarkable high-

colored, full-blooded look, with fiery black eyes and black curling hair which he wore cropped so that it fell just below the ears. In weight he was much heavier than he appeared because he was a muscular man of huge physical strength fashioned in such grandeur of proportion as might have been chosen by Fidias or one of the Greeks (sic). His brow was open and noble and his nose large and straight with elegant nostrils. These nostrils were always a little distended as I have remarked is the case with men of virility and passion of purpose. The lips were of a fine strawberry red and finely shaped though I have heard it said they were too full for some tastes. His hands were large and powerful, but of a beautiful shape, although hard and calloused from the powerful and heavy work which his truly Democratic (sic) nature craved warmly. Though he was but nineteen he had the mien and dignity of a well-developed man of forty.

"In his countenance there was already the light of Godhood. His were the flashing eyes of a man born to command as the Prophet of God. People on whom the Great Light had descended knew him at once as the leader sent by God to conduct His children out of the black slough of this world's sin and despair. A great light shone from his countenance. Many times since, the sight of him has called to mind those noble words of Solomon in describing God's love for the Church:

" 'His eyes are the eyes of doves by the river of waters, washed with milk, and fitly set.
" 'His cheeks are as a bed of spices, as sweet

*flowers; his lips like lilies dropping sweet-smelling
myrrh.*

*" 'His hands are as gold rings set with the beryl.*

*" 'His legs are as pillars of marble set upon
sockets of fine gold; his countenance is as Lebanon,
excellent as the cedars.' "*


Miss Bossert, perhaps through a modesty which
appears to have deserted her later in life, saw fit to
delete one sentence of the passage. She writes that
she saw him for the first time when she was standing
in front of Petersen's General Store, where she had
been sent to buy eggs by her afterward sainted
mother.

"While I stood watching him with all the curiosity which we in Valencia felt for each newcomer,
he lifted single-handed out of the rut into which it
had sunk a whole laden ox-cart which two oxen had
been unable to move."

Of that first appearance in Valencia there is no
further record, but from Miss Bossert's description
it is easy to see that he was no usual frontier youth.
It may have been that he had in Valencia one of
those adventures which later marked his progress
back and forth across the face of the Middle West,
but Miss Bossert, being at that time only seventeen,
would scarcely have heard of it. Her own adventure came much later.

From Valencia he went westward to sell what remained of his store of commerce and then for nine
years he appears to have been lost, like Saint John
the Baptist, in the wilderness. They were years
spent perhaps in trading and trapping. Throughout

his life he was surrounded from time to time by complete mystery. At the end of the nine years he appeared in Saint Louis, where he married Maria Trent and began his long career as a religious experimenter and itinerant preacher.

IV

For thirty years from the day the Mormons cast him out Cyrus Spragg and his ever-increasing family wandered the frontier country, appearing now here, now there, bringing with him excitement and romance and ecstasy where otherwise there was only poverty and work. As he grew older and more certain of himself, a kind of conscious glory came to envelop him, so that at times his journeying took on the aspect of a royal progress. Villages came to await his coming. Twice there were scandals that became known. Once in Mississippi he was forced to flee before the threats of an outraged husband across the border into Tennessee, leaving his family and his ox-cart to follow him. And each year the tired pretty woman who was his wife bore him another child until at length there were thirteen.

They were strong children, full of vitality, who thrived on the abundant food given by those to whom Cyrus Spragg had brought the light. He had other children, beyond all doubt—children like that of the plump yellow-haired woman who had disappeared seeking the Prophet. They were scattered throughout the borders of the Middle West. There were thirteen by his wife and three by the two deserted Mormon wives and countless others

not included among those he sired after he ruled as
God in New Jerusalem.

The wife, it seemed, could not bring herself to
leave him, perhaps because without him she could
not have fed all those mouths, perhaps because in
the end, after he had come to believe in himself, she,
too, began to believe that he *might* be God.  Or it
may have been a thing even simpler and less complex, that he had for her that fascination which he
had for other women, like Miss Amelia Bossert and
the yellow-haired wife.

The children had Biblical names—Jared and
Obadiah, Vashti and Uriah, Solomon and Bath-
sheba, Joshua and Isaiah, Boaz and Sulamith, Abraham and Ishmael—all save the last.  For some reason the tired woman rebelled against giving the last
a Biblical name.  Perhaps it was because she had
some foreknowledge that she would never have another child and so sought to have one that might
be her own instead of his.  Perhaps she knew even
before it was born that the last child was destined
to be strange and different from the others.

The child was born one hot August night in a
cottonwood grove in Iowa.  There was a clear sky
with a red moon that came up out of the flat prairie
as the sun disappeared.  The tired woman felt the
pains coming on and begged her husband to stop
for the night among the pleasant trees.  She could
not bear a child far out alone on that flat monotonous plain with not even a bush to hide her agony.
And when she had seen to it that the smaller children were asleep and the older ones had wandered
off among the trees, she went with Cyrus Spragg

deep into the grove until they came to a swamp
bordered round with deep thickets of witch-hazel,
and there in the wildest corner they made a bed of
leaves and blankets under the trees and Cyrus
heated water in an iron pot.

Her pain lasted all through the night, to the wild
accompaniment of frogs croaking in the marshes
and white herons moving about and chortling in
their sleep. A single coyote somewhere on the edge
of the marsh sat on his haunches and bayed at the
moon, long quivering wails that came surely from
another world. It seemed that the child would
never be born and that surely she must die, but when
morning came and the moon had disappeared and
only Venus hung red in the pale East, Cyrus Spragg
tore the child from its mother's womb. It was a
girl and it lived, but the tired mother knew she could
never have another child.

They baptized the baby in the waters of the
marsh, giving it the name of Annie, which was the
name of Maria Spragg's mother.


v


In the years that followed, revelations that were
false came from time to time to the Prophet. Once
he returned from meditation in the wilderness de-
claring that God had come to him in a pillar of fire
to say that mankind could alone be saved by turning
again to the ways of the birds and the beasts of the
field. There must be no more marrying or giving
in marriage and man must go about clothed only in
his skin, like the birds and the beasts. Sin, God told

Cyrus Spragg, was born of the garments with which man covered his body.

With his family and a little band of followers he set up a kingdom of Nature in the dunes and forests of Michigan. But two things he had failed to consider. The winter came and with it forty-seven Vigilantes from the nearest town. Together they dispersed the little band. Among the followers was Miss Amelia Bossert, the poetess, who early in the summer of the next year bore a son to the glory of the Prophet. The tired wife was released at last from the servitude of her body.

And then again at Cairo, Illinois, God came to him in the shape of a ram speaking with the tongues of angels to warn him against the new deluge. From the back of the great ox-cart he preached repentance and destruction, and beside it he and his followers set about building a clumsy barge that would have sunk as soon as launched. The great ship was finished in November and he settled himself to waiting for the rains to descend and the waters to rise. It is true that in that year the rains came and the rivers in the Middle West rose higher than they had ever risen before; but the Ark remained on dry land. No trickle of water touched it, despite even the prayers of all his band of followers. On the eighth day the river subsided again.

He did not wait for new floods, but told his followers that he had been guilty of error and sin and so had been blind to the true meaning of God's revelation, and packing his family into the cart, he disappeared again, moving toward the west with a small band of eccentric disciples. The Ark re-

mained, a curiosity which farmers drove miles to
see, and at last it was carried off piecemeal for fire-
wood by the negroes who lived on the riverbanks.

VI

In the spring of the following year the little cara-
van led by the Prophet came suddenly upon "the
spot where three rivers joined their waters." He
was no longer a young man and no longer quite a
charlatan. At sixty-one he had come to believe in
himself as others believed in him. The thing he
had created took possession of him. The site where
three rivers joined their waters was the spot indicated by him in a prophecy thirty years earlier. He
had not believed it then, and now it had come true.
It was as if God had chosen him, after all. Here
he unyoked the oxen for the last time. This was the
New Jerusalem.

It was a fertile country, green and well watered,
with deep black soil, though it was a flat country
and treeless and bare. The land was to be had for
the taking. At this time there were in his train
seven grown sons and nineteen followers, men and
women, and among them they claimed land larger
in area than all Judea. Cyrus Spragg became the
ruler and the patriarch and throughout the prairie
country those who had been awaiting a sign heard
of the New Jerusalem and left their homes and
flocked to join him. They came for days and weeks
in wagons and ox-carts, on foot and on horseback,
a restless, emotional people seeking the compensation of a romantic faith.

He built a Temple of which Miss Amelia Bossert's description remains. It was eight-sided, without windows, and possessed a single door. Inside there were no dividing walls, but only draperies and curtains. What light there was came through the roof, which rose to a height of a hundred feet in a gigantic dome-topped tower that was visible for miles across the flat prairie from any part of New Jerusalem. Near it he built the Ecclesiastical Palace, a rambling wooden house painted white, that was to shelter his wife, his six daughters, his seven sons and daughters-in-law and his eighteen legitimate grandchildren. It was the first house his tired wife had known in forty years and when it was finished she took to a bed placed near a window that gave out on the square before the Temple. There she lived, wearing out her tired life in watching with dimmed but uncomplaining eyes this strange thing built up out of nothing by the strange man she had loved and despised for nearly forty years. Neither the thing nor the man had she ever understood.

When the Temple and the Palace were finished there was a great service in the open air. Cyrus Spragg was photographed and took leave of his followers and entered into the Temple, to pass eternity in repose and meditation. God, he told them, would rule New Jerusalem through His instrument, Cyrus Spragg. He would send out revelations from time to time administering the sowing of crops and price of grain and the shearing of sheep. As God's instrument, Cyrus Spragg could not die. He would live forever in the depths of the

Temple watching over their good. There would be only virgins to serve him, virgins to carry forth his revelations into the light, virgins to feed him and attend his will. Then he entered into the Temple and no man ever saw him again. He became an Invisible Presence and there were converts to the faith and children born in New Jerusalem who had never seen Cyrus Spragg and so came to think of him as God.

But in New Jerusalem dissension and wrangling broke out even in the family of the Prophet himself, for his third son, Uriah, was unlike the others and would take no part in the plan, and went about muttering against his father. He and the Prophet's youngest daughter, Annie Spragg, who never left the side of her mother, talked bitterly against their father, even though their brothers upbraided and beat them, until at last the tired mother, with her favorite children, Uriah and Annie, left the squabbles of the Palace and went to live by themselves in a house on the borders of the colony. It was there the defeated old woman died at last calling on the Prophet to leave the Temple and visit her. But he never came, for God could not appear among his people. When she was buried, Uriah Spragg and his sister fled the colony one dark night, and with them went Miss Amelia Bossert and her four sons, for she was an old woman now and when the Prophet failed to choose her among those to serve him in the Temple, she uttered blasphemies that caused her to be driven from New Jerusalem. She went to Omaha to live and supported her four sons by sewing. One of them became a senator.

When the Prophet was sixty-eight God sent him a revelation saying that it was through his seed that the world would be redeemed and that all his children would be blessed unto the fifth and sixth generation as the chosen and the true Children of God. It became a great honor for any woman to be chosen as the mother of God's children.

## VII

There lived in a house not far from the Temple a young woman of twenty called Eliza Weatherby, the daughter of one of the Prophet's oldest converts. She was a pretty girl, devout and serious, but not without vanity. She sinned by wearing brooches and bright ribbons, and so she attracted many admirers. Her father's house adjoined the building where the produce of New Jerusalem was sold and the mail given out. Through this circumstance she made the acquaintance of a young man, the only unbeliever who was ever allowed within the sacred ground of the colony. He was tall and straight and lean and a Kentuckian. He was a hard rider and employed by the government to bring the mail from Omaha west across the prairies to New Jerusalem. For Miss Eliza Weatherby he conceived a romantic Southern passion which appears to have excited the girl, perhaps because it was so free of all the piety which surrounded the dour courtships of the Faithful. For New Jerusalem was a moral community where there was no dancing or gambling and no drinking of alcohol, and adultery was punished by expulsion from the sect. But the girl resisted him because she could not marry an infidel and urged him to become converted.

The suitor was a young man and quite out of his head with love and desire for the pretty Eliza Weatherby and at length, when she remained firm, he was driven beyond endurance. He expressed a desire to be converted and under Obadiah Spragg, eldest son of the Prophet, he began a course of instruction. What he learned there was never known, for the secrets of the sect were well guarded, but it caused him to violate the Temple. He discovered that Eliza was among the virgins chosen to serve the Prophet and on the day she was called to enter the sanctuary the Kentuckian broke in the door. A passing woman heard three shots of a pistol and saw him emerge and leap on his horse and ride off, not toward Omaha but toward the West. A little while later Eliza Weatherby ran screaming into the street crying out that her lover had murdered God.

A crowd gathered about the Temple, but none dared enter to violate its sanctity save the woman chosen to serve on that day, and as Eliza Weatherby had fallen into a faint that lasted until nightfall, she could not enter. So they waited, praying until morning of the next day, when the young woman chosen went into the Temple. All day they waited for her to emerge and when at last she came out she bore a revelation written by the Prophet. It read, "Fear not, my people. Thy God is immortal." The young woman told them that a darkness had descended upon the Temple and that she had not seen the Prophet's face.

There was great rejoicing in the colony, and out of death Cyrus Spragg wrung a greater faith.

But before six months had passed murmurs began to arise in New Jerusalem. The revelations of the Prophet had caused the crops to freeze out of the ground, and ewes to be bred too early so that the lambs died of cold. There came a great plague of grasshoppers which ate what was left of the wheat. Among the chosen women who served the Prophet other strange murmurs arose, that now he received them only in the darkness of the innermost chamber and that his manner was strange. Eliza Weatherby, who had become pregnant and seemed a little out of her head, made the hysterical statement that the Prophet no longer existed and that an impostor had taken his place. But they held her in disfavor for having loved an infidel and so having been the cause of all their misfortunes, and no one believed her. She was tried and, being expelled from the colony by the Prophet's eldest son for blasphemy, went to Des Moines to live, where she embraced a literary career and wrote book reviews for the newspapers.

But in the end it was a thing as simple and commonplace as jealousy that destroyed the strange kingdom of Cyrus Spragg. One day in the midst of worship before the Temple the wife of Obadiah Spragg rose and cried out wildly that the Prophet was dead and that an impostor had taken his place. And then turning upon one of the female followers who had been shown special favor by the Prophet she began to scratch and pull the woman's hair and call her all manner of evil names. When they had calmed her and Obadiah Spragg had bade her be silent, she turned and, pointing her finger, screamed at him: "There is the False Prophet. Him and his brother Jared. It took two of them to fill the place of the True Prophet. One wasn't good enough."

In their fear that God had chosen them for calamity the colony held a meeting in the open space before the Temple and four of the oldest followers of the Prophet, with prayer on their lips and despite the cries of "Sacrilege" from Jared and Obadiah Spragg, opened the door and entered the Temple. At the end of an hour they appeared again with terror in their eyes. The Temple was empty. There was no Prophet.

It was the end of the colony. Some sold their land and went away from the accursed ground and some stayed until better times brought prosperity. But the Spraggites were no more, and no one knows to this day what became of Cyrus Spragg. His son Obadiah declared that he had been taken to Heaven in a chariot of fire, but Obadiah was not Cyrus Spragg and he had neither the vigor nor the beauty nor the voice of Cyrus Spragg and none believed him.

In Des Moines the child of Eliza Weatherby was born. It was a boy and sickly, the child of the Prophet's old age. She christened it Alonzo for the Kentuckian and because she thought Alonzo a pretty name. But she refused to marry her lover. She died in the belief that he had murdered God.

## TWENTY YEARS OF DEVOTION

### I

AS MRS. WEATHERBY had explained, food meant little to her; it was rather the things of the spirit in which she found satisfaction. There were two reasons for this, one, that she really had no taste for food and could not distinguish good food from bad, and the other, that no matter how great her efforts, no matter the number of Yogi exercises which she practiced, it was impossible to keep her majestic figure within bounds. The trouble was with her glands.

The night after her strange callers had gone off in the black and red motor of the Princess d'Orobelli she and Miss Fosdick seated themselves to a dinner of veal and spaghetti and wilted salad served by the same Margharita who a little while earlier had been pinched by the chauffeur of the Princess. There was also a little of that acid wine which Italy produces in vast quantities. Miss Fosdick hated veal and from a too great familiarity detested spaghetti. She liked good food and only once in two years, when she had escaped secretly to a restaurant, had she tasted it.

But the meal was a little better than usual because Mrs. Weatherby was in high spirits over the success of the afternoon and the glory reflected upon her as the sole existing friend of Miss Annie Spragg. For Miss Fosdick this was a condition as rare as good food. The sweet disposition, the poise, the trained smile and the throaty voice, the sweet expression which Mrs. Weatherby exhibited to the world—all these were bought at a cost, paid in the beginning by Alonzo Weatherby and after his death by Miss Fosdick. All her ill temper was poured out upon their heads.

She observed to Miss Fosdick that Father d'Astier was a devout and charming man, that the Principessa was a woman of great distinction and that Mr. Winnery (although he had scarcely uttered a word) was a man of great intelligence.

"We must do something about the villa," she said, "now that we have begun to receive people."

She watched Miss Fosdick. She had a way of watching her companion as if to measure how much she might be told, for one could not afford to betray oneself to a companion. But as both grew older Miss Fosdick appeared to notice less and less what happened about her. She was, after all, (reflected Mrs. Weatherby) a perfect companion, docile and admiring, never intruding her own personality, and, most important of all, she was a companion who could not quit her place. Miss Fosdick no longer even gave in to those fits of hysterical weeping which had been so trying, or if she did weep, she wept in private where it would not disturb anyone. "What would the poor lamb have done without me?" thought Mrs. Weatherby. "She would have been helpless in this world, probably doing sewing by the day in Winnebago Falls. She is only a child, after all."

They sat in the grand salon with the superb view over the valley because as yet there was no furniture for the dining-room. From time to time Mrs. Weatherby would lean over and murmur, "Do Too-Too and Lulu want to eat?" at which the two Pomeranians, yapping, would spring into the air to snap at the piece of veal she held on her fork. The candles burned without a flicker in the still hot air and Margharita shuffled in and out noiselessly in felt slippers. It was the same night after night. This was the middle of August and it had been exactly the same every night since the middle of May. On the opposite side of the table Miss Fosdick stared out of her round eyes across the dark valley. The excitement of callers had made her a little seasick, so that she was uncertain whether she could eat or not. She thought, "I shall go insane. I can stand it no longer."

Mrs. Weatherby continued eating the tired lettuce. "You aren't listening, Gertrude. I said we must do something about the dining-room, now that visitors have begun to come."

"We might drive into Brinoë tomorrow."

"Not in this heat. You know how this heat affects you. I shouldn't mind it. If you could only *believe* as I do, the heat would have no effect upon you."

"Perhaps we'd better leave it until next year. It's so late in the season." (This, Miss Fosdick knew, was what she was meant to say.)

"Yes, next year," echoed Mrs. Weatherby, and then tartly, "You don't seem to take any interest in anything any more."

Next year (thought Miss Fosdick) they would come out here and live in the same dreary fashion.

Nothing would be done. And no one would come to see them except some crazy woman who would talk magnetism and spirit control. And next year and next year and next year. . . .

"If you can't listen I might as well go to bed. Considering all I do for you. . . ."

Miss Fosdick never heard the end of the sentence, for Mrs. Weatherby, in one of her sudden tempers, had rushed out of the door, followed by the yapping Pomeranians. On her way she knocked over her chair and the sound of it striking the stone floor echoed through the empty villa long after she had gone. Miss Fosdick's expression did not change. There was a buzzing in her head. The room seemed suddenly to swell to enormous proportions and then contract again. She lifted the tired lettuce to her mouth and ate mechanically. Everything was so still and breathless and hot. "I shall go mad," she thought. "I shall go mad."

It was the return of Margharita that brought her out of the sudden trance. She decided that she was glad of the quarrel, for it gave her a chance to be alone for a little time. If she stayed away long enough Aunt Henrietta would send for her and then when she came, Aunt Henrietta would sulk and refuse to talk. Anything was better than talking, feeding, feeding, feeding, the vanity of Aunt Henrietta. What the world failed to give her Miss Fosdick was forced to supply, and at the moment the world of Brinoë was simply ignoring Mrs. Weatherby.

Then suddenly Miss Fosdick thought with a pang, "I have been rude and ungrateful. We are two women alone together in the world. I must not forget that. I owe her everything in the world. But for her I shouldn't be here in this beautiful spot, in this interesting and historic country." But almost at once she was overcome with a loathing for the villa, for Brinoë, for all of Italy. She *had* to live there. She could see no way of ever escaping this alien, unsympathetic land where everything seemed romantic and untidy, fantastically beautiful and reeking with smells.

"If only I could speak Italian," she thought, "I could at least talk to the servants now and then. I must try and learn next winter."

But she knew she never would learn. She had never learned anything. There was nothing, she told herself, that she could do. She was not clever enough.

"I will go out into the garden until I've recovered my temper."

## II

In the garden the air seemed cool and there was a smell of fresh earth coming from the trench that had been dug for the cesspool. The moon had risen to the top of the sky and its light fell full upon the roof of fading plantain leaves, so that the carpet of moss below was flecked all over with a pattern of silver. Usually she was afraid at night in the garden, with that fear of darkness and the unknown that had paralyzed her timid nature since childhood. And there was something special about this garden. She always had a feeling of being watched by invisible eyes. It was too old, too haunted by its incalculable antiquity. But tonight the shadows seemed less ominous and the faint whispering of the leaves even friendly. It may have been the light showing from the servants' wing that gave her courage, or it may have been a sudden overwhelming conviction that anything was better than talking to Aunt Henrietta.

"I must not think that," she told herself. "Aunt Henrietta is right. It is evil thoughts that destroy us and make us old. . . . But what difference does it make whether I am old or not? Nothing can ever happen to me. I am thirty-eight years old and nothing has ever happened. I am getting fat and no man would ever look at me even if I had the chance to know one.

"Still," she thought, blushing a little, "that Mr. Winnery *did* look at me today."

She found herself presently at a spot in the garden where the jasmine climbed over the pitted stone balustrade that overhung the deep valley. A few pale blossoms still gleamed in the moonlight and the fragrance drifted through the still air under the colonnades of trees. The scent came to her vaguely, awakening and sharpening her senses and drawing her thoughts away from herself. Leaning over the balustrade she broke off a blossom and smelled of it, half dreaming. "That Mr. Winnery who was her today. . . . He was polite to me. But I shan't ever see him again."

She turned away and wandered down one of the long *allées*, but after a few steps she halted and thrusting the jasmine blossom into her hair, patted it smooth again and then set off, following the wall.

She walked a long way half-dreaming, half-aware that far down in the bottom of the valley on the opposite side there was an automobile moving along the lonely road toward Monte Salvatore. The distant sound of the motor drifted up from the valley below, and then all at once she was aware that the sound had stopped and that the car was not moving. It sat quite still at a point almost directly opposite the villa. It seemed an odd place to stop, in the very midst of an empty valley where there was no inn, no house and nothing but rocks and olive trees.

Watching it, she thought again of Mr. Winnery. He was a small man and not handsome, but he had nice manners and a kind face. It would be nice to know that. . . . It would be pleasant to feel safe. . . . Her thoughts went silly and muddled and she found herself blushing in the darkness. Surely she was going mad.

How long she stood there dreaming she did not know, but presently she was aware of the familiar terrifying certainty that she was no longer alone. The light in the servants' wing had gone out. It was as if something were watching her out of the shadows. A wild impulse stronger than her own terror compelled her to turn and look fearfully over her shoulder, and then she discovered that she was standing a dozen feet from the new-found statue. It lay against the black ilex, white and glistening in the moonlight. She saw the face with an extraordinary clearness and all the too rich beauty of the voluptuous body. For a time she remained fascinated and chilled with terror, and then in the most unmaidenly fashion she gathered up her skirts and ran toward the darkened villa. Once inside the door she fell upon the stone flagging and lay there so overcome by panic that she was unable to rise.

### III

At ten o'clock, sitting in the vast empty room which she called her boudoir Mrs. Weatherby lost patience and began ringing the great brass bell with which she was accustomed to summon the servants. Not only was she out of patience, but disturbed. Miss Fosdick had never before remained away sulking for so long a time, and there came to Mrs. Weatherby that faint and unlikely suspicion which sometimes raised its head, that her companion might have run away.

She had not gone. There was a timid knock on the door and Miss Fosdick entered, looking, Mrs. Weatherby thought, pale and agitated.

"It seems to me, Gertrude, that you're old enough not to sulk."

"I wasn't sulking, Aunt Henrietta."

"I've finished my exercises long ago. I thought you were never coming."

Miss Fosdick did not answer, but took up the hair-brush and began her nightly task of soothing Mrs. Weatherby's frayed nerves. The large empty room was lighted by two candles and an oil-lamp which stood on the dressing-table before an antique mirror in which Mrs. Weatherby's countenance gazed out, blotched and hazy, from the age not so much of Mrs. Weatherby's face as of the quicksilver. The great religious experimenter had changed into a white peignoir trimmed with white maribou. The exercises to which she referred were a series of facial contortions which she practiced each night for forty-five minutes in order to give firmness to the muscles of the face and sweetness to the expression. "Everything by nature," was her creed, and "the power of mind over matter." No flake of powder, no morsel of rouge, no cream of any sort, had ever touched her face and so her skin had that weather-beaten, tough look that marks the skin of those firm women who are above vanities.

Miss Fosdick, brushing the hair slowly (eight strokes to the minute was Mrs. Weatherby's formula) was having bitter thoughts. "Why," she asked herself, "should *she* want to keep young? Certainly it is not to attract men. She hates the attention of men. Maybe she wants people to remark how young she looks for sixty-five." And almost at once she reproached herself for having thoughts so lewd, disloyal and cynical.

At the same time Mrs. Weatherby was thinking, "Now is a time when I wish Gertrude had some sense. I'd like to talk over this conversion affair, but I can't risk it."

It was one of the times when the indomitable woman was put to rout by the very simplicity of her companion. She spoke again without turning, "You haven't changed your mind?"

"No, Aunt Henrietta. I tried praying but I got no answer."

Mrs. Weatherby answered her with a snort and the pair fell back into silence. Presently Miss Fosdick, looking out of the window, saw that the motor on the road far down the valley had not moved. Someone had dimmed the lights. She thought of calling Aunt Henrietta's attention to it, and then changed her mind through a desire to spite her by keeping this bit of excitement a secret.

IV

Mrs. Weatherby kept thinking of her approaching conversion. It was a subject which had occupied her a great deal lately; indeed, ever since she had abandoned the idea of founding a new religion out of her experience with new faiths. The idea of an "eclectic" faith combining the best points of all religions had come at length to die for lack of energy and any sense of organization. She was a muddled woman and being very rich she had no need of the material gains which commonly reward contemporary prophets. Indeed, the whole idea had been rather a failure. She had come to Brinoë to pass her twilight ("old age" was an expression she never used), expecting something of that triumph and that notoriety which had come to her in Winnebago Falls and later at Carmel and Los Angeles; and now it seemed that she had drawn a blank. No one noticed her, even when she drove to the town dressed all in white carrying tuberoses. There was, she told herself, too much competition among eccentrics in Brinoë. It was worse, even, than Los Angeles. (At the moment, as she sat before the blotched mirror, she experienced an actual jealousy of the posthumous notoriety of Miss Annie Spragg. That queer old woman had succeeded where she had failed.)

She wanted notice and flattery and no one in
Brinoë noticed her and no one flattered her save a
little group of Marchesas, Principessas and Contessas, all old and dowdy and poor who thought
they might get something from her. At first the
mention of their titles pleased her and then she
made the disillusioning discovery that Marchesas
and Contessas were as thick as flies in Italy, and her
natural shrewdness told her that they were simply
leeches. People in Brinoë seemed not to be interested in Messages and clung stubbornly to conventional forms of religion. Two years of campaign-
ing had brought her nowhere.

Being entirely without sensibility she was never
bored and so could not understand boredom in
others. She did not know into what depths of boredom she had plunged her three visitors that very
afternoon. She never imagined the depths of boredom in which poor Miss Fosdick had spent the better part of twenty years,—depths so profound that
at times she goaded Mrs. Weatherby into abusing
her simply for the sake of change. It had never
occurred to her, who had known such triumphs in
Carmel and Los Angeles, that in Brinoë she was
regarded simply as a colossal bore from whom people fled after one meeting as from a plague. She,
the imposing Henrietta Weatherby!

She had a passion for knowing what she called
"interesting people," and Brinoë, she felt, must be
alive with "interesting people"—writers, painters,
musicians and others who were simply "characters."
It was simply a matter of meeting them. She firmly
and naïvely believed that parties made up of people

who were "doing things" instantly became charged with fascination, wit and brilliant conversation. It never occurred to her that in groups musicians are vain and egotistical, painters hostile and technical and writers envious and mean-spirited. To her they were all just fascinating.

For months she had given thought to the question of how to make herself interesting. Being as devoid of talents as of sensibility, she could not suddenly become a singer, writer or painter, and being mean by nature she could not bring herself to buy her way to the things she desired. So in the end she had fallen back upon her great asset—her interest in religion. At last she had hit upon a plan. She would be converted to the Catholic faith and become a pillar of devoutness. Perhaps she would even gain a place for herself in that Papal party referred to in mysterious whispers by the Marchesa as the Blacks. Religion, she told herself, was her sphere. She had spent a lifetime studying religions and this very fact would give to her conversion a certain sensational interest. Having been much in the public prints in America she thought of each new adventure in headlines. "Famous experimenter of many faiths turns to bosom of Mother Church."

From the moment she reached a decision she had set about with energy planning the conversion. The Marchesa, to whom she expressed a casual interest in the Roman faith, advised her to be instructed by Father d'Astier as the most fashionable of worldly missionaries. She let it be known to Miss Fosdick that a conversion was expected from her at the same time, but Miss Fosdick, who had followed with docility through the mysteries of Christian Science, of Theosophy, of Bahaism, New Thought and Self Expression, suddenly rebelled at Rome. Something in her with roots deep in New England and Congregationalism stubbornly refused to undertake what she referred to crudely one day as Popery. She was so firm, so amazingly fanatic on the subject, that even Mrs. Weatherby was thrown down in defeat.

Sitting before the mirror while Miss Fosdick brushed her hair Mrs. Weatherby turned over in her mind the idea of becoming a Papal Countess. In her imagination she tried over the title, "Countess Weatherby . . . Countess Weatherby." It sounded a little ridiculous. Still she had heard of other Papal Countesses with names that sounded more absurd—Irish names. If only there was such a title as "Lady." "Lady Weatherby" sounded quite distinguished. And then she frowned as she thought that such titles were purchased for good solid money, not bought really, but given in exchange for rich gifts to the Church. And giving money was to her like cutting off a piece of her own flesh.

That is probably the reason, she thought, why Father d'Astier came all the way out here in the heat. He knew that she was rich . . . that and his curiosity about the miracle of Miss Annie Spragg.

At the thought of Miss Annie Spragg her eyes narrowed a little. She wished that she knew exactly how the Church meant to treat the miracle. If the Church canonized Annie Spragg it would be a great help to her (Mrs. Weatherby). She could bathe in the glory of having been the only person in Italy (except Gertrude, who did not count) who knew the queer old woman. She could indeed pose as the best friend of the saint. That would advance her a long way, further, indeed, than any amount of money. Perhaps they *would* make Annie Spragg a saint. They'd probably never discover that she was the daughter of old Cyrus Spragg the Prophet, nor ever hear the scandalous stories that had gone the rounds of Winnebago Falls, nor all those things she herself had chosen not to reveal. Father d'Astier had refused to commit himself. Father d'Astier, her shrewdness told her, was a clever man who would need managing if she were to get from him what she desired.

She yearned passionately for a confidante with whom she might discuss all these things, but with Gertrude it was impossible. In her stupidity she would not understand their complications. Undoubtedly she would put upon them the wrong interpretation.

v

In the placid bosom of Miss Fosdick there was a fury asmoulder and with each stroke of the brush it blazed and gained in strength. She had reached a pitch of boredom and irritation wherein she no longer asked herself whether she was being disloyal. All such self-inquiry was being buried under tides of long-pent-up resentment. It was as if all her softness had for twenty long years concealed a core of inflexibility. She was at that moment giving birth to a character, bringing decision into a soul where before there had been no decision. And it

was such a small thing that kindled this great flame
—the fact that Mr. Winnery had looked upon her
as if she were a woman. She had not actually seen
him do it. She had *felt* him looking at her while
Aunt Henrietta was telling that interminable and
inaccurate story of the villa. She was aware that
in the look there was admiration, perhaps even desire. It was years since such a thing had happened
to her. Not since that organist at the Bahai Temple. . . .

Above Mrs. Weatherby's grey head she saw her
own reflection in the mirror and she noticed presently many things that she had forgotten to notice
for a long time past—that she had pretty hair,
smooth and shiny and still a mousey brown, that her
eyes *were* blue and attractive and that her nose was
red and shiny. She thought, "I will buy powder the
next time I go to Brinoë, and I will use it whether
*she* likes it or not." (She had suddenly ceased
thinking of Mrs. Weatherby as Aunt Henrietta but
merely as *she*.) Miss Fosdick even wondered if
her hair would be becoming cut short like the Principessa's flaming locks. "No," she told herself, "I
am too fat. I must try to lose weight. I must write
for one of those diets advertised in the *Ladies' Own
World.*" Having been born with a fine high color
which needed only toning down, she had no need of
rouge. "Still," she thought giddily, "a touch on
the lips—just a touch."

Mrs. Weatherby interrupted her. "Don't pull
so hard. You know how it affects my nerves."

Miss Fosdick had a wild impulse to say "Humph"
and, giving the grey hair a good pull, to throw the

brush on the floor, but the force of habit was stronger than her new-born character and she went on with her task. When one had done the same thing at the same hour three hundred and sixty-five times a year for twenty years the effect became paralyzing. She tried to calculate how many times she had brushed that hateful grey head. Twenty times three hundred and sixty-five (sometimes three hundred and sixty-six) times one hundred and eighty strokes. But the problem was quite beyond her. She was very poor at figures.

A sense of power rose in her with the knowledge that she had refused flatly to become converted and that *she* had taken it quietly. One had one's right to a religion. Nobody could command you to change your faith, thought Miss Fosdick. People had been burned for refusing to change, by that very Church which Aunt Henrietta was considering. "I could never meet my mother in Heaven with her knowing I had taken up with Popery." It was the first time she had ever refused Aunt Henrietta anything.

Memories of ancient wrongs began to well up in her soul. Clarence Hazeltine she might have married but for Aunt Henrietta, who said she was too young to marry and carted her off to California. Clarence—she saw him again through mists of sentiment—thin, a little bald at thirty, round-shouldered and round-eyed. Timid he was. If he hadn't been he wouldn't have let her be carried off.

Again Mrs. Weatherby interrupted her. "Really, Gertrude, I don't know what has come over you. You know what a sensitive scalp I have."

Again Miss Fosdick had an impulse to hurl the brush, this time through the blotched old mirror. Again habit chained her.

"And you needn't sulk, either," added Mrs. Weatherby.

Sulk! Sulk! thought Miss Fosdick. If she only knew what I was thinking. By now Clarence probably owned the drugstore and had a family that might have been her own family. And there was that young organist at Carmel who played in the Bahai Temple and came to call night after night. He might have married her but for something *she* did. She suspected Aunt Henrietta of telling him that if he married Gertrude neither of them would ever get a cent from her. Maybe he *did* mean to marry her for Aunt Henrietta's money. "Well," Miss Fosdick thought, "what of it? At least I'd have been married. Something would have happened to me. It would be better than being a fat old maid. Something has got to happen to me! Something! Anything! Anything at all!"

Mrs. Weatherby was speaking again. "I'm afraid I have one of my headaches again. Some enemy is directing ill will toward me."

Again Miss Fosdick made no answer. She knew what the speech meant. In a moment Aunt Henrietta would ask her to sit by the bed all night exerting her will against the currents of malice being projected at Aunt Henrietta by some unknown enemy. If *she* only knew that on those occasions Miss Fosdick never stayed awake at all but slept roundly sitting upright. Nothing ever kept Aunt Henrietta awake when she felt like sleeping.

"Oh, I mean to escape," Miss Fosdick kept telling her interiorly, as if to break down the chain of habit. "Oh, I mean to escape, all right." She gazed malignantly at the image of Mrs. Weatherby, who was doing her nails and practicing her expression of sweetness at the same time. "Ah, if *she* only knew." But Miss Fosdick hadn't the least idea what she meant to do.

All this time she had been watching the clock and counting the strokes of the brush with a part of her mind that seemed immune from that wild torrent of rebellious thought. One hundred and forty-two, one hundred and forty-three . . . eight strokes to the minute according to Mrs. Weatherby's schedule.

Aunt Henrietta was speaking again. "I'm afraid, dear, that I'll have to ask you to sit by me tonight."

It was not possible that it was coming so surely, exactly as she had known it would come. This time she might have thrown down the brush, but before she had time to act there rose in the still air the sound of a voice calling in Italian, "Hello! Hello in there!" and the sound of vigorous knocking on the main door.

For a second the gaze of the two women, so hostile and now suddenly frightened, met in the blotched old mirror.

"Who could it be?" whispered Mrs. Weatherby, who was always afraid of something. "At this hour of the night?"

They listened for a moment and then the knocking was repeated and the shouting.

"Go to the window, Gertrude."

Miss Fosdick, with the hateful brush still in her hand, went timidly to the window on the opposite side of the room. Below her the graveled court-yard lay drenched in moonlight and bordered by the lean black shadows of the cypresses. She was aware that the motor with dimmed lights still stood on the opposite side of the valley. At first she could see no one, and then after a moment a tall man stepped from the shadow of the portico into the moonlight and called up to her in Italian. Miss Fosdick under-stood only the word "telephone," and partly in ges-tures, partly in bad Italian, explained that there was no telephone. The stranger at once began speaking English in a deep melodious voice with scarcely any accent.

His companion stepped into the moonlight and Miss Fosdick recognized him. It was dirty old Pietro, who kept goats and lived in a hut among the olive trees half-way up the mountain.

The stranger explained that he was motoring from Siena to Brinoë and that he had had an acci-dent. Some thief had charged him for forty litres of petrol and put only twenty into the tank of his motor. If they had no telephone he was lost, un-less by some miracle they had a few litres of petrol.

Behind Miss Fosdick Mrs. Weatherby had crossed the room and was standing discreetly in the shadow, peeping from the shelter of a curtain.

There *was* a miracle and the miracle was the Ford which Giovanni used for going into Monte Salva-tore. There must be some petrol in the tank. It stood in a part of the vast ruined stable built by the Spanish Ambassador to house his Arab horses.

"I suppose," whispered Mrs. Weatherby, "we must help him, but I don't like people who wander about in the night." She moved to the window and called down, "Young man, turn the light on your face."

"Old Pietro is with him," murmured Miss Fosdick hopefully.

The stranger did as commanded. He was not a young man though his figure was trim and slender. He might have been forty-five. He was distinguished and certainly handsome in a dark, almost Moorish fashion. The humor of the situation had caused him to grin.

## VI

Trembling with excitement, Miss Fosdick, still carrying the hair-brush absentmindedly in one hand, took up a candle and clattered down the stone stairs in her slippers. She was so excited that she even forgot to be afraid of the garden and made her way without a tremor through the tunnel that led into the courtyard. There the stranger met her murmuring a thousand apologies made with all the overwrought extravagance of Latin courtesy. He was dressed in beige tweeds and wore a cap and yellow buckskin gloves. The wind from Africa had died away at last and the candle burned in the still air without a flicker. By its yellow light Miss Fosdick saw that he was older than she had believed and of an aspect even more romantic than she had imagined. Thinking in terms of Aunt Henrietta's speech she told herself that it was Force that he had

. . . Personal and Magnetic Force. She thought, "Things are beginning to happen to me. He is exactly like the hero of 'In a Winter City.' "

Despite herself, her manner became overwrought and arch. She explained that Mrs. Weatherby was afraid of Italian servants. . . . She had heard stories in Carmel . . . and that all the servants slept in a pavilion near the stables. She led the way to the stables, followed by the stranger and old Pietro, who limped as he walked and kept muttering to himself. The miracle at the stables was even greater than she had hoped. In the shadows and among the ghosts of the Spanish Ambassador's Arab horses they discovered the battered Ford. The gasoline tank was full to the brim.

The stranger appeared in such great haste that he threw himself down without a thought into the dust and grease beneath the Ford and set to work filling the two bidons he carried with him. When he had finished he rose and insisted upon seeing Miss Fosdick back through the shrubbery despite all her fluttering protests that she was not afraid. In the thickest part of the shrubbery he even touched her arm gently with an old-fashioned courtesy. The implication that Miss Fosdick was so fragile that she might easily slip in the darkness and injure herself flattered her vanity, and made her feel very small and feminine. At the door he took out a soft leather wallet and taking from it a card gave it to her. It was then that she discovered for the first time with embarrassment that in one hand she still held Mrs. Weatherby's hair-brush. Strands of Aunt Henrietta's grey hair still clung to it.

Bowing, the stranger said, "This is my name. I will send a cheque tomorrow. Whose name shall I put on it?"

She wanted to say, "Oh, no. Don't think of it," in a grand and generous manner, but she knew Aunt Henrietta would insist upon being paid for the petrol. She should at least have answered, "Mrs. Henrietta Weatherby," but in an insane burst of unmaidenly behavior, she murmured, "Miss Gertrude Fosdick," and spelled it for him as he wrote it down. "F-o-s-d-i-c-k."

He took off his cap and bowed elaborately once more and disappeared, and then for the first time she was able to look at the card. Being far-sighted and not having her glasses, she had to hold it far from her. She read,

> ORESTE VALMENTE
> EL DUQUE DE FUENTERRABÍA
> EL MARQUÉS DE SANTOBAN

For a moment she feared her knees would give way. It was just like a novel, she thought. Just like a novel. It was like one of those stories of Ouida, one of the things you got in a paper-backed edition. Just like "In a Winter City." The hand trembled with excitement and the flame of the candle trembled too. Her shadow trembled on the ancient wall so that it looked as if she were dancing. Presently she shut the door and shot the huge iron bolt, but as she closed it she caught a sudden glimpse of the statue gleaming white in the moonlight and felt suddenly frightened again.

A voice from the top of the stairs brought her back to the horrid reality.

"What on earth are you doing, Gertrude? They have gone long ago."

Then Miss Fosdick remembered that there were still thirty-seven strokes of the brush to be done.

VII

When she re-entered the bedroom, Aunt Henrietta was awaiting her in a cold fury. She exhibited all the signs of what Miss Fosdick described to herself as "a tantrum." She had been working toward this point ever since dinner-time. Miss Fosdick knew the signs—the look of fury in the eye, the distended nostrils of the large, fleshy nose, the fat hands clasping the foot of the bed, the heavy breathing. With her thin grey hair hanging about her face, she was a terrifying sight that caused all the flame of rebellion burning in Miss Fosdick's bosom to turn to water and flow away.

For a moment Mrs. Weatherby stood regarding her in a cold silence as if choosing how she should begin. Then suddenly she found what was needed.

"What on earth have you got in your hair?" she cried out. "I think you must be crazy lately . . . an old maid like you putting flowers in her hair, as if a man was going to look at *you*."

Something exploded in Miss Fosdick's brain. She hurled the brush and the candle on the floor. The card of Oreste Valmente, Duke of Fonterrabia and Marquis of Santoban, fell with them.

"I'll put what I like in my hair and you can go to Hell."

For a moment Mrs. Weatherby recoiled as if Miss Fosdick had struck her a blow. "Oh! Oh!" she cried in a stricken manner, and then firmly, "Take care what you're saying."

"I'll put what I like in my hair. I'm an old maid because you made me one."

"You're a ridiculous sight."

"No more than you and your silly religions. You've spoiled everything for me."

Mrs. Weatherby gave a throaty laugh. "Spoiled everything, have I? And where would you be without me, pray? You'd have nothing except for me. You'd be a pauper."

In Miss Fosdick a hundred respectable New England ancestors rose and ran riot. "*You.* Everybody laughs at *you.* Nobody ever comes here but a lot of old women who want a meal." She choked and began to cry hysterically. "And a lot of old fools with silly religions."

Suddenly with a groan Mrs. Weatherby collapsed full length on the floor. She lay there crying out, calling upon Heaven to witness the ingratitude of this creature she had protected for so long. Miss Fosdick understood only fragments. "After I'm dead you'll remember. . . . After all I've done for you."

But Miss Fosdick felt suddenly seasick and ran from the room. The screams followed her along the corridor until she was in her own room with the door bolted behind her.

Sobbing, she seated herself at the dressing-table.

There was a light in her eye. At last the suppressed hatred of twenty years was satisfied. She had told Aunt Henrietta what she thought of her. The feeling was like a fresh cool breeze. It was all over. She was free . . . free with one hundred and thirty-two lira in the world, the savings of twenty years of slavery. Free, and there was nothing she could do, not even sew properly. But she was free. She could scrub floors. She was free.

In all the confusion the sprig of jasmine had come loose from her hair and had fallen into the V that revealed her plump white throat. She took it out and laid it on the table. Then when she had grown more calm, she regarded herself in the ancient mirror and fell to trying new ways of doing her hair. She couldn't go out into the world dressed in the ridiculous fashion that *she* had always commanded. Her hands trembled. She was afraid of herself and of this madness which had swept her without any effort of will into revolt. This was a strange woman who looked out of the mirror at her. Who was she? This creature born of the fires of hatred.

Then she let her hair fall down. It reached to her waist. Her hair, she told herself, had always been her great beauty even as a girl. She could not cut it.

Presently she rose feeling weak and shaken, and after drinking half a bottle of Fiuzzi water, went to the window for air. Far down below in the valley she could see a tiny light moving through the olive trees toward the stalled motor. Presently it reached the road, the lights of the motor flared up.

There was a sudden wild impatient roar and the car shot away toward Brinoë. As the lights disappeared around a curve of the valley, she suddenly felt seasick once more. The romance was gone and with it all the intoxication of her wild hysterical outburst. She was an old maid with one hundred and thirty-two lira in the world. She had not even a friend and there was no work that she could do. The fascinating Duque de Fuenterrabía would never even think of her again. She was quite certain now. The twenty years had driven her insane at last.

## VIII

For an hour Mrs. Weatherby lay on the floor waiting for Miss Fosdick to return and beg forgiveness. When at last the floor had grown impossibly hard and there seemed to be little chance of her companion coming back, she raised herself, and picked up the brush and the candle. Then for the first time she saw the card of Oreste Valmente, Duque de Fuenterrabía and Marqués de Santoban. Twice she read it through with awe and then thrust it reverently into the side of the blotchy mirror. Doing her thin hair into a knot, she walked down the corridor to Miss Fosdick's room, where a line of light showed beneath the door. For a moment she stood thoughtfully and then, knocking gently, she called out in the voice of a dove, "Gertrude. Gertrude *dear*."

There was no answer and she called again, "Gertrude. Gertrude."

Again only silence.

"Gertrude *dear*. Listen to Aunt Henrietta. You've broken her heart."

Still no response.

"Gertrude *dear*. Aunt Henrietta is willing to forgive. You wouldn't let a little quarrel like that break up all the love of twenty years?"

Not a word.

"Gertrude *dear*, let Aunt Henrietta go to bed knowing that you are sorry for the awful things you said."

In the end she went away, and in the morning when she went again to Miss Fosdick's room, she found it empty. Margharita, with a malicious gleam in her eye, said she had seen Miss Fosdick at dawn walking along the road to Monte Salvatore. She was carrying a handbag.

## A PRAIRIE IDYLL

### I

IN THE seventies the town of Cordova straggled its length along the highroad which once had been a trail across the prairies into the Far West. There were a few houses built of sawed timber, a few of the log houses that were remnants of its early days, a few shanties that served as dwelling-places for the negroes along the river, and the pretentious brick buildings of the Primitive Methodist Divinity School. The village sat pressed against a flat prairie so vast that it seemed to extend to the limits of the known world. The only break in the even line of its monotony was the sluggish meander-

ing river whose waters were red with the fertility
of the earth. To the south there extended a great
area of land that had once been only a vast marsh,
but with the passing of centuries the slow-moving
river had cut itself deeper and deeper into the soil,
draining the marsh and leaving it dry with a caked
peat-like surface which burned slowly with the
flameless intensity of rotten wood. In the seventies
there was so much rich land to be had that no one
paused on his way west to claim any of the bog,
and when the peat-like surface took fire it was allowed to burn until drowned by the flood-like rains
of the spring. Always there was some part of the
bog asmoulder, sending up great columns of white
smoke. The sight provided variety in a landscape
that otherwise was insanely monotonous. Sometimes the soil burned in a dozen places at once so
that the whole countryside to the south of Cordova took on the aspect of Hell, and sometimes
in the fantastic damp heat of the prairie summers
there appeared in it the mirages of lakes that
seemed made of smouldering brimstone. The water
in wells of that flat country was stale and flat and
without life.

It was to this town that Uriah Spragg and his
sister Annie came on the death of their mother, for
Uriah had set his mind on becoming a preacher of
the Primitive Methodist faith and to thus atone for
the colossal sins of his father, the Prophet. And
Uriah Spragg was no longer a young man and he
knew now that there was much to atone for. He
planned after he was ordained to go from place to
place in a wagon as his father had done, preaching

in villages and crossroads, wiping out the evil spread by the Prophet.

The burden of his father's sin was a thing which never left him.

He was a tall man, raw-boned in the parlance of the country, with great wrists and knuckles and knee-bones. Save for his great strength—he could straighten horseshoes and bend bars of iron—he had nothing in common with the Prophet. It was as if Nature had taken an impish delight in making father and son so unlike each other. Uriah's hair was sandy red and sparse; Uriah's lips were thin and always drawn a little, as if there was some pain forever gnawing him from within. His skin was pale and dry and covered with freckles; and his beard, which he shaved, was thin and scraggly. In his face there were deep furrows that seemed cut there by a careless chisel. His pale blue eyes had a way of wavering and shifting restlessly, so that they appeared never to be looking directly into the eyes of any person. It may have been the sense of his father's sin, the shame of being a son of the Prophet, which made him fearful and uneasy, for he was a sensitive man who suffered agonies. It was the soul of a woman in the body of a giant. And he was shy and silent and had no friends, for he believed that people were forever whispering about the doings of his father.

He came to Cordova to learn what he must learn, a man already on his way to middle age, to listen to sermons and read the teachings of Wesley with adolescent boys come out of the prairies and corn-fields, all like himself believing themselves chosen by God to spread His word. There were boys among them scarcely more than half his age and none of them was as old as his youngest sister Annie.

There was between Annie and Uriah a mysterious feeling which bound them together, as if they had been twins born of the same cell rather than brother and sister separated by twelve years with many brothers and sisters between. It may have been the knowledge that they were the two most cherished by the tired long-suffering woman who had borne them, or that they alone of all the thirteen understood the long agony of her lifetime. And they had known now for a long time, without once speaking of it, that their father was neither God nor God's Prophet nor even a good man, but only a lustful old reprobate who deceived himself into believing that he was God. It was a thought neither of them had ever uttered. They knew it. And when their mother died they went quickly away because Uriah was in haste to begin the atonement.

It had never occurred to either of them that on leaving the Saint's colony they should go separate ways. Having lived always a little apart from the world in the strange migratory life of the Prophet, having been steeped always in religion and Bible reading, they came to believe without knowing it that they were strange marked creatures who did not belong to the world as others did. As far back as they could remember the world had treated them as curiosities. There were always crowds about the wagon of the Prophet staring at him and his children . . . as if they were wild beasts.

II

At the time they came to Cordova Annie Spragg
was possessed of a strange wild beauty that passed
for plainness among the women of the place because
it had none of the chromo-like prettiness for which
their starved souls had a craving.   More discern-
ing and worldly critics would have discovered in her
figure and in her sly face a mysterious excitement
that stirred what was deepest and most carnal in
man.  Of all the thirteen legitimate children of the
Prophet she alone appeared to have been touched
by the same unholy power which he came to understand so well and to exploit with such profit.  The
two eldest sons had it not, for their joint imposture
of the Prophet had been discovered soon enough by
the women of the Saint's colony.  They were not
men enough to fill their father's shoes.

She was of middle height with red hair, not the
nondescript sandy red of Uriah's hair, but a deep
flaming red as her mother's hair had been on the
day the Prophet first saw her in her father's cabin
at St. Louis before she had borne thirteen children
in fifteen years; and her skin was not pale and
freckled like Uriah's, but of that waxen green-white
to be found in the women of Titian.  Her figure at
twenty-four was slim, but possessed of curves which
even stiff skirts and coarse black cloth could not
conceal.  Her eyes were greenish and of an odd
almond shape, slanting upward at the outer corners;
and her mouth was the mouth of the Prophet himself, red and full-blooded and voluptuous, with a disturbing power of excitement.  She had a gliding,

sinuous walk. Yet because love had not touched her, she went her way all unconscious of her power. Like Uriah, the dark unspoken things which they knew but never mentioned had made her afraid even of herself. Elsewhere, outside the lost village, she could have had what she wanted from the world, but in Cordova desire and the flesh were things to inspire horror. And always like a warning against the pale sky of that flat country rose the clouds of smoke from the burning bog, always the mirage of lakes of burning brimstone.

They rented one of the decaying log cabins from an old pioneer woman who had gone to live with her grandchildren, and when Uriah had stopped the holes in the roof and the walls they settled themselves in it until Uriah should be ordained. Though it was a thing never spoken of between them, they understood that neither of them should ever marry. Uriah had no desire to marry. Women had made his mother's life a long and passionate tragedy. She alone of all the women in the world was pure and good. He was afraid of women and hated them. There were even times when he hated his sister Annie for being a woman and the root of sin. He hated her for her fine shining hair and red lips, and for her sinuous walk.

III

Among all those who came to the seminary at Cordova believing they were the elect of God, there was a youth named Leander Potts, one of the nine sons of a farmer on the plains west of the Missis-

sippi. He had come in a way as an offering to God
from a father who was grateful for nine sons, but
he would have come whether his father permitted
it or not because he had seen visions while turning
the sod and knew that God had chosen him. And
his mother was a religious, who was half insane from
the loneliness of a prairie where there were no other
women. Leander was her darling and the one
chosen by her to follow God. To him had been
given the richest food. He alone had been given
books and the time to read them. When he came
to Cordova he was still an adolescent, chaste and
tempted, troubled by visions and dreams, carnal and
celestial. He was, too, a strong youth.

He was handsome in the florid way of Anglo-
Saxon youths, with curling blond hair and bright
blue eyes with long dark lashes like those of a girl.
At forty he would be ruddy and perhaps bloated.
At twenty he was like a young Florentine painted
by Leonardo.

It was Leander Potts who became the only friend
of Annie and Uriah Spragg. It was a slow thing,
this friendship, for Uriah with his pride and sense
of difference from the rest of the world, could make
no advances. And Annie stayed much at home, save
for solitary walks along the sluggish river when she
was happy, noticing the ways of the birds and beasts,
the trees and the flowers. Uriah acknowledged the
greetings of his fellow students, but chose never to
be the first to exchange a word regarding the
weather or the sermons. He had the sensitiveness
of a boy too old and too big for his schoolfellows.

He was all joints and knuckles, ashamed and flush-
ing easily.

But from the first day when he saw Leander's
curly yellow head before him in the chapel, he felt
drawn toward the boy. The sight of Leander was
like a ray of sunlight piercing the gloomy depths of
his soul, illuminating and warming it as no man or
woman save his mother had ever been able to do.
And Leander was, too, a sort of an ideal, a symbol
of all that which Uriah might have been save for
his age, his uncouthness and the scar upon his soul.
Leander seemed in truth the chosen of God—
comely, confident, young and, in a community made
harsh by fear of a terrible God, a creature bright
with charm. On the day he first spoke to Uriah,
the older man felt the skies open and saw the sun
pour through.

In Leander the first impulse to speak arose from
a sense of pity for Uriah, who even in that queer
community seemed strange and awkward and out
of place. It was Uriah's loneliness that touched
him, almost without his knowing it.

From that moment onward the older man came
to look for the boy's greeting as one who lives in a
dour climate looks for the sun. He plotted, without plotting, that he might encounter Leander during the day. To Annie, waiting for him at home, he
seemed to grow more cheerful and talkative. She
wondered at the reason, but she never asked him
and Uriah could not have told her why the world
seemed a better place, less black with sin.

As for Annie, she cooked and baked, and in order
to help Uriah with money she began to do sewing

for the women of the village. She even made an
entrance into that trade which all small towns as-
sociate with fast women. She became a milliner.
But the people of Cordova did not take kindly to
her. Her silence and aloofness disturbed them.
They came to know presently that she *was* the
daughter of the Prophet Spragg and so they gave
her a name for immorality and evil, a reputation
which her appearance, despite all her plain and ugly
clothes, could not deny. No matter how black her
dresses, there was something in the green slanting
eyes, the pointed nose, the red hair and the white
skin which made women draw together in little
groups like hens as she passed and caused men to
look after her as if their wills had turned to butter.
The wall of her isolation grew higher and higher,
shutting her in from all the world. And so she took
to going more and more on those solitary walks
along the river-bank. The river was the only relief from the monotony of that smoke-hazed world.

Because human companionship was denied her
she came to make friends of the birds and the tiny
beasts, the flowers and the rare trees of that flat
country. The very rabbits came to know her and
the birds along the river-bank awaited her coming
with the crumbs she brought from her table. It
was a happy life and she seemed content with it,
living only in dread of the coming of winter. Sometimes when she had gone a long way and could see
across the flat land that there was no one within
miles of her, she would take off her ugly black dress
and tight stays and bathe in a warm sluggish
stream, warming her naked body sinfully in the sun-

light. And all the while she drifted further and further from the dreadful God of Cordova. Uriah noticed it and reproved her. He saw her sit dreaming in the House of God, deaf to the harsh words of the Reverend Mr. Simpson, her mind wandering far from "a Hell paved with the skulls of unbaptized infants." And his fear for her would be shadowed at times with a strange dark cloud of hatred and envy, as if he understood somehow that she was secretly escaping him and the sins of their father and the justice of a vengeful God.

His friendship with Leander grew, bringing with it a disturbing and incomplete happiness. As the older of the two he gave Leander timid advice. Together they had long talks of the future, rising into a flame of passion at the glory of spreading abroad the Kingdom of God as taught in Cordova. They went on long rambles across a country where each mile was exactly like the last and the one before and talk could be the only diversion. Uriah always walked bent forward a little, his great bony hands clasped behind his back. And one day Uriah in a burst of fire proposed timidly that when they left Cordova they should set out together in a covered wagon carrying their message to remote villages and crossroads where men of God seldom came. Annie, his sister, said Uriah, could go with them and cook and mend their clothes. Life seemed to become a bright and beautiful thing.

Leander said, "But your sister. I have never seen your sister. I will go home with you tonight and see her."

But Uriah's face grew dark and he was silent.

torn between a desire to take the beloved Leander
to his home and an obscure and nameless fear of
having Leander lay eyes upon his sister Annie.

IV

Leander did come to the house, not that day but
another, one evening just after the long prairie sunset. Uriah was not there and Annie asked him in
to await her brother's coming. The meeting disturbed them both, but in Leander's feelings there
was no pity for Annie as there had been for Uriah.
He was confused and frightened. For a long time
now he had been aware of women, but he had never
been aware of one woman, and there was something
about this strange girl which seemed to be the
apotheosis of all women. He watched her, afraid
but fascinated, while she went quietly about her work
in the kitchen, making polite and halting remarks
about the weather or the corn or the sermon of the
Reverend Mr. Simpson. It was all outwardly cold
and meaningless and inwardly charged with disturbing things. Leander was aware of her in every
nerve and muscle. Annie, watching him stealthily,
was aware of a new beauty come into her life. Of
late during the long walks by the river life had
seemed to be opening like a flower, petal by petal,
in a loveliness she had never suspected. And now
came this beautiful young man with blue eyes and
fair curling hair like an angel.

Uriah came at last, dark-browed and forbidding,
and when Annie suggested that his friend stay to

supper, he could not send Leander away. Leander did stay and all through supper Annie sat modestly with eyes cast down while her brother and his friend talked of the church and of God.

After that Leander came more and more often, though there was little talk between him and Annie. Evening after evening she sat quietly apart in the darkness by the fireplace while the two men read the Scriptures and interpreted them. Sometimes she sat watching Leander's golden head from under her long lashes without being seen and sometimes when he was reading she stole sudden quick glances at his odd disturbing beauty. Always Uriah took care that the atmosphere should be saturated with the words of the Bible. He fought his battle in silence, filled with a corroding jealousy, knowing always that Leander was there because of Annie and not because of himself or of God. Craftily he chose to read and expound passages filled with sonorous warnings against unchastity, of the evils of the flesh and of desire. He read always in the cold tight voice of one in pain.

And presently Leander came to look ill. The high color left his cheeks and there was a tired look in his blue eyes. At night his visions and dreams grew more and more fantastic and troubled, filled with strange beasts like those out of the Apocalypse. Annie gave him pennyroyal tea to drink lest he be coming down with the fevers that swept the hot, damp prairies, and as he drank she watched him closely out of the green, veiled, slanting eyes. Leander knew now when she was watching him. It

was as if her gaze burned into his flesh and set his
blood on fire. Slowly Uriah grew confident again,
believing that he had won and kept the soul of
Leander unstained by the sin of desire that had
damned his own father. Annie said nothing, for
they never spoke of such things.

v

Six months after Leander first came to the cabin,
a tenth child was born in the house where he lodged
and there was no longer room for him. Nor was
there any room in all the village save in the house of
Annie and Uriah Spragg. He came there with his
carpet-bag and tin trunk to live in the extra room,
and after that there was no longer any peace in the
house, but only smothered passion and hatred and
jealousy. Uriah, more terrified than before, talked
much and hysterically of their mission, saying that
they must give themselves in chastity to God alone,
looking neither to right nor to left. Leander de-
voured himself with desire and a sense of sin.

One night in midsummer when the heat and stillness of the country was intolerable, the three of
them sat as usual in the single common room. It
was Leander's turn to read the Scripture and he
chose to read from the Song of Songs which is Solomon's, showing the Mutual Love of Christ and his
Church. He plunged deep into the middle of it as
if he had been reading it again and again and knew
each verse, and he read in a loud and terrible voice
shaken with his inward illness. Crying out, he read,

"How beautiful are thy feet with shoes, O Princess: the joints of thy thighs are like jewels, the work of the hands of a cunning workman.

"Thy navel is like a round goblet, which wanteth not liquor: thy belly is like a heap of wheat set about with lilies.

"Thy two breasts are like two young roes that are twins.

"Thy neck is as a tower of ivory; thine eyes like the fish pools of Heshbon, by the gate of Bathrabbim: thy nose is as the tower of Lebanon which looketh toward Damascus.

"Thine head upon thee is like Carmel, and the hair of thine head like purple; the king is held in the galleries.

"How fair and how pleasant art thou, O Love, for delights.

"This thy stature is like to a palm tree, and thy breasts to clusters of grapes.

"I said, I will go up to the palm tree, I will take hold of the boughs thereof; now also thy breasts shall be as clusters of the vine, and the smell of thy nose like apples.

"And the roof of thy mouth like the best wine for my beloved, that goeth down sweetly, causing the lips of those that are asleep to speak.

"I am my beloved's, and his desire is toward me."

In her corner Annie Spragg stopped seeing. She clasped her hands together lest their trembling betray her. Uriah Spragg sat upright and very still, his bony hands hanging at his side, his furrowed face ashen and drawn and strangely like the

head of death.   He looked neither to one side nor
the other.   It was as if he did not hear the passionate voice of Leander, torn and twisted by the
dark things in his soul.

And Annie Spragg *knew* now, for the words of
Solomon had made her aware of her body.

When Leander had finished and put down the
book, Uriah without a word reached out a knotty
hand and took it from him.   In silence he turned
the pages and then in the cold strangled voice that
was so different from the warm, rich voice of the
Prophet, he read,

"We have heard it said of them of old time, Thou
shalt not commit adultery.

"But I say unto you, that whosoever looketh upon
a woman to lust after her hath committed adultery
with her already in his heart."

When he had finished, he closed the book without a word and, rising, went into his own room, leaving them alone.   Leander rose and in silence rushed
through the open door out into the cornfields.   And
Annie, sitting alone in her corner, heard the voice of
her brother raised in prayer.

VI

All the next morning the three in the cabin went
the mean small round of their existence betraying
no sign of recognizing the thing that had happened.
Life went on the same as if by denying the thing
they could annihilate its existence.   But at noonday

neither Leander nor Uriah came home for dinner. Annie waited for them and when at last she gave up all hope of their coming, she locked the house and set out for a walk along the river.

It was a hot still afternoon, damp with the smell of growing corn turning to milk in the ear, and she walked slowly, stopping now and then to rest in the shade of the feathery willows and witch-hazel that grew in the fertile soil by the edge of the stream. Two little birds followed her, twittering and flying from bush to bush. Once while she was resting three quail came out from among the rows of corn to eat the crusts she brought them. The mud turtles, instead of slipping in alarm from logs and stones into the water, watched her with staring beady eyes, unafraid. The bluejays out of vulgar friendliness kept up a wild screeching and calling.

She wandered on and on, sadly and in a kind of dream, not knowing why it was she felt so tired and so confused, knowing only that the heat and the smell of the corn seemed to fill her with an over-powering desire to sleep. She had walked for miles and miles when she came at last to a spot which long ago she had chosen for her own. It lay in a wide bend of the meandering stream so that the fragment of earth was almost an island. In an-other year the spring floods would have cut through the narrow neck and isolated it, leaving it to be washed away bit by bit in the years that followed, into the distant ocean that Annie had never seen. No one had ploughed this land and it lay overgrown with a thicket of golden-rod and sumach and gen-tians. Here she had come alone many times. There

was a kind of bower where she lay whole after-
noons watching the ways of the birds and the
beetles, the turtles and the ants. Sometimes she fell
asleep, to awake only when the afternoon sun had
fallen low on the prairie and the cool of evening
had begun.

Today she pushed her way through the briars
into the bower and flinging herself down yielded to
the hunger for sleep.

## VII

It was late when she awakened slowly, aware of
a faint pleasant sound of splashing somewhere near
her, a sound that was cool, as if the water touched
her own hot troubled brow. Slowly she sat up and
looking out from the bower, she saw the cause of
the noise. On the log in the midst of the stream
sat Leander with his back to her, quite naked. He
was splashing his feet in the water and sending it
high in the air to fall down in glistening drops over
his blond head and white body.

A strange, voluptuous weakness filled her body
so that she could not rise. She felt that she must
be dying. She knew that if she did rise she could
not escape lest he notice her and know that she had
seen him thus. She was frozen to the earth, fascinated and helpless, and suddenly Leander slipped
into the reddish water and swam away toward the
far shore. She tried to cover her face with her
hands, but she could not move them to her face.
On the sloping bank opposite Leander was lifting
a great stone high above his head. She saw the

muscles flow beneath the white skin as he lifted it higher and higher until with a gesture of triumph in his own strength he hurled it from him into the midst of the cornfield. Then he ran and leaped and turned cartwheels on the thick red-black soil, and Annie, burying her face in the thick grass to shield it from what she kept seeing, felt a sudden wave of sickening beauty, of a kind she had never known before. It was a new world, as unknown to her as it was to the people of Cordova. Beauty and delight in life flowed in upon her, dazzling and blinding her, and with a great sense of freshness and freedom, as if she were herself for the first time, she pressed her face against the earth and wept.

When she raised her head again he was gone, and pulling herself to her feet she pushed her way through the bushes and ran along the edge of the high corn, keeping close against the willows and sumach for fear that he might see her and know that she had seen him in his nakedness. When she had run a long way, she fell from exhaustion and lay panting.

"From this day," she thought, "I am a lost woman." For she knew now that she was sick with desire for Leander.

In the south the bog was afire and the white smoke drifted slowly up in a great cloud against the prairie sky. In it the lakes of brimstone swam and flickered in the heat.

## VIII

She found Uriah waiting for her, his narrow eyes dark with suspicion and accusation, but neither of them said anything. They waited for Leander to return and at last at dark when he had not come in they sat down to eat without speaking to each other. It was nine o'clock and Uriah had been many times to the door looking out into the darkness when at last Leander appeared. He was hatless and in his hand he carried Annie Spragg's sunbonnet. Looking at her with a queer expression in his blue eyes, he said, "I found it by the bend in the river. I knew it was yours."

It was a strange accusing look as if he believed that she had been spying on him. Behind it lay a mist of shocked and confusing thoughts. She took the bonnet and ran into her room, closing the door and bolting it.

But she did not sleep. It was as if a demon had taken possession of her. She heard Uriah and Leander talking, talking, talking, still as if nothing unusual had occurred. She heard them reading the Scripture, Uriah in his tight pinched voice, Leander in his low warm soft one. She heard one of them go to bed and then the other. The light disappeared and all the house fell into darkness. She lay thinking, "I am an evil woman. I am cursed as my father was before me. I had better die. I had better kill myself at once."

Her love for Leander was so great that she could no longer breathe in peace. And he had said nothing. Perhaps tomorrow he would go away and she

would never see him again. They could not go on
like this. Perhaps if she did not kill herself, Uriah
would kill her. She had thought of late that there
was a look of cold murder in his eye. They could
not go on like this.

She did not know how long she lay thus tormenting herself, but toward morning she rose, thinking
to go into the kitchen for a drink of water from the
pail that stood there. It was not clear sparkling
water, but the dead stale water of the flat country.
In the darkness she made her way through the common room into the kitchen. She found the pail.
She was raising the dipper to her hot parched lips
when there was a sound of a door opening. She
pressed against the wall listening and presently
someone crossed the common room and entered
the kitchen. She thought, "It may be Uriah coming
to kill me." And then with a sudden sick feeling,
"It may be Leander. He, too, could not sleep."
But in the blackness she could not make certain.

She heard the figure in the dark fumbling at the
latch of the kitchen door. The door opened against
the blue of the prairie night and she saw that it was
Leander. He was dressed and in his hand he carried his carpet-bag. He was going away and she
would never see him again. She grew cold and
trembled and wanted to cry out, "Don't go,
Leander. Don't go. I am here waiting for you.
Nothing makes any difference." He must not go
away. He must not go away.

And then, although she had not cried out, he
hesitated for a moment as if he had felt her standing there in the darkness, and putting down the bag

he turned and made his way toward the water pail. He was coming nearer and nearer. He was beside her now, he would see her in a moment. In a low voice, she said, "It's me, Annie. Leander, you mustn't go away."

She heard him make a sudden quick movement of terror and echo, "Annie," and then it seemed to her that they were enveloped by a flame.

IX

In the morning he was gone and he did not return all that day though she went a hundred times to the door of the cabin to look for him. And he did not return the next day or the next. On the fourth day they found him. It was Uriah who made the discovery. Leander was lying at the bend in the river a little way from Annie's bower. He was dead and his gun lay beside him. He had shot himself through the head.

It was Uriah who brought her the news. He told the story simply, as if he did not know the reason why Leander had destroyed himself or that it meant anything at all to her. There was only the look in the pale blue eyes, so cold, so full of hatred that Annie Spragg turned away and hid her face. Uriah Spragg had now to atone for the sin of his sister as well as the sin of his father. They never spoke of it again, for it was their habit never to speak of sins but only of sin. And they never spoke again of Leander.

But they had to leave Cordova before Uriah was ordained because people began to whisper that they were evil because they were children of the Prophet, and that Annie was a witch and a bad woman. They even whispered that between them the brother and sister had made way with Leander because of the things he knew. One morning Annie found under the door a crude, misspelled letter warning them that if they did not leave the town before nightfall they would be tarred and feathered and driven out. They left and took up a life of wandering, for there was no place in all the world where they belonged.

## A SENTIMENTAL PASSAGE

### I

WHEN Anna d'Orobelli left Father d'Astier before the door of the tall house where he stayed when in Brinoë, their parting was a simple good-night. There was not even a pressure of the hand, for a curious and unfamiliar restraint had taken possession of them both. All the way from the Villa Leonardo, they had driven side by side in silence while the big motor roared up hill and down through the yellow dust. At the door she did not even wait for him to mount the steps and disappear, but turned the car and rushed away across the Piazza. She was late already and at forty-nine a woman could ill afford to keep a lover waiting. But she was driven, too, by a fierce desire to escape the quiet eyes of Father d'Astier. He had, she thought, come at last to make a truce with life, and so he was calm and filled with peace. He had rest and that was a precious thing.

She fled from him as she might have tried to flee
her own conscience. Father d'Astier *was* all the
conscience she had, and now he had turned up in
Brinoë when she wanted least to encounter him.
Who could have expected to find him there in the
horrible heat of August when everybody fled Brinoë?
(In her mind echoed the shadow, "Anybody who
is anybody." Not seedy people, of course, like
those she had encountered this afternoon.) Oh, he
knew well enough why she was there and what she
was doing. That was why he had been so silent, as
if she were betraying him. But he had been reasonable enough, all things considered; he had never reproached her but once and then only by the inscription on the fly-leaf of the Thomas-à-Kempis. He
had kept silent, which in a way was worse than if
he had spoken, especially when you had loved him
for nearly thirty years.

At the door of the Palazzo Biancamano, she
turned the motor over to the chauffeur. "At five
tomorrow, Enrico," she said, looking a little away
from him. Enrico, too, knew why she was in
Brinoë. He knew why she had driven through the
dust and heat all the way from Venice in August.
She would not need the motor until five because she
and Oreste would spend the heat of the day in the
apartment.

As the motor drove off she turned and looked up
at the windows of the apartment with that sudden
feeling of sickness and ecstasy which always over-
came her at such times. The windows were still
dark. She was in time. He had not come yet.

II

It was not her own apartment. She hated Brinoë because she thought the people who lived there dull and stuffy and full of gossip. It was an apartment loaned her by Nina de Paulhac, Nina knowing well enough what it was to be used for. A great many people knew, she thought, and yet what difference did it make? Your friends were your friends no matter what you did, and the others did not matter. Only she must not make a fool of herself. When women were old, love sometimes made them silly. She mustn't be an old fool like Mrs. Whitby, running after gigolos and dubious dukes at sixty.

The apartment was strange to her and there was only Ottilia, the *femme de ménage*, to show her about. Ottilia knew why she was there. Well, better that she did know. Then there wouldn't be any violated innocence. She wondered how many times the apartment had been lent to others for the same purpose.

Swarthy, moustached, with ox-like eyes, Ottilia showed her the bedrooms and the two baths.

"I am hard," she thought. "But what of it? God knows I've reason to be hard. Only where love is concerned, I am not hard. It's always me that suffers. You can't be really hard if you go on being hurt again and again."

She told Ottilia to keep the supper hot. "It's impossible to ruin Italian food," she thought. And aloud, "I'm expecting a friend to dine with me."

Yes. Ottilia knew. Signora de Paulhac had written her.

She wished Ottilia wouldn't smile like that with her eyes. Was she smiling just because she took that friendly interest which all Latins have in an intrigue, or because she thought it ridiculous in a woman of her age to have a lover? She must be about the same age as Ottilia, although Ottilia looked ten years older. Would Ottilia be going downstairs to regale other servants below with the tale? What did it matter? What did anything matter? "It is silly," she thought, "for a woman of my age and experience to behave always as if it were the first time, always worrying what people might say, always afraid of being caught." There wasn't anybody in the world who cared if she was caught, certainly not Faustino. A husband like that could be made *cocu* a thousand times in public and he wouldn't care at all so long as she gave him money for electric toys and a train to run by real steam around the garden at Venterollo—"like the children in the Bois riding to the Jardin d'Acclimatation the way I used to do. My God! How long ago was that? I mustn't think of it. I mustn't think. Perhaps that's why I've always kept my lovers so long, because it's always like the first time, always a renewal, a rebirth of love, rising from its own ashes. It was always exciting when it was like that. There was no growing *blasé*."

For a long time she lay in the hot water, allowing it to soothe her, to set loose all the nerves made taut by the wretched visit to the Villa Leonardo. When at last she rose and dried herself, she covered her body with a scented powder made for herself alone, and then fell to regarding it in the mirror.

It was not an old body, but firm and young, and the face was not old.

"Nina looks old sometimes, because she gets tired. It's vitality that counts in this world. It's the only thing. I'm never tired. Faustino was old and tired at thirty-four when I married him."

Her hair, cut short but not too short, was a fine artificial red. "Thank Heaven," she thought, "I've dyed it for so many years that no one remembers it was ever any other color. It's swimming that preserves the figure. Swimming and sun and exercise. If women would only learn that." She thought of Oreste and of the many women who envied her, and she grew warm with triumph. Oreste was at least five years younger than herself, only he didn't know. "I am carnal woman," she thought, "and quite pleased with myself." She thought suddenly of the curious piece of sculpture found in the garden of the preposterous Mrs. Weatherby. The memory of it gave her strange and voluptuous excitement.

Then she put on a pale green peignoir the color of sea-water and a collar of pearls.

### III

There was a loggia off the salon which hung above the river. It was quite dark now and the moon had risen above the circling hills. The air was still hot, but the insane wind from Africa had died away at last.

"It is after nine," she thought. "He is late. He counted on being here by seven."

She walked out into the loggia and leaning on the

stone balustrade looked down.   Below her the river
flowed in the moonlight a pale golden yellow,
shrunken by the drought to the size of a brook.   It
smelled badly.   Save for a pair of lovers the long
bare quai was empty.   The lovers leaned against
the river wall, two small black figures melted into
a single passionate shadow.   Presently on the
bridge just beneath appeared the dimmed lights of a
motor.

"There he is now," she thought.   The motor
turned slowly into the street below and moved toward the Palazzo Biancamano, and the old feeling
of sickness swept over her.   He was coming nearer
and nearer.   He would stop now at the door— She
waited, but he did not stop.   The motor went slowly
on.   Perhaps he had mistaken the way or did not
know the house.   But that could not be.   He knew
Brinoë well.   He knew Nina's apartment.   Perhaps
he had had a small accident on the way, an accident
that had delayed him but not injured him, and he
had telegraphed, only they had failed to deliver the
telegram.   Things like that happened in Italy.   It
wasn't any better with the Fascisti, no matter how
much they said to the contrary.   You couldn't change
the whole character of a race overnight.   In
America. . . . What was America like now?   It
was eighteen years since she had last been there.
Queer that she always thought of it as "home"
when she had lived in Europe more than half her
life.

In one of the apartments below someone had begun to play a piano and to sing.   It was familiar

music but she could not place it. The voice of the
soprano was young. It sang a little uncertainly.

Newport. What was Newport like now? Who
lived in the old house with the ugly stone turrets?
Her room had been the one in the turret above the
porte cochère . . . the room she had left to marry
Faustino, Principe d'Orobelli, Conte di Venterollo.
Well, it had sounded splendid enough to suit her
mother—her mother, who was having an affair with
a dentist years younger than herself. Wilkins was his
name, Herbert Wilkins. We are bad blood (she
thought). But there were plenty of other girls willing to take her place. Faustino was getting money
and she was becoming a Princess—Princess d'Orobelli. A fool she was, knowing nothing about anything . . . nothing about life. Thank God, girls
today were different, especially American girls; they
knew what they were doing.

There was another motor coming across the
bridge. It wasn't Oreste. It was a camion, rumbling and rattling through the stillness of the night.

"I mustn't watch for him," she thought. "If I
watch it will only make him later."

The voice belowstairs kept on singing. She knew
the music now. It was the Rosenkavalier—the
music of the Feldmarschallin in the first act. The
voice was singing in French and not too good
French. Probably an American girl studying in
Italy. A Viennese opera sung in French by an
American in Brinoë. The world was getting like
that. She, an American married to an Italian, had
a Spanish lover. What did it matter? What did
anything matter except staying young, like that fresh

uncertain voice and the dark pair of lovers on the quai. The voice was like silver.

"*Mais comment est-il donc possible que l'enfant que j'étais jadis puisse un jour connaître la vieillesse? Etre une Vieille! La Vieille Maréchale! Voyez, c'est elle, la vieille Princesse.*"

A bell rang somewhere in the apartment. She listened. Surely it was the telegram, perhaps explaining why he was late. A door opened. There was the sound of Ottilia's voice talking to someone with a man's voice, and then a laugh and then the door closing again. Ottilia would be coming now in a moment with the telegram. She stepped inside from the loggia, but Ottilia didn't come. What was keeping her? When a telegram came she ought to bring it in. All Italians were the same—hopeless.

Suddenly she rang with a too great violence, thinking at once, "I have lost all control of myself. I mustn't do that." There was another thought in the back of her mind which she kept pushing from her so that she might not even recognize it for what it was.

Ottilia was standing before her.

"The bell rang, Ottilia. Was it something for me?"

"No, Eccellenza. It was my cousin coming to pay me a visit."

Eccellenza! Eccellenza! Where had Ottilia learned that absurd method of address? If I watch for him he will never come. I must not be cross with Ottilia. Being rude to servants is a worse crime in the eyes of God than adultery. Most

Latins are horrible to their servants. Faustino
treats them like dogs.

She found herself in the loggia, watching, watching. "Well," she thought, "I'm here again, watching, without knowing it. There's no use going back
now."

She began to see herself all at once as another
woman whom she regarded from a great distance.

It was a funny thing what life did to you. Who
would have thought that the girl being married in
the garden at Newport would have turned into the
woman waiting in the loggia for Oreste? One
would have said that there was no connection between the two, but the chain was simple and clear
enough. It fitted together link by link, beginning
with Faustino. If a woman had a husband like
Faustino what could you expect of her? It wasn't
in her nature to be a *religieuse,* wearing black and
doing good deeds. After what had happened with
Faustino she wanted only life and more life. He
hadn't broken her. Only three months she had
lived with him, but that was long enough—too long,
because it was long enough for her to conceive a
child, not a child, but a monster, an idiot. Her own
good blood hadn't been strong enough to overcome
the taint of Faustino's life and blood. It wasn't
easy to think that your first-born was a cripple and
an idiot, and a grown man now. He must be twenty-
six, shut up always at Venterollo with his father.
She hadn't seen him in years. How many? Well,
she wouldn't think of that. After all, he wasn't
much more insane than Faustino himself.

She'd think instead of Victor because Victor was

a boy to be proud of, with red hair, people said, like
his mother's.   Only her hair had never been red.
It was the red hair of his father—not Faustino,
praise God, not Faustino but of Nigel.   Victor
wasn't a d'Orobelli.   He wasn't even Italian.   He
was son of Nigel Burnham.

Another automobile was crossing the bridge.
No, that wasn't Oreste either.   His motor was grey
and long.   If I watch for him he'll never come.   Ottilia said her cousin.   More likely it's her lover.
I can't go inside and sit there alone.   O God, don't
let anything happen to Oreste!

And Faustino didn't care that Victor wasn't his
son, even though he knew it.   Victor was the heir,
the next Prince d'Orobelli.   He had saved the line,
Victor, the son of an English father and an American mother, Victor, product of six happy weeks in
Malta.   I was young then.   I thought I wanted to
dabble in archæology instead of life.   Maybe it
would have been better; I shouldn't be standing
here now, suffering.   Six weeks in Malta.   No, that
was worth all this suffering when you thought of the
happiness, even the happiness of thinking about it
now, years afterward.   I am old, she thought.
Everything is measured in years now instead of
months.   There had never been anything quite like
Nigel, nothing so young and clean and unspoiled.
It was probably his first affair, and mine, O God,
mine was with Faustino, my husband.   A clean affair like that with Nigel must be better in the eyes
of God than legitimate marriage with a beast like
Faustino.   Odd how she thought of him always as
he had been in Malta in his uniform as officer of

His Majesty's Navy and never as she had seen him last in Monte Carlo, middle-aged, an admiral, with two daughters growing up into tall blonde English girls. Nigel was young, all youth. And she had been young then, too, young save for the stain of Faustino. And Victor was like Nigel, as if Nigel had never grown old at all but simply changed into a son. That was why she loved Victor better than Amadeo, Jim Cain's child.

"*Le temps,*" sang the voice, "*est subtil comme un poison; on ne le sent pas, tant qu'on s'aime; mais soudain, un jour, on ne sent plus que lui. Il est autour de nous, il pénétre en nous-même. En nous sans cesse il glisse; dans le miroir il coule; il ride nos pauvres visages; même entre nous son onde coule encore, sans bruit, silencieuse. Oh, mon ami! . . .*"

O God! Stop her singing! Send Oreste safely to me!

Odd how you could love in so many ways. Love with Nigel was like the morning sunlight streaming in at the windows. And with Jim Cain it was mixed with pity. Jim Cain, who thought himself a gentleman because he hadn't vitality enough to be positive. It was queer how quickly families went to seed in America, in three generations. Jim thought that doing nothing meant being a gentleman. He *was* a gentleman, but only by environment and accident. I could have married him instead of Faustino, but I'm glad that I didn't. I should have died of boredom with him. And I could not have betrayed him. I'd have been so sorry for him. Jim would worry a great deal about his honor, because he thought that

was one of the marks of a gentleman. And he was
dead now for three years. And Amadeo was like
him. Nobody had ever suspected Amadeo but Faustino. Faustino *knew* Amadeo wasn't *his* child. And
Jim's cousin Sabine, who suspected everything and
everybody . . . she even dared to speak of Amadeo
as "my cousin."

"I mustn't think these things," she told herself.
"It's a bad omen, as if I were *really* an old woman
looking back over my life. I mustn't act as if everything was finished. It *isn't* finished. It *isn't* finished."

The thought kept pressing in upon her closer and
closer. I must push it away. I mustn't even let it
take shape. It's nearly eleven now. O God, send
him to me. O God, just this once more. Don't
make me an old woman. I'm still young. My heart
is young. My soul is young. O God, don't take
him from me.

A motor-horn was sounding somewhere across
the river in the direction of the Palazzo Gonfarini.
It's a German horn, like the one Oreste has. If I
wait, if I cross my fingers, it will turn into Oreste.
Such miracles may happen, only we never know
about them. He might have taken the road by
Monte Salvatore. No, it isn't Oreste. It sounds
farther away now. It was going the other direction.
It was *climbing* the hill *toward* San Marco. How
high the moon is, at the very top of the sky.

Jean could have saved me. Jean was the only
one I ever loved. Queer that never once in twenty-
five years have I called him Jean, but always Father
d'Astier, politely, respectfully, as if there was noth-

ing between us.  He was the only one before whom
I'd have grovelled on the ground, kissing his feet
because he was a man and a good man.  And it was
his *goodness* that spoiled everything.  We could
have run away, anywhere, giving up everything, even
though he was a priest.  What difference would it
have made in the end?  Who would have cared?
And now he is an old man with peace in his soul
who thinks me a harlot.  It is your fault, Jean.  It
is your fault.  You could have taken me when you
wanted me, that time at Caporolla in the garden or
at Nina's or the night at Brufani's when Fate
brought us together alone.  You could have saved
me, Jean.  You could have saved me!  I'd have
been with you tonight happy to sit by you, instead
of here in the loggia waiting for Oreste.  But you
turned your back and contented yourself with writing pious sayings in a book and looking at me in silence out of your black eyes.  God understands.
God must know that what you did was a sin.  And
still you can have peace and faith, shutting me out.
Shutting me out.

(The thought was near now, far too near to be
put away.)  The city is quiet.  There isn't even the
sound of a motor-horn or the faint music from the
Piazza.  The moon has passed the zenith and
everyone is in bed . . . everyone but me who stands
listening and watching in the loggia.  Even the
lovers have gone away.  They are young, happy
creatures, they are young.  There are years before
them, and before me—perhaps a single night, a
week, a month.  O God, send him to me.

(The thought cried out aloud.)  He is not com-

ing now. It is too late. He is never coming. It is
all over now. I am too old. Tomorrow he will
write me giving excuses and letting me know that
it's ended and again I shall be hurt as if I'd never
learned anything. O God, dón't let me be hurt this
last time, this last time when I am saying good-by
to youth, to love, to everything. Love, God, that's
all I've ever had. I'm not a clever woman. I'm not
a good woman. I've never had anything but love.

She found her nails digging into the stone of the
balustrade. "I must go in now," she thought. "I
mustn't stand here any longer. I'm being a fool,
an old fool like Kitty Whitby. I mustn't do that.
I've always been discreet. I've been dignified. O
God, if only You had given me faith and peace like
Jean. O God, it was You and the Church who took
Jean from me. I'd have been a good wife to him.

*He's not coming now. He's never coming at all.
It's too late. It's all over.*

She went inside and threw herself down on the
sofa, where she lay for a long time not knowing
what she thought, or even whether she was alive.
And slowly when she had wept and wept she began
to feel calm again and cool.

I must not be a fool, she told herself. It's over
now and there's nothing to be done. I must make
the most of it. Perhaps if I pray God will send me
peace and faith. I must be an old woman now. I
must go out in dignity. It's time now. Victor is
a man now and he mustn't hear people laugh at his
mother. The past is the past, but Victor is old
enough now to understand. Victor, Nigel's son.

Nigel, who was like the morning sun streaming in at the windows. He is getting old, too.

She rose and rang the bell and standing in the shadow so that Ottilia should not see she had been weeping, she told her to serve the supper and then go to bed.

I must not let her know that he is not coming. I must not let her know that it matters to me. Aloud she said, "You can leave the supper on the table. I'll serve myself."

Ottilia knew that he wasn't coming. You could tell by the look in her ox-like eyes. They weren't smiling any longer. They had in them a gleam of sympathy. That was because the "cousin" was a lover. Ottilia understood. To be pitied by a servant! In love women were all of one kind. There were no princesses and no servants.

When Ottilia had placed the supper on the table and gone away, the Princess rose and going into the bathroom disposed of the soup and a portion of the vegetables so that in the morning Ottilia would not think that she had been unable to eat. She did this in the proper order so that if Ottilia came in suddenly she would not find all the food disposed of miraculously at once. But Ottilia did not return.

Then she drank coffee, thinking perhaps if I stay awake and pray all night God will send me faith and peace like Jean's. She took out the Thomas-à-Kempis that Jean had given her long ago, and tried to read it. It was a thing she carried with her always, more precious than her pearls, not because of what it contained, but because he had given it to her. He had held it in his hands and had written

in it.   He had beautiful hands.   She always saw
them when she read out of the Thomas-à-Kempis.
She read *from* what he had written with his beautiful hands.

*Dans la damnation le feu est la moindre chose;
le supplice propre au damné est le progrès infini
dans le vice et dans le crime, l'âme s'endurcissant,
se dépravant toujours, s'enfonçant nécessairement
dans le mal de minute en progression géométrique
pendant l'éternité.*

                                        *Michelet.*

That was true, but its truth did not change the
ways of humanity.   It went on just the same.   It
was a clever thought, but not strong enough to
overcome and subdue the body that shut you in, a
prisoner.   I will wear black, she thought, and de-
vote myself to hospitals and the poor.   Perhaps a
legend will grow up about me—the woman who had
given all to life and turned in the end to God and
the church.   That would be a fitting end to the
story, a fine way to end it, and it was only the end
that mattered now.

She wept a little, pitying herself, and then read
some more out of the little book, passages which she
had read many times.

"O Lord, let that become possible to me by Thy
grace, which by nature seemed impossible to me.

"Thou knowest that I am able to suffer but little,
and that I am quickly cast down, when a slight ad-
versary ariseth.

"For Thy Name's sake, let every tribulation be
made pleasant and desirable to me: for to suffer and

to be disquieted for Thy sake is very wholesome for my soul."

"Jean sought to cure me," she thought, "by giving me a book when he should have given me himself."

Perhaps if I read now God will reward me and send Oreste, after all. But that is foolish. I have never prayed to God except when I am unhappy. He must remember that. I only come to Him when I want to beg something of Him. No, the end must be in black. All great harlots become pious in their old age, as if faith could take the place of love.

She tried to read, but she did not know what she was reading. She kept thinking of the excuses Oreste would write tomorrow and thinking, "If I wear black I had best go to Worth. He will make me look discreet and respectable and chic. I shall be able to wear black without becoming an old horror. Satin I shall wear and black velvet. How people will talk when I am no longer seen about, when they hear that I have shut myself up at Venterollo with Faustino and my idiot son. Perhaps they will come and see me there. Surely God won't mind that. I can have Nina come. I can even have people to stay. God wouldn't mind that.

"But he that is wise and well-instructed in the Spirit is raised above these mutable things: not heeding what he feeleth in himself, of which way the wind of instability bloweth; but studies only that his mind may be directed to its supreme and final good.

"For thus he will be able to continue throughout one and the selfsame, and unshaken. . . ."

She tried to read on and on, calming her soul with

the long, quiet, beautiful periods, but she could not
see the page for the feeling of sickness which came
over her. People, she thought, must feel like this
when they are condemned to death. For me to be
old is to die.

Suddenly she flung herself down once more on
the sofa and began to weep. It was no use. It was
all over. She hadn't it in her to shut herself away
from life. And she never loved Oreste as much as
she had loved him tonight. O God, send him to me.
No, I must not do that. (She sat up.) I will
be courageous. It is all over. Tomorrow I will
go to Jean and ask him where I can go into retreat,
to begin another life. I will break completely with
the past and never see any of them again, not even
Nina. (She rose and walked to the mirror.) I am
old now. I should never weep. It makes me look
weary like Nina. It's only then that I look *really*
old. I am old. I am finished. I must find peace
now in God. I must go out in a beautiful dignity.
If I say it over and over again, I will believe it and
have peace . . . peace such as Jean has. I am old.
I am old. I am old.

It did make her feel more calm, more peaceful.
She sat down once more and opened the *Imitation
of Christ,* but as she opened it she saw again the
beautiful hands of Father d'Astier.

I am calmer now, she told herself. I will read it
through each day and in the end I will be saved.

"Prepare not thyself for much rest, but for great
patience.

"Seek true peace, not in earth, but in heaven: not
in men, nor in any other creature, but in God alone.

"For the love of God thou oughtest cheerfully to undergo all things, that is to say, all labor and pain, temptation, vexation, anxiety, necessity, infirmity, injury, obloquy, reproof, humiliation, confusion, correction and scorn."

Perhaps it was true. Perhaps there was such peace to be had on earth. In the end she would find it, like Jean, and be content. It was all over now. I am old, I am old.

"Nevertheless in all these they bore themselves patiently, and trusted rather in God than in themselves; knowing that 'the sufferings of the present time are not worthy to be compared with the glory that should be revealed in them.' . . ."

There was a bell ringing again, distantly, ardently. Perhaps it was he. O God, send me Oreste! Just this once . . . this last time. Why isn't Ottilia answering it? O God, send me Oreste!

She rose, thinking, "This is not true." It is a nightmare. In the hall she thought, "I dare not open the door. If I open it, it will change into someone else. I dare not touch the handle. I will call out his name. Then it can't change into someone else."

She stood trembling, making a great effort, and at last she was able to say in a weak voice, "Oreste."

From the other side came his voice, *the* voice.

"Anna. Let me in."

She tore open the door and he stood there telling her that he had had an accident in a remote valley. And she thought, "I must not cry. When I cry I look old." But her whole body was shaking with sobs. For no reason at all she was suddenly aware

again of that strange statue found in the garden of
the Villa Leonardo.

The book slipped forgotten to the floor, where
Ottilia found it the next morning when her "cousin,"
the green-grocer, had gone.


## THE CRIME OF MEEKER'S GULCH

### I

FROM the day that Annie and Uriah Spragg left
Cordova their existence drifted into a strange
state that was something more and something less
than human.   In all their obscure wanderings it
appears that they were hounded like the figures
out of a Greek tragedy by some fate which gave
them no peace, shutting them further and further
away from the world into the solitude of their own
souls.   It may have been that the consciousness of
their own queerness set them apart, or it may have
been as Signora Bardelli, the janitress, believed long
afterward—that Miss Annie Spragg sold her soul
to the Devil, a bargain she made perhaps on the
day that Uriah found the body of Leander Potts
lying in her bower by the bend of the river.   Perhaps she preferred the Devil to such a God as
Uriah worshipped.   The same strange thing that
shut them in from the world bound them to each
other in a lonely solitude.

On fleeing Cordova they fell back once more into
that life which they had led so long as children of the
Prophet.   From town to town they went and from
village to village and crossroad to crossroad, carry-

ing the word of Uriah's harsh God into the wilderness. But it was a life neither as pleasant nor as
comfortable as life had been in the days of the
Prophet, for there was nothing about the voice or
the face or the body of Uriah which stirred men to
tears of repentance and women to frenzies of hys-
teria. Uriah was merely repellent and cold. Gifts
of money and of food must have been slender and
infrequent and Annie, it appears, beyond pumping
the wheezy melodion for the services, did nothing
to help her brother. Nevertheless in those days a
man of God was looked upon as touched by a Divine
fire that set him aside from other men, and so Uriah
was tolerated and respected.

They accomplished most in remote and lonely
communities where the arrival of a traveling
preacher was the peak of excitement from one year's
end to another, where souls were craving salvation
as a change from the monotonies of harsh weather
and dreary landscape. But Annie Spragg contrib-
uted nothing save that uncertain touch upon the
melodion. Even that disturbing power of seduction
come down to her from the Prophet she seemed to
have armored and locked away in the depths of her
wounded soul. More and more she became a solitary, more and more she wandered through woods
and fields, taking for her friends only the birds and
the animals.

At some period during their long wanderings
(and they went as far west as Boise and as far east
as Carthage) Uriah came at last to be ordained a
legitimate preacher, qualified by his church and fit
to be given a flock and a house where he might rest

a little from his long and wandering atonement.
But even then God saw fit to give him only a little
peace, for wherever he went, he was driven on again
in a little time.    People disliked him and they distrusted the queer Annie and her silent, mysterious
ways.    Uriah's hatred of women grew with advanc-
ing age and as women were the best defenders of
priests he failed in his mission, for his female
parishioners came to look upon him as a poor thing
who was a feeble preacher with a harsh, weak voice
in which there was only the monotonous grey and
bitter scale of denunciation.    The women of a
parish were the natural antagonists of a preacher's
wife and she of them, and Annie Spragg was worse
than the most helpless clergyman's wife.    The
women she ignored.    She did not call upon them or
go to the Ladies' Aid or make mother hubbards for
the missionary society.    She merely sat at home,
mysterious and silent, surrounded by the outlandish
wild things she had made her pets.


II


    And so at last when Uriah Spragg had passed his
fiftieth birthday, they came to the church at Winnebago Falls, a miserable and dying parish worthy only
of one whose life had been a failure.    The building
itself was a primitive affair of unpainted wood, long
in need of repair, which stood in a poor part of the
town between the railroad yards and the river, and
his flock was made up of the remnants of a migration of poor whites who, abandoned by their
strength in the course of a western migration, had

settled down in apathy along the mud flats. They were a poor lot, undernourished, superstitious and fearful. Most of them could not read or write, but they were all Children of God who possessed souls, and Uriah, whose only ambition was atonement, took up his task without complaint.

The preacher's house stood on the outskirts of the town, a poor wooden affair like the church, half hidden from a highway which was neither city street nor country road, by great cottonwoods and a thicket of untended lilacs, syringas and woodbine. Great clumps of burdock, emblem of poverty and the sordid, had taken possession of the yard and grew close against the old house. Beyond it stretched an abandoned terrain grown over with sumach and wild cherries, which in summer served mercifully to hide the fragments of old buggies and baby-carriages, tin cans and bicycles, dumped there when they ceased to be any longer of use to the citizens of Winnebago Falls.

Into this house Uriah and Annie Spragg moved the few primitive things which made up their household furniture. The pay was three hundred dollars a year and "contributions," but "contributions" from a flock which itself lingered on the fringes of starvation could not have been great. Still they were for a little time secure and safe from change, since it was impossible to assign Uriah to a lower charge.

Not long after they had moved in, Annie Spragg was discovered foraging along the river and on the fringes of the dump heap, collecting bits of wood. With these she constructed by her own hands a crude

enclosure which she began to fill with pets. To the
members of her brother's new flock she remained a
mystery, since no one spoke to her even when they
came to the house, unless by chance she happened
to open the door and usher them in silence into a
parlor furnished with three chairs, a worn carpet,
two religious chromos and a rubber-plant. People
saw her sometimes in the town, wandering along the
street, peering into shop windows at things which
she could never afford to buy. She had begun even
at that date to appear extremely eccentric. Her
clothes were queer and out of date, with a skirt
which always trailed far behind her through dust or
mud, regardless of the weather. But she was very
clean, and even in those days wore white cotton
gloves. People who encountered her at the door of
Uriah's house noticed that she wore them even when
opening the door, and Mrs. Bosanky, the drunken
old Irish woman who came up sometimes from the
flats to help her clean the house, said that Miss
Annie wore the gloves even when cooking and clean-
ing and doing the washing.

Within the crude enclosure among the burdocks
at the back of the house there came to be sheltered
rabbits and guinea-pigs, three or four stray cats, a
crow with a broken wing and an old and bony mon-
grel dog whose broken leg Miss Annie Spragg had
mended with great care. The thicket about the
house had long been a refuge for birds and after she
came their numbers increased. People said it was
strange that Miss Annie Spragg's cats never annoyed the birds and that even bluejays and sparrows

lived in the thicket in peace with more timid winged things.

And then one morning old Mrs. Bosanky arrived leading on a string a young he-goat that had been left behind by an Irish family which had set out for Oregon. He was a fine creature, with black intelligent eyes and a long fine shining coat as black as night. And after a time the town became used to a new sight, more extraordinary than any of the others. It saw Miss Annie Spragg walking in the evenings after her work was done along the road toward Meeker's Gulch, a lonely and almost impenetrable marshy thicket some four miles to the north. The he-goat walked beside her in the most docile fashion without even the constraint of a leading string, and when dogs ran out from the houses along the road to bark at the queer figure of Miss Annie Spragg, he arched his back prettily and bent his head and beat the earth with his pretty shining black hoofs. She took him there to feed upon the wild sweet clover that grew high on the edges of the country road. Sometimes when people passed along the road while the goat was feeding, they encountered the green eyes of Miss Annie Spragg watching them through the black veil she always wore, and they hurried on, filled with the nameless and ancestral fear that attacks children in the dark.

### III

Uriah, too, sometimes walked along the county road that led to Meeker's Gulch, but never at the hour of sunset. He chose the morning and the mid-

dle of the day.   Heat seemed to have no effect upon
his great shambling body, not even the thick damp
heat of the fertile prairies.   He was fifty-one and
then fifty-two and life and the atonement he had
planned seemed only to withdraw further and further from him.   There were men and women who
presently had stopped coming to his church and
others who, for reasons he could not understand,
hated him.   He had done his best, his duty; he had
been hard and conscientious toward Annie as well as
toward himself, yet none loved him, none asked his
aid.   He still possessed his gigantic physical
strength, but he was becoming an old man, with hair
turning white.   The bitter chiselled lines in his face
were becoming great hard gashes that gave the
countenance a perpetual look of anger and hatred.
The pale blue eyes sank deeper and deeper into their
cavernous sockets.   And the ungainly body, denied
since the beginning the pleasures for which nature
intended it, began like the bodies of those who abuse
the pleasures of the flesh to be racked with obscure
but devastating pains.   At times he could no longer
stand erect for the pain in his spine.   People saw
him day after day walking along the country road,
his body bent with pain, still in the same old posture,
with the great bony hands clasped behind him,
composing his bitter sermons as he walked or calling
fiercely upon God for strength.

There had never been much love in the harsh body
and even the little that there had been appeared to
have burned itself out in the flame of his strange
passion for Leander Potts.   But neither was there
any hate in him, but only that thing which is less than

human—duty and the sense of atonement for the
sins of his father the Prophet and for the sins of his
unchaste sister.   He came at last never to walk in
the town but always in the open country.   Once a
year he went away to attend for three days the convention of his church.   It was his only diversion.

## IV

Among the farmers who lived along the road to
Meeker's Gulch there was one of German descent
called Ed Hasselman, who kept cows and supplied
milk for most of the citizens of Winnebago Falls.
He was a hard-working man, but the curse of drink
was on him.   Sometimes he would stay sober for
months and then one day the appetite would take
possession of him and he would become like a mad-
man, staying drunk for days and weeks.   Sometimes
it was whiskey and sometimes it was only hard cider,
but his drunkenness possessed always the same wild
quality of bestiality.   At such times he was seized
with nightmare visions and went out of his mind,
and then a woman called Maria Hazlett who kept
house for him would have to deliver the milk in
Winnebago Falls.   When she appeared the whole
town knew that Ed Hasselman was drunk again.
She was a fat, blousy woman with a moustache and
Ed Hasselman had never married her, but she was
accepted as next best to being his wife.   No one
knew her well, for she was a silent woman who appeared to accept all that life brought her without
comment or complaint.   She was never heard even
to complain of Ed Hasselman's drunkenness and

the long hours of back-breaking work which it imposed upon her. She seemed content with him. She had been an illegitimate child, brought up on the county poor farm, and at eighteen she had gone to work for Ed Hasselman when his wife was still alive. When the wife died Maria Hazlett simply stayed on.

One morning, a day or two after Uriah Spragg had gone off to the annual church convention in Dubuque, Maria Hazlett appeared delivering the milk and as she went from house to house she spread a strange story, telling it alike to hired girls, housewives and men she met in the street. It went through all the town.

She said that in the early morning when Ed Hasselman had gone out to the barn to help her with the milking, he had seen the figure of Miss Annie Spragg black against the sunrise hurrying across the open fields from the direction of Meeker's Gulch and with her was the black he-goat. She was not going toward Meeker's Gulch, mind you, but away from it, back to town. Ed had been drinking a little, Maria Hazlett said, but not enough so that he didn't know what he was seeing.

Some put the story down as a drunken hallucination of the milkman and others guarded it, turning it over in their minds, savoring all its possibilities, but in the end everyone came to know it and it served only to deepen the isolation which surrounded the strange brother and sister. They came to be looked upon a little as though they were strange animals brought from a far country, which might be regarded safely from a distance. Here and there in

the town, but mostly among the members of Uriah
Spragg's own flock, murmurs began to arise against
them, and strange rumors that they were both mad
and that Miss Annie Spragg at least deserved being
shut up.   Surely it was not respectable to have such
a woman as the sister of one's preacher, and sometimes people who belonged to other churches—
Methodists and Baptists and even the haughty Congregationalists—treated the Reverend Uriah Spragg
and his sister as comic figures.   But worst of all, the
old black story of the Prophet, leader of the Spraggites, never long dead, raised its head.   It was a
story never far distant in the memories of all the
prairie people and in the years since the Prophet's
mysterious end it had grown in exaggeration and un-
wholesome detail.   Uriah and Annie Spragg were
two of the products of the Prophet's colossal lust
and as such were the accursed of God and the beloved of the Devil.   There was even talk of riding
Uriah Spragg out of town upon a rail, and there
were dark stories that Annie Spragg was much more
to him than a sister.

It came to a crisis one hot Sunday morning in
August when Uriah Spragg went as usual to preach
to the remnants of his flock in the decaying wooden
church, and he found his own church door locked
against him.   Across it had been nailed three planks
and on one of these was fastened a bit of paper on
which was written in half-illiterate handwriting:

*To the Reverend Uriah Spragg,*
  *We want none of the spawn of Cyrus Spragg.*
  *We want no more of you.*

*We want a good preacher or none at all.*
*We are sick of being laughed at.*
*Until further warning the church will be closed.*
*Take warning and do not try to force yourself*
*where you are not wanted.*

(*Signed*)
John Hemphill.
Darius Curtis.
Alexander Bostwick.
(*Committee.*)

He did not attempt to tear loose the planks and
force an entrance to his church.   For a little time he
simply stood quite still in the high grass staring at
the paper, and then, turning slowly, he walked away
with his head bowed and his great cruel hands behind his tired back.   As he left the churchyard,
passing through the rusted gate, there arose behind
him from the thicket of sumach a loud derisive
laugh.   The committee had been hiding there to
watch him.

It was the end.   There was nothing left.

v

At two o'clock in the afternoon of the same day
Maria Hazlett, drowsing in the heat with the
reins hanging loose over the dashboard of the milk-
wagon, was roused sharply.   Her team had shied
at something that lay on the edge of the road and
very nearly threw the wagon into the ditch.   Stirring herself to action, she halted the team to find
that almost beside her, among the high sweet clover,

lay the body of a man. Being a courageous and un-squeamish woman used to hard farm work and butchering, she got down heavily and turned the body over on its back. She saw then that it was the Reverend Uriah Spragg, and that although the body was still warm he was quite dead. It needed Maria's calloused nature to regard the sight without turning ill. His face was no longer the face of Uriah Spragg, but she recognized him by the white hair, the rusty black clothes and the great hands that were like the cruel claws of a bird of prey. He had been beaten savagely from head to foot by some sharp instrument. Even his clothing had been ripped and torn in the mad fury of the attack.

There was no one in sight. The murder had been done at noonday on the county road in the very midst of the flat prairie where there was neither tree nor bush nor dwelling to hide the murderer.

VI

All that day and during most of the night crowds streamed out the county road to stare morbidly at the spots of blood in the dust at the edge of the tall sweet clover. Crowds hung over the fence of the old house where they took Uriah's broken body back to his sister Annie. Crowds trampled the vulgar burdocks into the ground. No one saw Miss Annie Spragg save the sheriff and two sweating and stupid policemen who said that she received them in white gloves and took the news calmly enough—"Although that maybe was because she was cracked."

After three days they buried him, and Miss Annie

Spragg, who did not take the trouble to put on black or put off her flower-trimmed picture hat, tacked up a notice on the front fence that she was going away and that her furniture was for sale. She would have gone perhaps overlooked and in solitude as she had always been, but for the dark rumors which began to be heard. It was said outright that she had killed her brother and that everyone knew that crazy people were far craftier than sane ones. At last a committee from Uriah's own church, feeling perhaps that they were not above suspicion, called upon the sheriff to make an investigation and "clear the honor of Hanna County by fixing the guilt for the murder of the Reverend Uriah Spragg." People, moved perhaps by some dark mistrust, began to hint that the black he-goat had played some part in the crime. No one had found the weapon with which Uriah Spragg had been beaten to death and Joe Hutton, the undertaker, told a story that the wounds on his body were like those that might have been made by the twin prongs of a pair of horns. It was true that since the day of the murder no one had seen the he-goat.

And so they arrested Miss Annie Spragg and questioned her, although they could draw no intelligible story from her muddled and perhaps crafty answers. Next they searched her, calling in two women from Uriah's church to strip her naked. She made no resistance, only looking at them quietly out of her disturbing green eyes. At the very beginning when they took off the white cotton gloves they made a strange discovery. On the palms and the backs of both hands there were red scars, as if

dropped the case and annoyed her no more, and the mystery remained unsolved, an epic in the history of a town where little ever happened.   Some even felt a little sorry for her when the stories got about that she had been beaten and branded by her brother, but none approached her save drunken old Mary Bosanky.

She went away at last, so quietly that no one knew she had gone until long afterward.   Only Mrs. Bosanky knew where she had gone, for she had asked her and received the answer, "To Italy."   And when Mrs. Bosanky asked her why, she had answered, "Because I lived there once."   And Mrs. Bosanky, who could neither read nor write, thought Italy must be a town in the next county and took no more notice of it.


## FATHER D'ASTIER'S STORY

### I

HE WAS born of mixed blood.   On his father's side he was French and on his mother's Italian, and the two bloods had been at war within him since the day he was born.   Until the day he died they would battle there in his body and in his mind.   In youth the struggle had been incomplete and confused, but with age the two demons came to divide, each withdrawing a little into his own corner, and with the clearness of division there had come a certain peace, for Father d'Astier understood that he was two persons and not one and that there was no merging the one into the other.   The one man was a mystic, and gullible and sentimental, of that blood which painted smiling Madonnas and miraculous children seated in fields starred with impossible flowers beneath throngs of pretty angels. The other was of the blood of the philosophers, of Voltaire and the eighteenth century, a creature inquiring and restless, skeptical and touched with the despair of those who stand in awe of that which they are too proud to believe. All that was French in him found satisfaction in facing the truth and knowing it however unpleasant it might be.

There was in him, too, a monster, born perhaps of the long struggle in his soul. This, too, at sixty he knew well. He had known it for a long time now. It was a monster not easy to tame, perverse and cruel, which sometimes claimed possession of his very soul and destroyed what he loved best.

He was thinking of these things when the Princess dropped him before the door of his own house, a great house which he owned, for he was a rich man, and in which he kept for himself only two small rooms under the eaves looking down upon the square beneath the lovely tower of San Stefano. Of those who occupied his house he knew nothing. They lived their lives beneath him, lives that were tangled and complex, tragic or comic, pathetic and nondescript. He preferred not knowing his tenants. And he owned, too, the old rookery called the Palazzo Gonfarini where this strange woman Miss Annie Spragg had died. But as he climbed the stairs, a little wearily, he was not thinking of Miss Annie Spragg but of his own life and the life of Anna d'Orobelli.

He was tired. That long motor ride had worn
his nerves. And then the discovery of that obscene
but beautiful statue had been disturbing. A thing
like that was better hidden forever in the dark earth
of that ancient garden. It stirred up the demons.

"I am growing old," he thought. "Yet she seems
as young as ever. She is a remarkable woman."

She had not tricked him. He knew well enough
why she had been in such haste. Had he not known
her for nearly thirty years, better perhaps than any
man, better even than any of her lovers, for there
was a side of her known to him which they would
never know? She was a woman, he thought, born
out of her time, a woman who might have been a
*grande amoureuse,* or a great courtesan. She was
always in haste, always unsatisfied, like a flame, always seeking, seeking, seeking something. What
could it have been? Love, perhaps, or something
more than that, if indeed there were anything
greater than that. Perhaps she had been seeking
always a man whom she could find worthy of her,
to receive all that she had to give. Such a man
might have saved her, but it was too late now. She
would never find him. She was growing old and to
seek love when one was old was to be ridiculous.
The thought hurt him, as it had hurt him many times
during the past year or two, when he had heard her
name mentioned in jest, when people had told stories
against her. Women did not like her and that was
natural, but men had come of late to talk of her. It
was like an audience of dolts witnessing a great play
which they had not the capacity to understand. A
whole life wasted. They did not know her as he

knew her.   They could not understand why it hurt
him when they laughed.

He turned the key and let himself into the two
small rooms.   They were like twin cells, sparsely
furnished, with plain oak tables and chairs, a cupboard. . . . It was here that he came when he
wanted peace and rest from the world, when he had
need to retire and fight the demon that sometimes
claimed his soul.   This time he had come all the way
from a country house in Shropshire so that he might
be alone.   And now he was to have no solitude because he had found Anna d'Orobelli in Brinoë and
because Fulco chose to torment him with all the nonsense about the Spragg woman being a saint.   He
was to have no peace because he had found there
the two people in all the world whose presence tormented him most.

He did not bother to send for a hot supper.   He
ate the cheese and wine and bread which he always
kept in the cupboard, eating in a room that was dark
save for the splashes of moonlight on the floor.
Fulco would be coming in a little while.   It would
be time enough then to have a light.

He thought again, "People do not know how it
hurts me when they laugh at her.   They do not
know that I shall die wondering if I was not the
one chosen by God to save her."   Perhaps saving her
would have been in the sight of God more worthy
than all the souls he had brought to the Church,
cowardly, worldly, sniveling souls, most of them.
But who could decide a thing like that?   Certainly
not the Church, filled with men no nearer to God
than himself and most of them far more stupid.   It

required charity to understand such things and only God had charity. And who could know that there was a God? He had been honest with the Church, he told himself. He had never let men know that he doubted these things.

The struggle was beginning again. He saw it now. He was too old to fight against it any longer, but there was a part of him that would not leave him in peace—that part which would not lie down shamelessly in the calm which appeared to envelop those who never asked questions.

He did not see Anna now as he had seen her a little while before in the loggia of that preposterous woman at the Villa Leonardo. He kept seeing her as he had seen her years before when they were both young, when—(why did he keep on tormenting himself?) when it could have happened. And now it was too late. There was no living life over again. There was only that single straight narrow groove, the record of each life, which was soon worn away and forgotten when you were dead. Who would remember you when you were dead? Who would care what you had done, what pleasures you had known and what sorrows? What difference could it have made? It would not have been an easy thing, what with his having been Father d'Astier and she the Princess d'Orobelli. Could they have dared such a thing, and faced life confident in each other, finding in each enough to throw away all else? She would have gone in recklessly, greedily. Perhaps her way was better, after all, taking life as it came, squeezing it for the last drop of color and fire and beauty.

His agony was that it was too late now. He would die without ever knowing. If he had taken the wrong turning, it could not be undone now. And she had gone on and on all these years, wasting herself and all she had to give prodigally and without restraint. Perhaps in the eyes of God he had committed the greatest of sins. If God and Nature were one, he was the greatest of sinners. The Church taught otherwise, but the Church, the Church. . . . The Church had far less in common with God than Nature had. As it grew older, the Church seemed to have less and less. For forty years he had been serving the Church like an honest servant, no more, no less. For forty years he had been atoning for the first sin, and surely by now he had atoned. Had he not brought souls to God? *Souls to God?* The phrase echoed bitterly inside his head like a phrase spoken aloud in an empty room. *Souls to God.* Souls who had wanted to come to God because they were worldly or because they were afraid of life and needed to believe in a pretty story that was considered holy and could not be denied. And at the end there was always Heaven, not a fine, noble, splendid Heaven, but a Paradise like the Primitives', filled with pink and blue angels and God in a blue robe. He had brought souls to God, but not his own soul. It was still the same as it had been at seventeen before he had known anything of life, a little more placid, perhaps, and more resigned, but not much different. Sixty years of life had not proven anything. He was no nearer the mystery now than he had ever been. Sometimes he fancied that God was perhaps on his side smiling at the antics of all the others.

And suddenly he thought with shame of what he had written on the first empty white page of the Thomas-à-Kempis he had given Anna so long ago.

*Dans la damnation le feu est la moindre chose; le supplice propre au damné est le progrès infini dans le vice et dans le crime, l'âme s'endurcissant, se dépravant toujours, s'enfonçant nécessairement dans le mal de minute en minute en progression géométrique pendant l'éternité.*

*Michelet.*

*He* had written *that.* He who could have saved her.

What did it all mean, what did it all matter? There was Anna a little way off with Oreste Fuenterrabía searching, searching for what Oreste Fuenterrabía could never give her, and what she could never find now. Soon they would both be dead. Ten more years. Twenty more years. The sooner, the better now for Anna. She was not made to be old. For himself it did not matter. Nothing could happen to him now. He was tired tonight and he had yet to deal with Fulco and all his stupidity, to keep Fulco from making a fool of himself. Fulco, who would not see that the world was what it was and that Christ had come too soon. There were those who believed that Jesus would come again. Perhaps when he came again the world would not reject him—this world of priests and preachers, of statesmen and barterers and politicians and cheats and idle women, a world ridden with greed and ambition. He knew the world. He had lived in it for a long time. He knew those who ruled the world. The poor were humble, but the poor in power would be no different. No, he had seen too much of the world, years and years too much.

There was a sound of footsteps on the stairs and he put down the glass of wine to listen. He knew the steps. They were Fulco's, shuffling, timid, uncertain. He knew the creaking boots. For some reason Fulco's boots always creaked. He rose and lighted a candle, wearily, for he would rather have received Fulco in the dark. There was a knock on the door, a timid, apologetic knock. It was his past knocking. It was his fiery, unhappy youth. There were people, he thought bitterly, who said that youth was the time of happiness.

The door opened and his son stood there, fat and squat and awkward in his priest's clothes, and ill at ease like a peasant, with red swollen peasant's hands and a round face covered with pimples. Only the eyes were her eyes, great, brown, gentle, sensitive eyes, like a doe's, in which the shadow of pain was mirrored so easily. He had wanted it dark so that he could not see those eyes.

He tried to speak kindly. "Sit down, Fulco. Where have you been?"

The man sat down. (He must be nearly forty-one, thought Father d'Astier.) His hands clasped his hat. It was not the proper manner for a priest, but rather the manner of a timid commercial traveler trying to sell an article which no one wanted. (He will never rise in the Church, thought

Father d'Astier, because he does not understand the
world.  He is too simple.)

Fulco spoke in a weak voice, rather too high-
pitched and a little grating.  "I have been to the
Palazzo Gonfarini praying there.  There was a
great crowd of devout.  Surely the Holy Virgin has
vouchsafed a miracle in your own house."

How round-eyed he was and how credulous, how
exactly like her!  Father d'Astier tried to be firm
and kind.

"It is true, Fulco, that the woman died in my
house, but that means nothing.  You must not hope
for vain things, Fulco.  Nothing is known of her.
People always come like that to seek relics the minute anything strange occurs.  People want to believe
in miracles, and among the poor, relics are valuable.
The poor can turn them into money."

It was odd that he found himself speaking to this
man of forty as if he were a child.  It was odd and
revolting.

"She was a good woman, Father d'Astier.  A
*religieuse*.  She came daily for years to worship the
pictures of Saint John the Shepherd.  I have seen
her there day after day with my own eyes.  The
very doves in the Piazza loved her, and the little
birds sat by her when she was dying.  Sister Annunziata swears to that.  And the janitress.  I saw
them too, but you need not take my word; there is
the word of the others."

Father d'Astier interrupted him.  "The janitress
is infidel and anti-clerical and Socialist.  She is malicious and intelligent.  We cannot take her word.
Besides, saints are not made like that.  We do not

even know that the woman had espoused the Church."

"She was a good woman," persisted Fulco. "The light of God was in her eyes."

"And how do you know the light of God?"

"I know, Father d'Astier, I know. I have seen it once before in the eyes of Sister Annunziata who they are beginning to say is crazy. I know the light of God."

Fulco went a little breathlessly, for the climb up the four flights of stairs to the top of the palace had taken his breath. He kept telling Father d'Astier all those things about Miss Annie Spragg which the older man had already found out for himself and knew better than Fulco. The old priest did not listen. He sat with bowed head as if he were listening, but he was thinking of other things. He was thinking of Brinoë forty years before when he had come to stay with his mother's people, not much different from the Brinoë that lay all about him tonight in the moonlight. The city was too old to alter much. And he was thinking of the villa on the hill beyond the Church of Monte Salvatore, a small white villa surrounded by an orchard of olive trees. And he was thinking of the fat widow of Professor Baldessare and their daughter. The Professor had been a remarkable man, raising himself from the level of the peasantry with a peasant wife, greedy and coarse and vulgar. But the daughter was a miracle. He saw her again with a sickening clarity, like one of the women of Botticelli. There was a room in the Uffizi that he had not entered in years because he could not bear to look at

a picture that hung there. (Fulco was talking, talking. He became drunk with words without ever
knowing their value.) Laura was her name, like
Petrarch's Laura. It was odd how long an old
wound could give pain.

He had been young then and strong, not this old
man tired of the world who sat listening to Fulco's
complaints against his fellow priests—young and
twenty-two, a boy who thought the world his for the
taking, a boy who sinned and then tormented himself with his sense of sin and then mocked at God
and the Church, only to begin again on the same
round in the order. He had been full of animal
delight at being alive, and the delight of delights
was Laura Baldessare. It was not the memory of
his sin with her that troubled him now, but of the
other sin he had committed, so much the worse, of
destroying her soul by tearing from it cruelly the
simple faith that had dwelt there. He had done it
with wild gusts of adolescent talk, and because she
loved him she had believed what he told her. She
believed anything he told her—he who stood in
awe of God at one moment and in the next felt
superior to God, a silly fellow strong enough to
doubt but too feeble to stand before the awesome
spectacle of a universe. He knew better now. He
was no longer defiant. He only waited for the end,
to see.

Fulco was questioning him. He raised his head
and murmured, "Yes, Fulco, but continue. Tell me
all your reasons first." Fulco was so certain that
the old maid was a saint.

He could not hear what Fulco said for the

memories that crowded in upon him, memories
which went back years before there was ever a potential saint in the Palazzo Gonfarini. In Fulco's
eyes there was that same fire of belief that had once
burned in her eyes. It redeemed Fulco, he thought,
from being an utter lout. "There is a demon born
in me," he thought, "that has always tormented
those I have loved best." Anna, too, he had tormented, long afterward.

Again he began to think what his life would have
been if at its beginning he had taken another turning. If he had married Laura. He could have married her even at the end before she died when Fulco
was born, but chance had brought him too late, an
hour after she had died, going out into the darkness
shaken and terrified because he had destroyed her
faith. That, he thought, was a real sin, a sin that
could torment one even into the grave. Her poor
faith did no one any harm and it had made her unafraid.

And now for forty years he had been atoning for
that sin since the day when in the midst of youth
he had turned to the Church to atone. He had
kept his vow. He had atoned. From that day on
he had never known love, and for him that was not
an easy thing. But others had been made to atone
as well, for life was a silly tangled thing. There
was Anna driving through the darkness like a mad
woman to meet her lover because she had never
found love and still believed that one day she might
find it. That was *her* faith, a good faith, quite as
good perhaps as the other though more easily
proven false. She would not believe that already

it was too late. And what good had this atonement brought to himself or to God or to the world? What had it brought him in the end but old age and doubt? It had not made Laura alive again. It had not restored her faith before she died, so that she might die in peace.

And here was Fulco raving about faith and saints and a peasant's Heaven filled with pink and blue plaster images and magenta paper wreaths. That was the cruel joke Nature had played on him—making Fulco not in the image of Laura or himself, so that he might have had a son to be proud of, but in the image of that vulgar and scheming old woman, Laura's mother, who connived at her daughter's sin because she saw her one day as the Marquise d'Astier. That was Nature's bitter jest, that and this stupid adoration which Fulco had for the man he did not even know was his father. If Fulco had not been stupid he might have guessed long ago that there was some reason for this stranger's interest in him. And Fulco had become a priest because he, Father d'Astier, was a priest. This fat, stupid, pimply little man was his son, his heir, who should have been the Marquis d'Astier. Suddenly he felt a sickening wave of distaste and hatred for his own son. He was stupid, stupid, and he could never be rid of him.

Then all at once he knew a fierce desire to beat his head against the floor. "I am proud and worldly like all the others. I have learned nothing at all. I am no different. O God, teach me humility."

Fulco's thin monotonous voice trickled through

the haze of memories. "Sister Annunziata is a woman inspired of God. . . ."

He could bear it no longer. He raised his head this time and looked straight into those trusting doe-like eyes. A kind of madness seized him. There was something in those eyes which he must destroy. He knew he must quench it forever. He could have no peace until he had done it.

"You are stupid, Fulco. You are stupid. You have lived in the world for forty years and have learned nothing. . . . Nothing. You complain because they do not give you a parish. Parishes are not gotten by faith alone. Men are not made princes of the Church simply because they have faith. You learn nothing. The Church has no need of a saint now, least of all in Brinoë. There is nothing to show that this woman has ever embraced the faith. Miracles cannot happen to heretics. There is no place for your simplicity in the Church. For centuries there has been no place for it."

In the eyes of the fat little man the shadow of pain and terror was mirrored. He sat on the edge of the chair, his fat red hands crushing the black hat. The sight of him sitting thus, so stupid and humble, only enraged Father d'Astier. He thought wildly, "He has neither courage nor intelligence."

Aloud he said, "You have lived too long among priests, Fulco, and superstitious peasants. Can you not see that the Church is no longer a power? It is only a shelter for the weak and fearful, all those who must have miracles and wondrous things, like children in the presence of a cheap magician."

He arose suddenly, as if possessed, and began to

pace the narrow room. The demon had risen now, alive and fearful. He told Fulco things which had long been hidden in his heart which he had told to no one since the day he entered the Church. The heretic churches were no better, he cried, because they tried to mingle faith with reason and that could not be done. All that the Church taught was a legend and a superstition. To believe, one had to be as simple as the most ignorant man. To believe, one must be stupid and afraid. Had he not brought souls to the Church? Had he not brought money to the Church? It was for that he worked and that alone. Did he not know these things? Had he not lived with the Church for nearly half a century? Not because he believed, but because it was a profession, a career.

And this whole affair of the Spragg woman was nonsense—the concoction of a half-insane nun and a malicious peasant woman who hated priests. And if even such things could be, if they were true, the Church would not make a saint of her, because it had no need of saints at the moment. The same miracle had happened to more than a hundred others. It was on record. They were always hysterical women. No great organization could saint every woman who saw fit to produce miraculous scars on her body. The Church made saints when it needed them and where it needed them. It was not an affair left to the Divine Will of God. It was geography and politics.

The Church was not rich and powerful because it was the instrument of God, but because the men in the Church had made it so. They were politicians.

Because men chose to enter the Church it did not make them different from other men. They were, after all, pitiful and human and insignificant like all the others. They made people believe in things which no man could prove. The Church had muddled and compromised and corrupted the teachings of Jesus. It had buried his teachings beneath a mountain of cant and theology and superstition. When it was powerful it had committed murder by fire and torture always in the name of God but always to increase its own power and wealth and stamp out its enemies. It was among the great criminals of the world.

"Go to your history, Fulco," he cried out. "Cease being a dolt. Read the records of its worldliness. It lives by gold more than by faith, taking the money of those who are afraid or who bargain with it. I *know*. I have brought it much money. It is my work to bring the rich and the powerful into the Church."

He halted suddenly, facing the frightened Fulco. "And your faith. What is it? It has been said that faith can move mountains, but no one has seen it done, save by the faith that man has in himself, in the steam shovels and the dynamite he has invented in the face of a hostile Nature. Man can save himself by faith, but not by a cowardly faith that pins itself upon conjurer's tricks, but by faith in himself and in Nature and in the teachings of Christ. The world and the Church have forgotten Christ, who was a simple man. What had Christ to do with the cheap tricks of an old maid, an insane nun and a malicious scrubwoman? All that should be beneath the dignity of God's church."

He moved to the table and took up the thin book which held for him all the peace he knew. He opened easily to a page to which he had turned a thousand times in the struggle to subdue the monster in his soul. By the yellow light of the candle he began to read.

*"For a man's worthiness is not to be estimated by the number of visions and comforts which he may have, or by his skill in the Scriptures or by his being placed in a higher station:*

*"But by his being grounded in humility, and full of divine charity; if he be always purely and sincerely seeking God's honor; if he think nothing of and unfeignedly despise himself, and even rejoice more to be despised and little esteemed by others than to be honored by them."*

He put down the book and turned his white face toward Fulco. "Where is humility in the world today? Where is divine charity? Who is it that purely and sincerely seeks God's honor?"

Then, quite suddenly, he felt weak and leaned against the window, his head in his hands, trembling. He was an old, tired man once more.

There was a long silence and then the timid voice of Fulco murmuring, "The world, the Church can be purified. If what you say is true. It can be purified."

"And who is to do it? The Church would have none of Savonarola. The Jesuits turned into politicians who said the end justified the means. It hanged Savonarola by the neck and burnt his body when he sought to purify the Church." He turned and looked at the cowering Fulco. "Go now. I can't talk any longer."

Fulco answered him. He was weeping like a little child. "I can't argue these things. I know too little. But the world can be saved," he repeated. "The Church can be purified."

To Father d'Astier it seemed impossible to remain any longer in the same room with this man who was his son. Turning, he went quickly into the bedroom and, closing the door, bolted it. . . . The room was tiny with only a narrow iron bed covered with coarse blankets. Upon this he flung himself down, feeling that he was ready to die. Fulco knew now. Fulco, his own son, was the only one who knew the truth. He had killed Fulco's faith as he had slaughtered the faith of Fulco's mother. The demon had won a second time. And faith was all that poor Fulco had in the world.

Presently he sat up on the narrow bed. "Tomorrow," he thought bitterly, "I shall go out into the world again and go to dinners and make flattering speeches to rogues and criminals and fools. It is too late now to change. I am too old. And tomorrow no one will know." Again he had betrayed the thing he served.

Tomorrow he would go again to the Villa Leonardo to continue the conversion of that silly woman Mrs. Weatherby, and from her he would get money for the Church. Oh, he had brought money to the Church—thousands, millions of lira and francs and marks and dollars and pounds. He had, he thought, bought himself a place in Heaven by now. He had

the right to ask a seat of God. He would tell God
he had bought a seat in Heaven and paid for it. He
would go again to dinners and to house parties and
great receptions. . . .

In the midst of these thoughts he seemed to hear
the voice of someone talking quite near at hand. He
listened and presently he recognized the voice. It
was Fulco's. He had not gone away after all. He
had been in the next room all the while, and now he
was down on his fat knees, praying to God for the
soul of Father d'Astier.


## STAY ME WITH FLAGONS

### I

THE citizens of Winnebago Falls came long before she died to think of Mary Bosanky
simply and primitively as a town character, placing
her in the category of those who were a little less
than human. Most of them thought of her until
her death simply as a drunken old Irishwoman who
worked a little when she was sober, who went along
the streets muttering to herself and who died in the
end at the county poorhouse. But none of them
had seen her as she stepped ashore from a sailing
ship at New Orleans in the year of the Great Irish
Famine. Then she was twenty-six, buxom, strong
as a man, and handsome with black hair and blue
eyes and a fine high color. She could neither read
nor write but she boasted when drunk that she was
descended from the Kings of Clare. Toward the
end it was a boast that she used more and more fre-

quently, in the fashion of those who invoke blue blood to compensate for the disappointments of this life. And with Mary Bosanky there was great need for compensation. There was the worthlessness of Michael Bosanky and the poverty of the shack in which they lived by the railroad, and most of all there was Shamus, her son, who was so beautiful to look upon and so different from other sons. She knew that all the blood of all the kings of Ireland could not brighten the wits of Shamus.

And all her life she had as well to bear the cross of her own stormy nature, which was that of one who never found life quite fine enough to satisfy her desires. In the beginning when she was young and had her strength and vitality she managed somehow to wrest from life a little of what she asked of it, or at least she was young enough then to delude herself into believing that she had. She found a strange excitement in everything—in the wharves and the river boats, the negroes and the markets of New Orleans and then for a little time on the river boat where she worked for the wife of the captain. She had a kind of rollicking good nature that was always hungry for adventure, and when adventure did not come she grew bored, and when she grew bored she imagined grievances which convinced herself that she was a creature abused and exploited, and this in turn gave her a reason for quitting the place where she worked and moving on to a new town or a new country. Before she was thirty she had been a chambermaid, a cook, a dishwasher in a Cincinnati saloon. She had cared for children and even worked in the fields at harvest time. She lived almost the

life of a man, save that she was always virtuous because rooted deep in her savage and superstitious
nature there was a fear of priests and of the life
after death.  She was terrified of thunderstorms
and of corpses and heard strange noises in the night.
There were no even, monotonous plains of contentment in her life.  Her mood was either one in which
she went all day singing ballads from her home
county or one in which she went about praying and
moaning and saying her rosary.  At the age of
twenty-eight she found herself washing dishes in
Rafferty's saloon and lunch-room on the edge of
Winnebago Falls where the tracks of the Iowa,
Nebraska and Western Railroad crossed those of
the Trans-Mississippi Freight and Passenger Company.  In those days they were building railroads
everywhere and it was always the Irish who did the
work, so Rafferty's saloon was filled a large part of
the time with wild Irishmen drinking and carousing
in the hours when they were not shoveling earth
and stone to bring prosperity to sleepy places like
Winnebago Falls.

II

Among the Irishmen was one Michael Bosanky,
a great red-haired giant of a fellow two years older
than Mary, who drank and roared and sought to
make life constantly more exciting than it could
possibly be.  He was a devil with the ladies and he
tried to be a devil with Mary, but she would have
none of him save on the terms that the priests held
holy and respectable, and in the end the banns were

published and they were married, drawn together by an attraction which had its roots in that mutual hunger for a life that was better than any life can be.

It was the beginning of Mary's real trouble, because she was tied to Michael by a force stronger than banns and marriage ties, stronger than her fear of priests and of Hell. It was a force that would not let her quit her job and go on to the next town. She was in love with Michael in her own passionate and possessive way and it was a love as violent as the very natures of herself and Michael. She could not imagine living without him. The sight of his great brawny figure reeling across the tracks from Rafferty's saloon gave her a kind of fine palpitating excitement she had never discovered in all her adventures. And it was thrilling to live with Michael because he was roaring drunk a great part of the time and he threw things at her and tried to beat her. But she was a strong woman and the attempted beating often turned into a brawl that ended in the wildest of love-making. She discovered almost at once that Michael was no good, but that did not vanquish the certainty that life with him was a fine and glorious affair.

He lost one job after another and presently Mary went back to working out, not this time at a regular job, but by the day, sometimes cooking, sometimes washing, sometimes scrubbing floors. She made a little money this way, but Michael always took it from her and went across the tracks to Rafferty's place. All of Winnebago Falls came to know Mary Bosanky. She worked for the best families like the Weatherbys and the Fosdicks. They grew fond of

her and they pitied her hard life, but it never occurred to Mary to pity herself.    Michael never
chased after other women any longer.    He seemed
to find her enough for him.

And presently when Mary became a little weary
of Michael's perpetual drunkenness she began, too,
to drink and life at once became brighter.    They
drank together and the fights they had were magnificent.    Sometimes one emerged with a blackened eye
and sometimes the other and sometimes both.    She
began  to  grow  undependable  among  the  best
families of Winnebago Falls and so to lose her
work.

When she was thirty-nine something happened
which Mary regarded as a miracle.    For nine years
she had prayed to all the saints of fertility and now
at thirty-nine she was going to have a baby.    On the
advice of the priest she even gave up drinking,
which was for Mary a great sacrifice.    The child
was born in the two-room shack by the railroad.
It was a pretty baby, a boy, curiously strong and
healthy, with black hair and blue eyes like herself.
He was strong enough even to survive the rough
treatment that was certain to meet any child born
into the world of Bosanky's Shanty.    She called him
Shamus after her father from whom she had not
heard in fifteen years.    As he grew older he was
slow in walking and in making himself understood.

But when Shamus was old enough to go to the
parish school it was clear that there was something
wrong with him.    He did not learn things like other
children and he could remember nothing of his les-
sons.    He was not an idiot.    It was more as if there

were a part of his brain that had never existed. The other children tormented him and so he came to play alone and to invent extraordinary games. At home his only playground was the railroad-tracks and there he found his way miraculously in and out among the locomotives and shunting trains. At nine he was still among the six-year-old children in the parish school. At ten he ran away four times within a month. Once he was missing for two days and Mary Bosanky, who loved the child with the love which mothers have for children who are different, wandered over the whole country-side searching for him. He was discovered at last on Ed Hasselman's farm by Maria Hazlett, Hassel-man's housekeeper, asleep in a thicket in the midst of a flock of sheep. After that they gave up trying to teach him anything and he was allowed to run wild. When he was thirteen he began to have visions. He would fall down in a kind of trance and remain unconscious for hours and when he awak-ened he told wonderful stories of having been to Heaven and seen the golden streets and the angels walking about. He heard wonderful music and his great friend was Saint John the Shepherd.

### III

Since neither Shamus nor drinking made life seem grand enough, Mary and Michael came to discover new ways of elevating their spirits. One way was their expeditions to a place called Lakeville, which was a sort of cheap summer resort for the Germans of Winnebago Falls. There was at Lakeville a

round deep lake of cold clear blue water where the
fishing was good. On its banks there was a grove
of trees with cottages that were little more than
shacks set in their shade. Mary and Michael
seemed to know without planning it when the time
had come to go to Lakeville for a carouse. Together they would set out on foot to walk the fourteen miles along the county road to the north past
Ed Hasselman's farm and Meeker's Gulch. A
friend of Mike's, the foreman of the road gang, had
a shack there where they could stay. They always
took plenty of whiskey with them and left Shamus
behind in the shanty. Sometimes they would sleep
out of doors on a sand-bar under the moon and
sometimes in a rowboat made fast among the lily
pads and the tall shaking reeds near the shore. And
always there was wild drinking and wilder love-
making, as if Mary were still a handsome young girl
instead of a middle-aged woman bloated and saddled
by drink.

And Shamus, left to himself, took to wandering
more and more often, and farther and farther. He
never slept under a roof. Sometimes if the weather
was warm he slept in a thicket or a ditch and if it
was cool, among the sheep or among the cattle in
the open sheds built in the fields to shelter the beasts
from the winter blizzards. The farmers of three
counties came to know him and to feed him when
he came their way. He was harmless and sometimes
he would help them in the fields without asking any
pay. He invented games for the children and made
them whistles from the willows that grew along the
streams and marshes. He did not make them sim-

ple primitive whistles but whole sets of pipes bound
together with willow bark on which they could play
tunes. He was skilful with his hands and gentle in
working about beasts. At sixteen he was strong as
a man and possessed of a strange dark beauty not to
be found among the blond heavy German farmers.
He went about in rags, his clothing torn by briars and
barbed wire fences. Sometimes a farmer's wife gave
him a shirt or an old pair of overalls. He had a
dark skin with a fine high color, black curling hair,
blue eyes and small ears that were pointed at the tips.
He knew about weather and could tell the farmers
when it would be safe to cut their hay and take in
their wheat. There was really nothing very strange
about him but the curious vacant look in his eyes,
his strange love for beasts and his way of not seem-
ing at times to understand when people spoke to
him.

The year that he was sixteen his mother came
back alone one morning from Lakeville and tried to
explain to Shamus that his father was dead. He
had fallen overboard from a rowboat and been
drowned. At least that was what people thought.
It was what Mary thought, for she didn't really
know what had happened. She had awakened sober
to find herself alone in the boat in the middle of the
lake. Michael had disappeared. They made an
effort to drag the lake but no trace was ever found
of Shamus's father. There was a legend that the
lake had no bottom; at least no one had been able
to reach the bottom with a sounding line.

For a time Mary, sobered a little, gave up drinking and went again to working regularly. She be-

gan too to find a compensation for Shamus's dull wits in the miraculous visions which he had. These were more frequent now and more complete in their details. She fancied that God had made her the mother of a saint. The stories of his visions went the round of the parish and all the county. But Shamus did not abandon his habit of wandering off into the open country for days at a time. When he was gone Mary found life insupportable and took again to the bottle.

They had been town characters for years when the Reverend Uriah Spragg and his sister Annie came to live in Winnebago Falls and old Mrs. Bosanky, when she was sober enough, went to work for Annie Spragg. Shamus Bosanky and his mother were the only people in the town poorer than Uriah and Annie Spragg and Annie Spragg was the only person in the place who would any longer give Mary Bosanky work to do.

Sometimes Shamus went with his mother to the weathered wooden house hidden by lilacs, syringas and burdock where the Spraggs lived. Miss Annie Spragg fed them and was kind to them and presently they came to be her only friends in Winnebago Falls. She showed Shamus all the animals and birds that lived in the wooden enclosure behind the house and after a time it was as if he became one of them. He would come day after day to spend his time there, playing with them and teaching them tricks.

IV

The rest of the tale comes from Ed Hasselman
and Maria Hazlett who kept house for him on the
farm near Meeker's Gulch.  Their part of it happened long after Uriah Spragg was murdered and
Annie, questioned and tormented, had been allowed
to disappear.

Since Shamus had first run off as a little boy he
had been friendly with Ed Hasselman and Maria
Hazlett.  They always fed him and took no notice
of his goings and comings, and from the first they
seemed to accept him without question.  Sometimes
he stayed about the farm for days sleeping among
the animals and helping in the fields.  He was a
great help to Maria Hazlett at the periods when
Ed retired into drunkenness.  At the time he told
them the story he was thirty-four years old.  It was
only a little time before his death.

It was at the beginning of one of Ed Hasselman's
spells and Shamus appeared one evening just at
dusk out of the woods back of the house.  They had
finished supper and the milking was over and Maria
was washing the cream separator and the milk crocks
outside the kitchen door under the great catalpa
tree that grew there.  As the sun had gone down a
great burning harvest moon came heavily up out of
the prairie and Ed on the doorstep with a flagon of
hard cider beside him sat playing on his concertina
snatches of half forgotten tunes that he had heard
as a child in Dorfsweiler, his father's village of the
Black Forest.  Maria got Shamus some cold ham
and some hard cider and bread and cheese and he

sat eating and listening shyly on the edge of the
stone coping about the spring.

He finished his supper and as it grew darker he
got up presently and began to dance, not any set
dance, but a series of steps which he had made up
himself.  It was a dance composed mostly of mad
leapings and caperings so violent that remains of his
ragged clothes fell apart leaving him naked to the
waist under the hot August moon.  Ed Hasselman
drinking more and more, gave Shamus more and
more to drink and played the concertina more and
more wildly while Shamus danced with his black
curling hair flying about his dark face.  And all the
while Maria, her work finished, sat on a milking
stool watching the whole scene with a face on which
there showed neither astonishment nor interest.
She accepted the scene just as she had appeared to
accept everything since she had left the poorhouse
as an orphan and gone out into the world.  Thus
she had accepted the long trial of Ed Hasselman's
drunkenness and the discovery years earlier of the
body of Uriah Spragg in the ditch by the county
road.

At length Ed Hasselman became too drunk to
play and Shamus grew weary of his dancing and the
two of them sat quietly drinking and looking at the
moon.  And presently Shamus told them the story
which no one in Winnebago Falls ever believed because they said that Shamus was a half-wit and that
Ed Hasselman was drunk.  But Maria Hazlett was
not drunk.  She never drank.  She simply sat there
listening quietly.  She was content with her world
as she found it.

It had happened years earlier before Uriah
Spragg was murdered and when he still lived with
his sister in the wooden house by the town dump.
Shamus was about twenty years old at the time and
he had been off wandering for days and was on his
way home because he felt one of his visions coming
on.  It was dark and he had been hurrying across
fields and through woods for hours when he reached
Meeker's Gulch.  It was a lonely marshy place overgrown with sumach and witch-hazel so dense that
even stray hunters rarely penetrated it.  But Shamus wasn't afraid of it.  In the depths of the wild
swamp he felt at home.  It was only people who
frightened him.

It was, too, a hot still night like the night he
sat telling the story under the catalpas to Ed Hasselman and Maria Hazlett, with a red heavy August
moon climbing the prairie sky.  There was not
a breath of air stirring, yet as Shamus penetrated the swamp he noticed an odd thing——that all
the leaves of the sumach and witch-hazel, the oaks
and the cottonwoods, were dancing with a gentle
motion as if stirred by a gentle breeze.  They kept
up a faint whispering and presently he was aware of
a faint prefume like that of wild honeysuckle and
he began to hear snatches of faint music which
seemed to come out of the very sticks and stones
and the trunks of the trees.  It was sweet low music
like the sound of the fifes in the Grand Army parade
on the Fourth of July, only it was softer and less
shrill.  He thought one of his visions was coming
on and so he hurried, pushing his way through the
thicket with such violence that most of his clothes

were torn from his body. He was looking for some
open grassy space where he might fall down and lie
for hours in a state of unconsciousness.

Then as he pushed through the witch-hazel he
came suddenly upon an open space where the thick
marsh grass had been trampled down in a wide circle and in the moonlight he discovered two dancing
figures, one very white and the other as black as the
shadows cast by the copper moon. One was Miss
Annie Spragg and the other was the black he-goat.
She was quite naked with her long red hair falling
to her knees. There was a wreath of honeysuckle
on her head. The black he-goat capering prettily
with his delicate black front hoofs raised in the air
followed her round and round the trampled circle.
For a little time Shamus stood watching them from
behind the trunk of a great oak tree and presently,
as if he could not help himself, he joined in the
dance.

It was sunset of the following day when he came
to his senses and found himself lying on the bruised
grass in the middle of Meeker's Gulch.

When he had finished his story he slipped quietly
to the grass and fell into a sleep beneath the catalpa
trees. Maria Hazlett rose and covered him with a
featherbed and then raising the half-conscious Ed
Hasselman got him into bed. In the morning she
had to deliver the milk on the milk route in Winnebago Falls, because Ed was taken again by one of
his spells.

V

It was two years after this almost to the day
when Shamus went off for the last time wandering
across the country. His mother had been sleeping
quietly in the shanty by the railroad-tracks when
she was awakened in the middle of the night by the
thunder that terrified her. Rising, she began to
sprinkle holy water about the shanty and to call
upon the saints to protect her. When she went into
the kitchen where Shamus slept she found his bed
empty. Despite her terror of the storm, she went
outside and called his name again and again into
the screaming prairie wind. But she got no answer.
In the flashes of lightning she found no trace of
Shamus but only thick black shadows and the distant lights of the railroad switches. He was gone
into the wild storm and she could not find him.

When the sun came up the next morning he did
not return and she went to the police, who laughed
at her craziness, not knowing what Shamus was to
her. They telephoned about the county but no one
had seen any trace of him. It was Maria Hazlett
who thought where he might be found. That evening when she went to fetch the cows from the pas-
ture by Meeker's Gulch she went into the swamp and
there in the thickest part she found him. He was
lying on the thick grass, which had been trampled
down in a wide circle. He lay on his back in the
shadow of the big oak with one arm thrown over
his head. His clothes were all torn and the rain
had plastered them close to his supple body. His
black hair lay in ringlets over the dark forehead.

She thought he was asleep at first or in one of his trances, but he was dead.  There was no mark of any kind on his body.

She picked him up and managed to carry him to the edge of the swamp, where she laid his body on the grass beside the brook until Ed Hasselman could come and help her get it back to the house.  Dead, he seemed to her more beautiful than ever.  It was odd, she told Ed Hasselman, that he had never appeared to grow any older.  He must have been thirty-eight when he died but he looked no older than he had looked at twenty.  Perhaps, she said, it was because he was half-witted.  People like that didn't seem to grow old.  They belonged to a world of their own.

## VI

The church buried him in consecrated ground, so Mary's soul was at peace.  After that she was never sober again and at last they took her out of the filth and squalor of the little shack, off to the poorhouse.  One morning three weeks after they brought her there the keeper found her dead in bed.  She was seventy-seven years old, a queer dried-up wisp of a woman who had once been the fine high-colored Mary Bosanky.  In all those seventy-seven years life had never once been fine enough for her.

## THE END OF AUNT BESSIE

### I

SHE was not a bad girl, not really. It simply never occurred to her that there was anything wrong, not very wrong, in the way she lived. And so she often remarked to Teena Bitts, "I'm not a tart proper, I never went off with a man that I didn't meet proper in Winterbottom's place." The pavement knew her not although she was well known to the patrons of the Pot and Pie, a sort of restaurant and public house and rendezvous of bookmakers on the city side of Bayswater. She had been ruined at sixteen in an areaway while her mother was away scrubbing the stairs of the Houses of Parliament, and when the same mother discovered Bessie's error and its impending result, she sought out the man and made him right the wrong. Technically Bessie's child (which died) had a father, but substantially Bessie had no husband, for he disappeared two days after the ceremony and was never heard of again.

But marriage did not make of Bessie an honest woman. She went her way as before and in a few months Mrs. Cudlip, her mother, reported to her charring friends that Bessie's husband had returned and that Bessie had lost her position at the Pot and Pie. In four months Bessie gave birth to what her mother called "a little girl," and Bessie went back to work leaving the baby to be cared for by a childless couple who lived in Hammersmith and later adopted it. Before Bessie was twenty-four the same

incident in all its details (even to the return of the
husband who appeared to visit Bessie after the mysterious fashion prevalent among the heathen gods)
was repeated twice more. At the birth of the third
child, Bessie very nearly died and after that she appeared to change her ways. At least the husband
did not miraculously reappear and she had no more
children.

At twenty-eight she was a plump, coarsely pretty
girl, whose high spirits never deserted her. With
a loud laugh she could bandy the coarsest jests with
any of the coarse patrons of the Pot and Pie. Her
round rosy face, her blue eyes, and the blond hair
that hung damp and curling from a huge pompa-
dour constructed over an elaborate apparatus of
wire, were among the stimuli which betrayed sober
men suddenly into the pagan knowledge that it was
best to live while one was alive. Without dreaming
of such a thing she conveyed this message to every
man she served with mutton pie and stout. And
Bessie was so carefree and good-natured that she
never imposed upon her admirers any sense of sin.
It was all a lark. She even came to be known in a
strange blend of good humor, affection and contempt
bred of familiarity as Our Bess and sometimes
Good Queen Bess. She was the toast and the joy
of the Pot and Pie and the men who came in with
pockets empty and spirits depressed went away after
a tilt with Our Bess feeling warmed and cheered.
She really loved humanity. She loved the smoke
and heat of the tap room, the collared looks of the
mugs of ale, the oaths of the cabbies and bookmakers and the sight of old Mrs. Crumyss, ginny

and happy, exchanging crackling witticisms with the gentlemen who baited her. She had, too, a liking, fatal to one of her tendency to plumpness, a great liking for the ale that came out of the shiny brass-bound tuns served by Teena Bitts. "That Mrs. Crumyss," she used to say in relating to her mother choice bits of that lady's wit, "She's a hot 'un." She had a way of emphasizing such remarks by a hearty slap on her round, well-covered thigh. There was all the zest about Our Bess that Rubens, who loved life, imparted to the plump rosy ladies who were so like her. Winterbottom, the proprietor of the Pot and Pie, understood her value to him. He did not even object to her enforced holidays.

But Bessie never had any money. It was not that she spent it, even in betting on the races, as might have been supposed. She had a 'orror of betting and of bookmakers as bookmakers. She never had any money because she never understood how it was people got money. Even Winterbottom underpaid her. Sometimes her "friends" gave her a cheap trinket or a pair of silk stockings or a few shillings but rarely more than that. Teena Bitts said scornfully that she had no character. But Our Bess only laughed and asked Teena what *her* character had got her beyond a reputation for being coldblooded and stingy.

II

The development of character in Our Bess—that change which turned her in the end into Aunt Bessie of Bloomsbury and St. John's Chapel—dated from the twenty-fourth of December, 1905, a cold foggy night with snow falling that melted as it fell. She had been standing in the doorway watching Teena Bitts draw ale from the fine brass-bound tuns and listening with hearty appreciation to the sallies of old Mrs. Crumyss, who was trying to drink through her veil, when the door opened and in out of the fog came a small thin man with a pinched face as white as wax. He had no overcoat and the collar of his coat was turned up about his thin throat. None of the others appeared to take any notice but the sight of him did something to Bessie. Perhaps it was pity that struck her down, for he was everything that she was not. He was sickly, white and shivering, with a wild look in his near-sighted brown eyes. She marked him at once for her own, filled with a strange emotion that sometimes took possession of her. To herself she called it, "feeling that she ought to brighten 'im up a bit," but it was really much more primitive and direct than that. Bessie felt sorry for anyone who could not see that the world was a fine and shining place, as fine indeed as the brass bands on Winterbottom's ale barrels. She could not see why everyone should not be as happy as herself.

He did not respond to her sallies as other men did. Even after she had served him with meat pie, a pitcher of stout, a gooseberry tart and some coffee, his spirits failed to show any signs of rising. Nothing, she discovered, seemed to have any effect upon him. He failed even to appreciate the excruciating sallies of Mrs. Crumyss. After he had eaten he began to drink brandies and sodas, drinks with a great deal of brandy and very little soda. The more depressed he became the more interested and curious became Bessie's attitude.   It was like a challenge to her, as if her record was to be smirched with failure for the first time in the eyes of Winterbottom and Teena Bitts and the others.   She noticed that despite the shabbiness of his clothes he was clean, and that his hands were white and soft.   And then suddenly she discovered that under his coat he had no shirt but only a frayed undershirt and she had doubts that he would be able to pay for all he was drinking.   But remembering that it was Christmas Eve she told herself that if Winterbottom made trouble she'd pay the bill out of her own money. Everyone else in the place was so gay and happy. Mrs. Crumyss was never in better form.   She was still drinking through her veil and seemed now to be managing quite well, as if, like the seventh child of a seventh child, she had been born with one.

A little before closing time when the noise was at its height the stranger suddenly fell forward on the table and Bessie, feeling that the time had come to act, pointed out to him that the pub was closing and that he had better pay for all he had eaten and drunk.   Her suggestion brought forth no response save a mumbling and moaning sound of which she could make nothing.   Winterbottom at last noticed her efforts and knowing her fatal sympathy for any customer who could not pay, came over to the table. He went straight to the point, searching the stranger's pockets hopefully, but he found only a half-penny, a soiled handkerchief and three damp woodbines.   He had already started for the door to

summon a policeman when Bessie stopped him.
"Leave 'im alone," she said. "I'll pay for it."

Winterbottom was content. It had happened before. He would rather have the money than see the
stranger arrested, even if the money came out of
Bessie's pocket.

"And what are you going to do when it closes?"
he asked her.

"Never you fret about that. I'll take 'im in
charge."

The revellers, singing, went out at last. Teena
Bitts put on her hat and went off scornfully to
spend a respectable Christmas with her parents in
Limehouse, and Winterbottom stood waiting to see
what Bessie proposed to do. In a moment she came
in from the washroom and gave the cynical Winterbottom a challenging glance. She was looking high-
colored and high-spirited as if she felt her reputation
menaced a second time in the same evening. She
was a strong woman, and after raising the stranger
to his feet she took him firmly by one arm and set
out through the fog. Winterbottom put up the
shutters, locked the door and put out the lights,
unaware that he had lost Our Bess forever.

Somehow, through fog and snow, through
crooked and winding streets, she got the stranger
back to her own room. Toward the end it was a
little easier because he began to see things following
him and that hurried him along.

III

The beginning of Bessie's character was a violent one, for she no sooner had the pitiful creature safe in her warm and shabby room than he went entirely to pieces. He began seeing things in her closet, under the bed and coming through the transom above the door. He saw all manner of strange beasts, even to unicorns, which Bessie knew well enough did not exist save on the splendid device of the British Empire. Under the stimulus of delirium the little man developed a superhuman strength which proved very nearly too much even for the stalwart Bessie. But she succeeded at last in binding him into the great double bed, and after rousing another indignant lady dwelling in the same house she secured morphine, which after a time reduced him to a stupor. She managed at last to get an hour's sleep lying beside him lest he should awake and become violent again. In the early morning she gave him some hot milk and when he fell asleep again she put on her hat and coat and set out through the slush for the Pot and Pie.

There she confronted Winterbottom and told him that she was in need of a holiday. He looked at her with a twinkle in his hard eye and asked, "What? Again?"

But Bessie denied his suspicion. She had a cousin, she said, who was ill and in need of care. Otherwise he would be sent to the workhouse and no Cudlip had ever darkened the door of a workhouse.

So Mrs. Winterbottom took Bessie's place at the

Pot and Pie until Bessie was able to return.   It had long since become an accepted system.

IV

The stranger not only became Bessie's problem; he took on the proportions of a crusade.   She tended him carefully, rarely leaving his side save to buy food out of her almost invisible savings or to come down on the heads of others in the house who disturbed his rest by becoming noisy.   She had in a cheap doctor and with the shrewdness of the poor she learned from him enough so that it was unnecessary to have him a second time.   Her patient, she discovered, was suffering not only from drink but from starvation.   She fed him up in splendid style and as he progressed toward recovery she experienced a new emotion—that of pride in the efficacy of her cure.   She even thought for a time of giving up her way of life and becoming a nurse, but learning upon investigation that such a change implied complications and a good deal of tiresome training, she abandoned the idea.

It was not until the third week that she learned the name of the stranger.   He had been well enough for some time to lie in bed watching her out of his dark eyes, but Bessie, feeling that it was indelicate to be curious about his name, did not mention the matter.   She simply continued to address him as "You" and refer to him to the others in the house as " 'im."   She stood in awe of hm, for her cockney shrewdness told her that he had come out of a world far above her, of which she knew nothing.   The

delicate hands, the beautiful accent, the dim weak
face with dark eyes under a high white forehead,
filled her with a strange pride. This was indeed a
rare flower that had fallen into her hands. Even
as she lay beside him on the bed (there was nowhere
else for her to sleep) she felt that she was com-
mitting sacrilege.

At length one day he looked at her and said, "My
name is Lionel Blundon. What's yours?"

She blushed and said, "Bessie Cudlip." It
sounded so cheap and commonplace beside the elegance of Lionel Blundon. "Lionel," she said to
herself, "Lionel." That *was* an elegant name.

He began presently to sit up weakly in bed and to
take a faint interest in things.

v

But Bessie soon found that her funds were vanish-
ing. Funds were a thing that never mattered before. There was always the Pot and Pie or she
could borrow from Teena Bitts or get an advance
from Winterbottom. But it mattered now; Mr.
Blundon was a responsibility. He could not be sent
out into the streets, white and ill and shaking with
fever. He seemed content with his lot and displayed no inclination to go.

So one night after Mr. Blundon had gone to
sleep, she slipped out to the Pot and Pie dressed in
her best clothes. She took up a place in the corner
and became the center of interest. The place had
not been the same since she left and they now received her with cheers. The men bought her drinks.

Even old Mrs. Crumyss was thrown into the shadow by her triumphant return and spent the whole evening neglected in the corner, mumbling and drinking. Teena Bitts, standing before her shining tuns, grew sarcastic and made bitter inquiries about the stranger whom Bessie had "picked from the dust bin." And Bessie, a little flushed and excited by her triumph, retorted that he had turned out to be a gentleman and the cousin of the Duke. But this gave Mrs. Crumyss her long awaited opportunity. From then on she kept making bitter remarks about "The Duchess" and " 'er Gryce," and won back a little of her prestige. The name stuck to Bessie. Our Bess became 'er Gryce from that day forward.

At closing time Mrs. Crumyss led the way with unsteady dignity, followed one by one by the others, and at last Bessie left too, accompanied by 'Arry, who, rumor had it, had just made a killing on the Newmarket. Teena, seeing her go, remarked that it was the first time Bessie had shown any character.

At dawn she returned before Mr. Blundon was awake and for several days she was in funds. Necessity had made her practical.

As Mr. Blundon (as she continued to call him) grew stronger, he appeared also to grow restless. Feeling that he was too proud and of a birth too noble to accept money from her, she left small sums about carelessly when she went out, sometimes on the table, sometimes on a shelf in the closet, as if it were crumbs for birds. Always when she returned it was gone. By this trick he was able to buy himself cigarettes and newspapers. He did not return to the Pot and Pie and showed no inclination to

drink so she came to the conclusion that his drinking was not a disease but done deliberately out of
despair.   Once in a burst of confidence he confided
to her that on the night he had come to the Pot and
Pie he had been contemplating suicide but that on
studying the chilly river he had decided instead to
drink himself to death.   He was a simple fellow,
she thought, who didn't pretend to be anything he
was not.

Then one day he asked her timidly if she would
do an errand for him.   He wanted some books and
he was still too ill to go into the city for them himself.   So Bessie dressed herself up and made the
excursion, bearing a slip of paper on which were
written the titles, because she could not possibly have
remembered them.   They were difficult names
which impressed her profoundly, such names as
Astaroth  and  Indo-Persian  and  Anaït.   They
seemed very rare books, for she was forced to trudge
from shop to shop to find them all, and they were
very expensive.   Later on she made other trips to
buy books until her room had quite the air of a
library.   Then Mr. Blundon bought ink and pens
and paper and went to work.   Each day he covered
a great many sheets of paper with spidery handwriting which she attempted without much success
to decipher when he was not in the room.   But even
those portions which she was able to read (and she
was none too good at reading and writing) she failed
to understand, and she had not the presumption to
question him about the whole affair.

But all this took money (she had even to buy him
new clothes) and so Bessie went more and more

frequently to the Pot and Pie, always as a patron, and only after Mr. Blundon had gone to bed.  Always she came in early before he was awake.  She was afraid that he would discover the nature of her excursions and forbid them.  She took great care not to disturb him on getting into bed, but once or twice she fancied that he was awake when she came in.  When he made no reference to her mysterious absences, she decided that she must have been wrong, though she was quite certain that once at least he had opened his eyes and looked at her.  She even managed to save up quite a bit of money.  Teena Bitts's sarcastic references to " 'er Gryce's lack of character" grew more and more mild and at length died away altogether.  Teena was outdone.

But Bessie had a plan that would require all her money.  Mr. Blundon had become to her more than a crusade; he was now a part of her life.  If he seemed tired, she began to worry.  If he did not eat she thought of calling a doctor.  She could not imagine her life without him.  And when his poor health lingered she decided that it was the air of Bayswater and that what he needed was a holiday at Brighton.

She was fearful that if she mentioned the plan, his pride might cause him to object to it and so until the day when she had saved enough to swing the excursion in style, she did not speak of it.  When at last she summoned up courage to propose it, Blundon accepted it at once as a splendid idea.  He would take his books and work in the sea air.

But she could not resist having a final triumph at the Pot and Pie and the night before they departed

she went there to let Teena Bitts and Winterbottom
and Mrs. Crumyss know in the most casual way possible that she and her friend were going to Brighton
for a spell.    Winterbottom eyed her shrewdly and
sadly, suspecting that the moment had come when
he was to lose Our Bess forever, and after she had
gone Mrs. Crumyss remarked acidly through her
veil that "the next thing they'd be hearing was that
'er Gryce had become one of them swell divorce co-
respondents."

VI

It was the first time Bessie had ever been outside
London and, as she said, "it made her feel lost."
Even the crowds and the music on the jetty did not
help much after she was used to them; they did not
make up for the gayety of the Pot and Pie with
Teena Bitts uttering coarse bitter comments and
'Arry and Alf drinking and Mrs. Crumyss giving
freely of her experience of life.    Without Mr.
Blundon Bessie would have been miserable, but his
presence gave her a purpose, something, as it were,
to steer by.    She had to plan the days and watch
over his health and see that there wasn't any noise
in the lodging house and buy him cigarettes.    Although she had long been Bessie to him, she never
presumed to call him anything but Mr. Blundon, and
although they shared the same room there had never
been even a suspicion of lovemaking between them.

It was in the second week of the visit that the
great meeting occurred.    Mr. Blundon, who was
working hard at the lodging house and was a bit
exhausted by Bessie's hungry attempts at conversa-

tion, suggested that she go and listen to the band concert, and as she always felt restless away from crowds, she took his advice. He would meet her by the fifth light out from the shore on the pier.

It was a soft fine evening and all Bessie's smouldering hunger for life was fanned into a flame. Indeed her emotions had so thoroughly gotten the better of her that she began to wish Mr. Blundon wasn't so sickly and that he wasn't such a swell that she was afraid of him. She began to feel deep yearnings for the companionship of the Pot and Pie. She even wished that Mr. Blundon might miraculously turn out to be 'Arry or Alf. Lost in this strange mood of depression she wandered along the pier to the accompaniment of Pomp and Circumstance. She reached the fifth light and halted, lost in a slough of homesickness. And then someone pinched her and her spirits skyrocketed once more.

Turning, she planned to upbraid her insulter, since that was the conventional thing to do. "How dared he do such a thing to a lady?" (Indeed she had been acquiring airs lately through contact with Mr. Blundon's elegance.) But when she turned there was no possible suspect in sight but a kindly looking old gentleman in black who wore a black Homburg hat and carried a black umbrella. He looked a little, she thought, like a parson. Thinking that the pinch must have been administered by some mischievous person who vanished in the crowd, she turned back to her reverie. Being pinched was not a new experience for Bessie. Her plumpness made her a tempting subject and she had developed a technique for dealing with the situation. Barely had her spirits fallen, leaving her to brood over the sea, than the pinch was repeated.

Again she turned sharply and this time there could be no mistake. It *was* the kindly old gentleman in the Homburg hat who had pinched her. She gave him an indignant glance, but not so indignant as it would have been if Alf and 'Arry had been nearer than Bayswater. He lifted his hat calmly and said, "Good evening, ma'am, it's a fine evening."

Her instinct told her at once that this was not a gentleman of Mr. Blundon's elegance. His clothes were rich but his manner and spirit were those which she understood.

"I've seen finer," she replied with some tartness, resolved not to give in too easily.

He was really a fine looking old gentleman, about seventy, she thought, with a fine ruddy face and a chin beard that was white and cut short and round. On his black waistcoat glittered a massive gold watch-chain. He had bland round blue eyes and an air of good humor. He asked her if she was alone.

"Not exactly," said Bessie. "I'm wyting for a friend."

Would she mind if he chatted a bit until her friend came? No, she said, but she'd have to stay there by the fifth light because that was where she was going to meet her friend.

"Nice music," he said.

"Yes, nice music."

"I've always liked Pomp and Circumstance. It's like the British Empire."

"You must be musical," she suggested.

"I like music."

"I'm from London," she said wistfully. "I came down here for the air and I ran into my friend.'

The mention of London appeared to make the old gentleman a little bolder. "Maybe I'd better tell you my name so you can introduce me when she comes along."

"It's a he," said Bessie, and then noticing the old gentleman's alarm, added, "But it's all right. We're only friends."

"Oh," said her companion. "Well, my name's Winnery—Horace J. Winnery."

"And mine's Cudlip—Bessie Cudlip."

Horace J. Winnery, she thought, was a beautiful name like Lionel Blundon, only it didn't fill her with awe. It made her feel quite at home.

The band blared into a potpourri from Faust and Mr. Blundon came into sight through the crowd. He was peering to right and to left with his near-sighted eyes. Bessie, being in a realistic mood, could not help thinking that her new acquaintance, even at his age, was more of a man.

"There's my friend now," said Bessie, and Mr. Winnery with a glance at Mr. Blundon looked relieved of some secret anxiety.

She introduced them and Mr. Winnery was very cordial, but Mr. Blundon seemed absentminded and concerned with his own thoughts. But she was proud of him and hoped that his accent had impressed Mr. Winnery. It would show him what sort she was.

"Let's go and 'ave some ale," said old Mr. Winnery, so they went and sat in the pavilion and drank together. It seemed to cheer Mr. Blundon. It was the first time he had had a drop since Christmas Eve.

Mr. Winnery, who wanted clearly to be friendly, relaxed a great deal more and began telling them the story of his life in a voice loud enough to compete with the Soldiers' Chorus. He was in Brighton, he said, for a spell and he didn't think much of Brighton. Frankly, it was getting on his nerves. In his opinion it was a poor place. London for him every time. He was lonely. It was funny but he'd been hoping he'd run into some young people. He was a bit of a gay dog himself and didn't feel a day over thirty. He'd lost his wife some months ago. That was why he was wearing black clothes. He didn't like black clothes but you had to wear them. Not that she wasn't a good sort. He'd been married to her for forty years and when you'd had somebody about for forty years you missed them when they were gone. Would they have another drink? Yes. It was a hot night. He was always thirsty on hot nights. He was a ship's chandler, and a good business it was, too. He'd made a lot of money at it. And now he was trying to enjoy himself, but he couldn't do it alone, not alone. You had to have somebody to enjoy things with you.

(At this point the band swept gayly into a potpourri from Cavalleria Rusticana and Mr. Blundon dropped into a quiet slumber.) "Like most drunks," thought Bessie, " 'e's got a weak head. It ain't that he drinks so much." She considered his behavior a proper breach of manners but she hadn't the courage to disturb him.

Mr. Winnery was still shouting above Mascagni's

best effort. Maybe if they weren't too busy they'd spend a little time with him. It would be his treat. He had plenty of money.

Bessie said Mr. Blundon was working in the daytime, but that she had nothing to do. He was writing a book, she explained impressively.

"Ah," breathed Mr. Winnery, impressed. "A book. What kind of a book?"

"I don't know," said Bessie. "It's just a book."

The band stopped playing and began putting its brass instruments to bed in green baize. Bessie thought it was time for them all to go home and awakened Mr. Blundon. Together the three of them walked to the end of the pier. She noticed that Mr. Blundon was a little unsteady. On the promenade Mr. Winnery bade them a polite good-night.

"Perhaps," he suggested, "we might meet in the morning. Say ten o'clock."

Mr. Blundon offered no objections. He did not even seem to hear.

"All right," said Bessie.

VII

Bessie liked the old gentleman. He was, she told herself, one of her sort, out for a good time. All the black clothes and Homburg hats and black umbrellas in the world could not dampen the twinkle in his blue eyes or the healthy pink in his cheeks. "When he was young," she speculated, "he must have been a wild 'un." She was growing a little bored with Mr. Blundon's quiet way of living. Bessie was one who could not do without her fun.

She met old Mr. Winnery the following day. She even arrived at the rendezvous a little before the hour agreed upon. It was the wedding of twin spirits. They walked the promenade together and rode in donkey carts and went to the cinema and drank ale in large quantities. (Both, unlike Mr. Blundon, were blessed with hard heads.) They had lunch in the showiest hotels and restaurants, such places as Bessie had never before dreamed of entering. Indeed, Bessie began to think that she was cut out for a grand life. Mr. Winnery was never awkward in such places; he had an assurance beside which the elegant Mr. Blundon seemed a cringing creature. Mr. Winnery could buy anything he wanted and going about with such a gentleman was a new experience for Bessie. He bought her trinkets—a barette set with brilliants for her taffy-colored hair, a spotted veil which she admired and which gave her a fast look. She kept thinking, "I wish that Teena Bitts could see me now." She squealed with delight in shooting galleries and places where she garnered gaudy vases and trinkets by throwing hoops over them. She and Mr. Winnery came to think Brighton the gayest place in the world.

Meanwhile Mr. Blundon worked uninterrupted in the daytime and accompanied them at night to the band concerts. Sometimes he drank a little too much and Bessie was forced to steer him home. It was all very gay and everyone was very happy until one day Bessie, who seldom thought of such things, looked in the old stocking where she kept her money and found that there remained only three pounds and ten shillings. The Paradise of Brighton was at an end unless she found an Alf or a 'Arry, and that, she told herself, was difficult with Mr. Blundon on one side and Mr. Winnery on the other taking up all her time. Mr. Winnery might have been an aid but he, like Mr. Blundon, showed no interest in love-making, that is, if you discounted an occasional furtive pinch or shady joke. There seemed to be no way out but to bid old Mr. Winnery a sorrowful farewell and conduct Mr. Blundon, whose health seemed much improved, back to Bayswater where she knew her ground.

The next morning while she and Mr. Winnery were drinking together she told him that her visit was at an end, and old Mr. Winnery very nearly caused her to faint by asking her to marry him. She did not accept at once for she had, of course, to consider Mr. Blundon. She could not turn him out abruptly into the world to fall back into poverty and drunkenness. Besides, she would miss him. He would leave a hole in her life. So she told Mr. Winnery the whole story, out and out, even to the fact that although they had long shared a room there was nothing between them. She gave it as her opinion that Mr. Blundon was too sickly to be interested in such things. She told the story regretfully, feeling that she was driving the last nail into the coffin of her adventure with Mr. Winnery.

But Mr. Winnery proved himself a gentleman in every sense of the word. He believed the story, he told her, moved perhaps by the certainty that Bessie was too guileless to have invented such a tale. Her generosity, he said, made him care for her all the more deeply. As to Mr. Blundon, he could go on in his present state until he was well enough to fight his own battles in the world. Mr. Winnery would pay the expenses. Oh, yes, it would be a pleasure. He had plenty of money. And in that way they could be married at once. He implied a little sadly that he probably hadn't long to live and now that he'd found a companion that enjoyed life the way he did, he didn't want to waste any time. He told her about his house in Bloomsbury, his victoria and his brougham and his horses and his business. They would travel, he said. He'd always wanted to travel and find out about the world but he never had been able to get away from the docks, and Amanda —that was his late wife—had always made such a fuss when traveling.

She said she would speak to Mr. Blundon. She couldn't say yes or no until she found out how he took it.

### VIII

When she regained the lodging house she found the room in disorder. The books were mostly lying on the floor and Mr. Blundon's precious manuscript was scattered from one end of the room to the other. There was an ominous scent of brandy in the air. At first she did not see Mr. Blundon. It was only after she had set about putting the room in order that she discovered him. He was lying half in, half out of the closet, entirely hidden by the open door. Only his feet were in view. And he was dead to the world.

She thought, "It was that first drink at the pavilion. It got 'im started again."

After she had lifted him into the bed, she picked up the books.   No, she could not marry Mr. Winnery and desert poor Mr. Blundon to drink himself to death.   It was like turning a puppy out into the cold.   Still maybe she owed it to herself to be hardhearted and forget him.   She couldn't go on forever. . . .

Then as she was sorting the numbered sheets of illegible manuscript, she found among them a bit of paper that did not belong there.   It was a sheet of mauve paper and there was a purple coronet in the corner and under it was printed Narkworth Abbey, Middlebox, Surrey.   The letter began, "My dear Cousin Lionel" and was written in the crabbed and trembling hand of an aged person.

Bessie began to feel a little sick but curiosity pressed her and she read on.   "I have taken up your case with your cousin, the Duke, but he is unwilling to do anything.   He remains firm in his belief that you have disgraced the family and the name of Blundon not once but many times and that you have been at all times stubborn and unregenerate.   I believe I am quoting his own words correctly.   I have done my best to soften him, but as you know, he is a hard man.   The Blundons are always hard.

"I have disobeyed him in writing you.   He forbade any communication whatever unless, of course, you are willing to go to Africa or Australia.   You know he is extremely close and allows me barely enough money to run the two houses, the one here and the one at Prince's Gate.   Therefore I am able to spare you only the small amount enclosed."

(The cheque, thought Bessie, which he had spent in getting drunk.)

"I am glad to hear that your health is better and that you are working. I hope you will continue in the same condition, living quietly and respectably and that your health will not again be affected. I have never been to Brighton but hear that the air is good except for those who have livers.

"I am, with best wishes, your aunt

"LETITIA,
*"Duchess of Narkworth."*

For the only time in her life, Bessie felt faint. She sat down and read the letter through a second time. So the lie she told Teena Bitts had turned out to be true. Mr. Blundon *was* the cousin of a duke. She felt suddenly dizzy and to steady herself took a drink of what remained in Mr. Blundon's bottle. Then she stared for a time at the frail small figure sleeping on the bed with its mouth open. She thought of Mr. Winnery asking her to marry him. "It ain't true," she told herself. "It's like any blooming nightmare." It was like something she had made up. It was like a cinema. That little thing on the bed was the cousin of a duke.

Overcome with emotion she began to blubber. No, she couldn't turn Mr. Blundon out into the cold—not 'im, the cousin of a duke. He wasn't made to get on in the world. Somebody would have to look after him. Well, she'd explain to Mr. Winnery how she couldn't desert Mr. Blundon.

IX

But when Mr. Winnery set his mind on a thing he got it, so the unfortunate collapse of Mr. Blundon made no difference. When Mr. Blundon had recovered a little, the three of them went back to London, only not to Bayswater this time, but to Bloomsbury, where Mr. Blundon was put in lodgings near enough at hand so that Bessie might keep an eye on him. Bessie herself, with the new-found airs acquired from Mr. Winnery at Brighton, went to a temperance hotel. She objected to this and it was only later that she understood the subtlety of this move of Mr. Winnery.

It had never occurred to her that Mr. Winnery had any relatives. He had always seemed to her a gift from God sent to destroy the fit of misery which had seized her that night by the fifth light on the Brighton pier. It was only when Mr. Winnery announced the banns that the relatives came suddenly to light, filled with fury and indignation. There appeared two pious and rather dreary maiden sisters older than Mr. Winnery who lived at Scarborough on his largesse, and an orphan nephew who lived in Italy. The two sisters made the first move by telegraphing in distress to the nephew, who came all the way from Italy to London.

The interview took place in the common sitting room of the temperance hotel and Bessie acquitted herself with dignity. The nephew, Mr. Winnery of Brinoë, was smallish, about forty, with a bald spot and an air of condescension toward his uncle. It appeared from his insinuations that he was a su-

perior, cultivated and literary figure. Bessie, who
had only one standard in judging gentlemen, thought
him rather a poor thing. He had been educated at
Oxford by old Mr. Winnery and had an accent a
little like Mr. Blundon, a fact that helped to put
Bessie at her ease, since instead of awing her it now
seemed quite familiar.

She put on an air of style, taking care to point out
that it was old Mr. Winnery who wanted the marriage and not herself. In fact he had *insisted* upon
marrying her despite the fact that she herself had
raised many objections. She knew, she said, that
she could make him happy in his declining years.
They had already discovered that.

Although she had developed a great deal of
"character" since she left the Pot and Pie, she was
not to be tempted by promises of money to be paid
after the two sisters and Mr. Winnery of Brinoë had
come into the old gentleman's estate. The idea indeed made her indignant. She pointed out that she
was a friend of Mr. Winnery and not of his money
and that she would have married him just the same
if he hadn't had a penny, which was quite true. She
felt in his debt for the good time at Brighton and
she was one of the few whose happiness is scarcely
affected by money.

There was nothing to be done and in the end the
Italian Mr. Winnery went back gloomily to Italy
and the spinster sisters returned to Scarborough to
tell day after day the story of how their respectable
brother had been kidnapped by a cheap woman
young enough to be his granddaughter.

X

Bessie was married to Mr. Winnery at the registry office in the presence of three employees of the ship chandler's firm of Winnery and Company. Mr. Blundon managed to leave his book long enough to be present. He looked very nice in the new clothes Bessie and Mr. Winnery bought him for the occasion.

And Bessie, dressed in the finery lavished upon her by an adoring bridegroom, went on her bridal tour to Paris. They stayed at the Grand Hotel, where Bessie had but to open her window at any hour of the day or night to look out upon the crowds and gayety of the boulevards. They went to music halls and dined each night in a different restaurant and climbed the Eiffel Tower and visited the races and were astonished by the chocolate splendor of the opera. Mr. Winnery was happy as a boy and Paris became for them only a glorified Brighton.

It was only when Bessie went back to the house in Bloomsbury that she became aware for the first time in her life of that mental state known as temptation. The house bore the imprint of the late Amanda Winnery, a religious woman and a stout believer until her death in the professions of the Plymouth Brethern. The furniture was mostly of black teakwood and red plush embellished by a large amount of inlaid funereal marble. In each room framed legends set forth such thoughts as REPENT LEST YE FALL INTO THE HANDS OF THE DEVIL, and HE THAT LOOKETH UPON THE WINE WHEN IT IS RED IS IN DANGER OF HELL FIRE. These had been

embroidered in appropriately sombre colors by
Amanda Winnery and long ago had turned faded
and dusty.  Bessie found them depressing.  During
the first few weeks, especially at those moments
when the cheerful Mr. Winnery was not in the
house, she was filled with a terrible desire to make a
visit to the Pot and Pie.  Alone in the depths of that
mausoleum, her soul cried out for the companionship of Teena Bitts, Alf and 'Arry and old Mrs.
Crumyss.

Then slowly, bit by bit, the presence of Amanda
Winnery's virtuous ghost began to give way to the
presence of the very living Bessie.  The framed
legends slowly disappeared, whither no one knew,
and in their place appeared bright chromos purchased in Mile End Road and a great deal of brass
work, for which Bessie developed a great taste.
And last of all, a gramophone, a parrot, two
canaries and a pair of white poodles made their appearance.  She loved food and drink with a passion
equalled only by that of Mr. Winnery and so they
gave themselves over to a perpetual orgy of eating
and drinking.  She gracefully allowed her natural
indolence to take possession of her, sometimes not
troubling to dress until the evening, and each day
she grew plumper and plumper and, to the taste of
the old-fashioned Mr. Winnery, more desirable.
Mr. Winnery beamed with happiness and for the
first time in all his seventy years, life seemed to be
what he had always believed that it should be.  In
his lodgings Mr. Blundon seemed to be content.
She visited him three or four times weekly and his
spells of drunkenness grew fewer and fewer.  He

lived quite comfortably on the money allowed him
by Bessie, and Mr. Winnery grew to have quite an
affection for him, and to share the pride which
Bessie found in supporting the cousin of a duke.

It might have gone on forever thus but that Mr.
Winnery was, when all was said and done, an old
man, and drinking and eating was certain to take its
toll. One night while Bessie sat in her wrapper
reading John Bull on the opposite side of the fire
from Mr. Winnery she noticed that the newspaper
with which he covered his face when he slept was
very still and that his hands hung down in a queer
fashion. She went over to him and lifted the newspaper. He was quite dead. He had simply gone
to sleep in the midst of his happiness, warm and content after a good dinner, with his Bessie sitting
opposite him.

XI

What might have been called the Last Phase of
Bessie began on the day after the funeral when the
will was read. Save for the money to continue the
income of the maiden sisters living in Scarborough,
the income of the entire fortune was left to Bessie
Cudlip Winnery. There was no provision made
for the nephew who lived in Brinoë, save the ironical
one that on the death of Bessie Cudlip Winnery, the
entire fortune was to go to him. And Bessie was
more than ten years younger than her nephew and
in the most robust of health and spirits. But she
was of a forgiving nature, and understanding perhaps the nephew's agitation at the time of her
marriage to Mr. Winnery, she arranged that

the usual income was to be sent to Brinoë out of her own money. So now, with Mr. Blundon, she supported two gentlemen instead of one.

She dressed herself in the thickest and blackest crêpe and then discovered something which she had not noticed before—that for nearly four years old Mr. Winnery had been her entire life and that without him she was lost. He had taken the place of Bayswater and the Pot and Pie and of Alf and 'Arry and Teena Bitts and Mrs. Crumyss and now she had neither the one nor the other. As she had grown immensely fat and very indolent, she did nothing about it for a long time. Even the temptation to return to the Pot and Pie seemed to have weakened, or at least taken another form. She wanted to return now on a single visit only to show Teena Bitts and Winterbottom how well she had done.

Her only diversion was an occasional visit to the lodgings of Mr. Blundon. Sometimes he was in and sometimes not and when she did find him there he received her with the same dignity and detachment that had marked their long friendship. But, as Bessie said, he was never much of a one for small talk and their conversation lagged. The dialogue consisted usually of inquiries about the book, the character of which remained a perpetual mystery to Bessie, and remarks about the weather. The regeneration of Mr. Blundon seemed well on the way to become an accomplished fact. He no longer got drunk, and in decent clothes appeared the gentleman he was by birth. He was fond of Bessie, but cold, and her own attitude toward him was a little that of a hen that had mothered a duckling. Only once had he ever lost his temper and that was on the occasion when she suggested that the book must be nearly finished and that surely it would be in many volumes. At which Mr. Blundon told her that it was a monumental and erudite work and that she wouldn't understand it even when it was finished. Bessie wept a little, not because her feelings were hurt (she knew he was quite right about her understanding any book) but because the book had not been finished before the death of Mr. Winnery. *He* would have understood it, she said. *He* was a wonderful man and understood everything. She was very lonely without him. Life wasn't the same. Perhaps, she suggested tearfully, Mr. Blundon would like sometime to drive out in the victoria with her and the poodles.

But Mr. Blundon told her that he detested riding in victorias and that the motion made him seasick. His refusal filled her with disappointment because at the bottom of her proposal lay a crafty plan. She had hoped that one afternoon they would make an early start and that suddenly they would find themselves as if by accident in Bayswater before the Pot and Pie. She had pictured to herself the triumph of calling out Teena Bitts and Winterbottom and even old Mrs. Crumyss, if she was still alive, to witness the spectacle of herself with horses and coachman, poodles and Mr. Blundon, the cousin of a duke. She wanted to know what Teena Bitts would have to say now about her lack of character.

But being of a philosophical turn she abandoned the triumphal plan and pushed out into another di-

rection in search of human companionship. She
simply wanted people to be friendly. She wanted
small talk, of this and that, spiced perhaps by sallies
like those of old Mrs. Crumyss. So she turned to
her own servants, the cook and two housemaids, but
the results were disastrous. After two weeks of
dreadful uneasiness, all three gave notice and sought
mistresses who would not seek to be intimate with
them.

In despair Bessie told herself that as the widow
of Horace J. Winnery she could not frequent public
houses. In any case she could not go comfortably
on foot and ladies who frequented pubs did not
drive up to the door in a victoria with a coachman.
It wasn't that she wanted to drink. She could do
that at home. She wanted simply an excuse for a
talk.

At last she hit upon the idea of going to Brighton
in the hope that if she did not find it gay she might
at least recapture memories of that lovely visit with
Mr. Blundon and Mr. Winnery. So with a great
effort she got off at last and at Brighton took a
gilded sitting room and bedroom in the showiest hotel in the place. She hired a victoria and went driving with the poodles. She sometimes went down to
the beach and sat under a black umbrella while they
yapped and barked for stones thrown them by the
children. She sat gloomily listening to Pomp and
Circumstance and potpourris from Faust, Carmen
and Cavalleria Rusticana. She sat drearily in dark
cinemas. She could not frequent places where you
could shoot at ducks and giraffes made of painted
tin nor toss hoops over Japanese vases. She found

that hers was a nature that could not live upon
memories. She was trying to enjoy herself but she
couldn't do it, not alone. You had to have somebody to enjoy things with you.

In the end she began again to hate Brighton as
she had hated it the first time she saw it. Only this
time it was worse because she didn't even have the
gloomy Mr. Blundon to sit with her in the evenings.


## XII

But Brighton appeared to occupy a prominent
place in the horoscope of Bessie, and two days before she planned to end her visit as a failure she
made by accident the acquaintance of a lady and
gentleman sitting at the next table to her in the
pavilion.

Bessie wouldn't have noticed them, for they were
quiet and drab and she had no taste for drab people,
but the lady took a fancy to Esther, the poodle
which she had in her lap. The lady asked Esther's
name and so opened the conversation. One thing
led to another. The lady and gentleman were Mr.
and Mrs. John Willis and their speech had that
faint cockney echo which always warmed Bessie's
heart. They were from London, they said, and
didn't care much for Brighton. It seemed a poor
place and much overrated. Bessie said she thought
so too. She was from London. Yes, she lived in
Bloomsbury.

Mrs. Willis, who was a dark, nervous little
woman of middle age, said, "Bloomsbury—well, I
never. That's where Mr. Willis and I live."

A glow emanated from Bessie's heart and took possession of her whole body. Bloomsbury, well, I never. Queer, and they lived quite near each other and never knew it. Funny how you could live in Bloomsbury for years and never know your nearest neighbor. It was an exclusive community. Mr. Willis, a little blond man with spectacles and a walrus moustache said that was the way life was, he'd found, and wasn't the music nice. That was the only thing they liked about Brighton—the band concerts. Indeed, they were about to cut short their visit and go back to London, where they felt more at home. They were going to stay two more days just to give the place a fair trial. It was Mr. Willis's first real holiday in fifteen years. Yes, he was a busy man. He had a linen shop and you could never trust people who worked for you.

Queer, said Bessie, she felt the same way about Brighton. She was going the day after tomorrow. Maybe they could go up together. How was she traveling? On the express, first class.

Mrs. Willis was afraid they couldn't travel like that. They weren't rich enough. When you've a shop you have to mind how you spend your money.

Perhaps then, suggested Bessie, they would travel with her, as her guests. She'd like it. She had plenty of money and she'd been hoping she'd meet someone to enjoy things with her. It wasn't any good trying to enjoy things alone. It would be a pleasure.

But Mr. Willis, who appeared to be cautious, said he'd have to think it over.

The band finished playing a potpourri from Ca-

valleria Rusticana and began putting away its instruments in receptacles of green baize. Mrs. Willis
thought perhaps they'd all better be going to bed,
so Bessie paid the bill for everything and they set
out slowly, for Bessie found it difficult to move very
fast. As they walked she said she had no children
(which was quite true) and so was very fond of
dogs. The Willises must see her other poodle,
Minnie. Minnie was at home because her chest was
weak and Bessie didn't think the night air at the
seaside was good for her.

Queer, said Mrs. Willis, they hadn't any children
either, although they'd prayed for them. But she
managed to fill in her time in church work. That
helped a great deal and it was sociable. Did Mrs.
Winnery go to any particular church?

Bessie said no, that she wasn't much of a one for
church. (Indeed, she had never seen the inside of
a church.) She'd come to Bloomsbury a stranger
and she'd never yet found her way about.

Mrs. Willis said she must come to their chapel.
She was sure that she'd feel at home there, and
Bessie said they must both come and have Sunday
dinner with her. At the end of the pier Bessie's
hired victoria was waiting and she drove them home
to their shabby lodgings. They parted the best of
friends.

"We might meet tomorrow," suggested Bessie.

"That would be fine," said Mrs. Willis.

"About ten-thirty at the end of the pier," said
Bessie. She waved back to them gaily as she drove
off to the splendor of her own suite at the George
and Crown.

The next day proved a great success, so great a
success that they all decided to stay five days longer.
Bessie it was who paid the expenses.  It gave her
pleasure, she said, and she had plenty of money.
And in the end they all went back to London on the
express, first class, with a compartment to themselves because Bessie felt uneasy when anyone like
Mr. Blundon was put in the same compartment with
her.

In Bloomsbury Bessie went to the chapel and Mr.
and Mrs. Willis came home in the victoria to Sunday dinner.  She did not care especially for the sermon nor for the boredom of sitting an hour and
a half in a hard pew, but she had found human companionship and she told herself that she couldn't
have everything.  Mrs. Willis admired the brass
collection and the chromos and Bessie sent her as
a gift a female white poodle.  It was the beginning
of a great friendship.  From then on Bessie attended the chapel regularly save on those Sundays
when she found the effort to dress quite beyond her
power of will.

She got used to the services and came to endure
them but she found her real pleasure in the meetings
of the ladies and all the auxiliary activities of the
chapel.  She could sit and drink her fill of amiable
talk.  And for the chapel she proved a godsend.
In a congregation of small linen drapers, green-
grocers and clerks, she appeared to be a female
Midas.  And because she wanted everybody to be
happy she bought a grand new organ for the chapel
and had new windows put in and presented it with
a baptismal font.  Out of gratitude the members

of the congregation had carved upon it, "Presented to St. John's Chapel by Bessie Cudlip Winnery." As for Bessie, she was happy. She had only one desire—that Teena Bitts might walk in some Sunday and read that inscription on the baptismal font.

It was Bessie, too, who established the famous August Bank Holiday Excursion and Annual Picnic. Oddly enough it was Mr. Blundon who suggested to her the idea. He thought it would be splendid if the children of the congregation could get into the country more often, so Bessie made it an annual affair. On the August Bank Holiday she hired char-a-bancs and, packing into them all the Sunday School children and as many of the parents as were free, set off into the country for the day. She herself occupied a seat in the back of the first char-a-banc, leading the way and filled with happiness. After the second year the excursions became so celebrated that people joined the chapel and sent their children to Sunday School for the sake of the single uproarious outing.

In the fourth year after Bessie met Mr. and Mrs. Willis, two momentous things happened. One was the death of the poodles. Esther died of old age and Minnie of the lung complaint which had troubled her for so long. Bessie bought two new poodles but they were never the same, she told Mr. Willis, because she had had Esther and Minnie while Mr. Winnery was still alive and their deaths were like the breaking of a chain that bound her to him.

In the midst of her grief she was sitting one afternoon in the window of the drawing room

(happily dressed) and listening to the gramophone
when an antiquated and high-pitched Rolls Royce
drove up and stopped before the door.  At sight of
it Bessie withdrew quickly behind the curtains but
not so quickly that she wasn't able to see that it had
on the door a coronet exactly like the one she had
seen on the letter found in Mr. Blundon's room so
many years before.  A footman rang the bell and
in a moment Briggs came in trembling, pale and
shaken, to ask if Mrs. Winnery could receive " 'er
Gryce, the Duchess of Narkworth."

"Now," thought Bessie, " 'es's done it.  E's gone
and told 'er the whole thing."

Peering from behind the curtain she saw a little
old woman dressed very queerly in black with a
black bonnet and parasol get down from the Rolls
Royce and come up the steps.

"She ain't so awesome," thought Bessie with relief.  "She looks just like old Mrs. Grubb that sits
in the third pew at chapel."

The little old lady came in and Bessie received
her with all the grace of manner Mr. Winnery had
taught her.  Would 'er Gryce sit down?  And did
she mind the poodle puppies?  No, it appeared, 'er
Gryce didn't mind, she kept spaniels herself—
cockers—and she was very attached to them.
Bessie told her about the death of Esther and Minnie, not without shedding a tear and explaining their
relation to the late Mr. Winnery.

And then 'er Gryce came to the point.  She too
had just lost her husband a little while before and
since he was dead there had been a reconciliation
between her and Mr. Blundon, the cousin of the

late Duke.  Indeed Mr. Blundon had gone to the
funeral and then came to Narkworth House for
lunch.  And a very changed Mr. Blundon he was
from the last time she had seen him.  He was even
cheerful and happy.  And after lunch he had taken
'er Gryce aside and told her what had happened to
him and how it was a Mr. and Mrs. Winnery who
had taken an interest in him and helped him when
his own family had cast him out.  (Not that Mrs.
Winnery must think the worse of the dear Duke.
He was a good man but hard.  The Blundons were
all hard.  And Mr. Blundon had given him, as the
head of the family, a great deal of trouble.)  So
she had come to thank Mrs. Winnery for what she
had been doing all these years.  If the dear Duke
hadn't been in his grave he would have come too,
out of thankfulness for seeing Mr. Blundon such a
changed creature.

Bessie said that what she'd done was nothing and
that it had given her and Mr. Winnery great pleasure and that they were very fond of Mr. Blundon
and couldn't have got on without him.

'Er Gryce said that now it was arranged for Mr.
Blundon to live in the dower house at Narkworth
and go on with his writing.  He had told her that
he was at work on a book which he would have finished shortly and would publish.  He had been reti-
cent about it.  Did Mrs. Winnery know what it was
about?

No, Bessie said, it was, she supposed, just a book.
But it was really too bad about Mr. Blundon going
to live at Narkworth.  She'd miss having him there
in Bloomsbury.  It would be a hole in her life.

But 'er Gryce said Mr. Blundon was going to keep the lodging in Bloomsbury to stop in when he came to town. He had grown fond of the place. She didn't suppose there was anything she could do for Bessie, but she wanted her to know how grateful the family had been for what she had done.

Then Bessie suggested that 'er Gryce have a drop of tea and the old lady lifted her veil and said she would be delighted to have some and, after the trembling Briggs had been sent to fetch it, they fell to discussing this and that and Bessie told her about the chapel and the August Bank Holiday Excursion and Annual Picnic. 'Er Gryce said she was interested in such ideas. She proved to be a very pious old lady and much interested in work among the poor. She would send Mrs. Winnery a cheque to help along her good work, which seemed to be growing at such a pace that Mrs. Winnery would soon find it beyond her means.

They drank tea together and became very friendly and 'er Gryce suggested that they might meet again and plan a place at Narkworth where tired girls could be sent for a rest. Mrs. Winnery might help her with the London end of it. Her daughter-in-law, the present Duchess, who was Miss Mazie Ffolliott of the Gaiety, had already been a great help in recruiting tired girls from the music halls. It was a plan she had had in mind for a long time. She could, she thought, house as many as twelve girls at a time in the old Abbey at Narkworth. She was having plumbing laid down. She had begun the day after the dear Duke's funeral. Perhaps Mrs. Winnery would come and have lunch with her one day at Narkworth House and they would talk it over. But Bessie said she didn't go out much and maybe 'er Gryce would come instead to Bloomsbury.

Bessie went with her to the door and was standing there when 'er Gryce drove off bowing and waving pretty as anything from the window of the antique Rolls. She was very nice, thought Bessie, and not a bit like a Duchess. She reminded her in a way of old Mrs. Crumyss if you forgot the way Mrs. Crumyss talked and drank.

That evening Bessie dropped in to see Mrs. Willis and gave her a finely detailed account of 'er Gryce's call.

The visit roused again the old temptation to return to the Pot and Pie. She was tormented by the desire to just drop in in passing to tell Teena Bitts about 'er Gryce. But she could not go until after the August Bank Holiday, which was only six days off. There was too much to be done in preparation for the Excursion and Annual Picnic. This year the crowd would need fourteen char-a-bancs. When that was over she would drive back to Bayswater in splendor just for one afternoon to show Teena and Winterbottom and Mrs. Crumyss.

XIII

The great day came and Bessie, sitting high in the back of the first char-a-banc, watched Mr. Willis twirling his walrus moustache and getting the crowd organized. At last they were off in an uproar of motors and a cloud of fluttering flags representing about equally the British Empire and St. John's

Chapel.  She wished again that Teena Bitts and old
Mrs. Crumyss could see her.

They went to Nottingham Forest and there under
the trees with the efficient direction of Mr. Willis
they spread out the food from great hampers.
There were all kinds of sandwiches, roast beef and
mutton, sausages, tarts and fruit, and quantities of
ice-cold beer, a real feast such as appealed to the
Gargantuan imagination of Bessie.  Then Mr. Willis organized a gymkhana in which all the children
and some of the grown-ups took part, and all this
led up in the end to the peak of interest—a race between the fat men of the congregation and the fat
ladies of the congregation.  There were twenty-
three entries in this event but when the lineup came,
Bessie was not among them.  At her absence a cry
went up from all present.  She, the fattest woman in
the congregation, was entered!  She, Mrs. Winnery,
who was responsible for all the fun!  It wouldn't be
any race at all if she didn't take part in it.  (Among
the fat ones it was already decided to fix the race
and allow her to win.)  The children gathered
around her crying, "Go along, Mrs. Winnery," and
Bessie protested and laughed, laughed until she became hysterical, but in the end she yielded and, removing her hat and jacket, took her place with the
others.

The race was to be run from the green char-a-banc
to the foot of the great oak that stood on the edge
of the road.  The whole congregation lined the edge
of the course.  Among the slim gentlemen bets were
placed as to the winner.  Shrieks of merriment
shattered the forest stillness.  And at last Mr.

Willis dropped the napkin that was the starting sig-
nal and they were off.   Bessie got off in the midst
and was making remarkable speed for so large a
woman.   Cries of encouragement went up from all
sides, for Bessie was the favorite, such a favorite as
there had never been in any race.   There was not
one who did not want her to win.   And Bessie was
doing her best, although very nearly helpless with
laughter.   Slowly she forged ahead into the lead.
Fifteen more yards and the victory would be hers.

But suddenly something happened.   It seemed
that she tripped over something, perhaps a root, and
fell to the ground.   A cry went up and fifty people
ran to help her.   But when they got to her side, she
seemed unable to rise.   She lay there quite still,
breathing with difficulty.   Six men carried her into
the shade of the great oak.   They brought water
and fanned her and from somewhere in the congregation there appeared an unsuspected bottle of
brandy.   They poured part of this between her
lips.   But there was nothing to be done.   Her
breathing stopped presently.   She had died of apo-
plexy in the midst of merriment.


XIV

At the chapel they gave her a great funeral.
Mr. Blundon attended it and 'er Gryce sent a wreath
made by the gardeners at Narkworth House.   The
preacher delivered a long sermon of eulogy, calling
attention to the new organ, the new windows and
the baptismal font, and most of all to the August
Bank Holiday Excursion and Annual Picnic.   In the

end he said, rather sentimentally, "For one reason, if not for countless others, she will always be remembered among us.   It can be said of her that she shared all she had and that her only desire was that others should be happy like herself."

It was Mr. Blundon himself who, as her oldest friend, consulted with Mr. and Mrs. Willis about the tombstone.   They decided upon it at last—a simple stone with the inscription:

HERE LIES

BESSIE CUDLIP WINNERY

WIDOW

OF

HORACE J. WINNERY

Died August — at the age of forty-six years
at the August Bank Holiday Excursion and Annual
Picnic of St. John's Chapel

HE PRAYETH BEST WHO LOVETH BEST
ALL THINGS BOTH GREAT AND SMALL
FOR THE DEAR GOD WHO LOVETH US
HE MADE AND LOVETH ALL

The two poodles went to join the poodle Bessie had given Mrs. Willis and the house was closed and sold, and the following week Mr. Blundon's book was published.   It was in two large volumes and was named A HISTORY OF PROSTITUTION, RELIGIOUS AND SECULAR.   It was an excellent and erudite book and received scholarly notices.   On the flyleaf appeared the dedication, "To Mr. and Mrs. Horace J. Winnery, whose Friendship and Aid Made the Writing of This Book Possible."

But Bessie died without ever returning to Bayswater. She died while the crowds stood in the hot street before the Palazzo Gonfarini in Brinoë looking up at the window where Miss Annie Spragg lay dead.

## SISTER ANNUNZIATA

### I

SIGNORA BARDELLI, concierge of the Palazza Gonfarini, had asked for Sister Annunziata and she stood there firmly waiting until she got what she wanted. It was always Sister Annunziata whom they asked for when they wanted a nun to come to the bedside of one of their dying. Sister Maria Maddelena, who stood in the small square room facing the agitated janitress, was in her heart a proud nun and when she thought "they" she meant all the poor who lived in the decaying old rookeries in the quarter about the Palazzo Gonfarini. Usually "they" asked for Sister Annunziata timidly but there was no timidity in the bearing of the stalwart Signora Bardelli. Sister Maria Maddelena knew her by reputation, a shrewd and a boastful woman, who mocked priests and the Church. The sister, who was human in her small way, could not resist murmuring, "But you do not hold with the Church, Signora Bardelli."

"It is not for me," said the janitress. "It is for the stranger living in my house. She is religious." She gave a shrug indicating that when she came to die she would not call upon the hocus pocus of the Church.

"Her name?" asked Sister Maria Maddelena.

"Signorina Spragg."

"Is she a foreigner?"

"It seems so. I do not know where she came from. She has lived with me for sixteen years."

"And you don't know anything about her?"

"She never talked. She did not speak much Italian."

"She has no money?"

"For three months she has not paid me anything. She hasn't any more money." Signorina Bardelli began to gesticulate. "What has all this got to do with it? She is sick. She is out of her head. She is dying. I cannot care for her and the whole house as well. I want to see Sister Annunziata."

"Sister Annunziata has just come in. She has been staying with the wife of Carducci, the butcher, who died two hours ago."

"It will not matter to Sister Annunziata. Tell her that Signora Bardelli wants to speak to her."

She was stubborn because she was thinking that she could not support the presence in her house of any of the others. They would be asking things of her and disturbing the other tenants. Besides she distrusted nuns as meddlesome creatures, only Sister Annunziata was different. She told herself she was not seeking aid from the Church. She was coming for Sister Annunziata as for a friend. She would not leave until she had seen her.

"The old woman may be dying now while we're talking," persisted the janitress, and then as if to intimidate Sister Maria Maddelena she added threateningly, "Without absolution, without the last

rites of the dying. And that will be your fault for
delaying me. I will not leave till I talk to Sister
Annunziata. It will be on your head."

"They" nearly always talked like this. It was
clear that the janitress was beginning to lose her
temper. Sister Maria Maddelena said, "Wait,"
and disappeared through a little door behind the
table where she had been sitting, and Signora Bardelli, feeling she had put to rout the entire Church
of Rome, seated herself solemnly on a bench against
the grey wall beneath the solitary crucifix, a Christ
that was elegant and prettified, half-clad in purple
and crimson garments with a crown of thorns that
was gilded.

When the door opened again Sister Maria Maddelena was followed by a tall malformed figure who
was forced to stoop a little to pass through the archway. It was Sister Annunziata. She was rather a
grotesque than a woman and her ugliness made her
seem no age at all, although you would have guessed
that she was forty-five. She had high cheek-bones
and a long enormous nose and one eye turned out-
ward a little so that it was impossible to know when
she was looking at you. Her great hands hung suspended from fantastically long arms. The nun's
dress suited her better than any other. One is not
taught to look for beauty as the first quality of a
nun. She seemed pale and tired.

At sight of her Signora Bardelli rose politely
and greeted her. The manner of open hostility
melted away. She told her story—how the strange
old woman who had lived with her for sixteen years
was ill and perhaps dying. Signora Bardelli had

found her in her bed unconscious when she failed to
appear during the day. She was fond of the old
woman. She had grown used to her. Sister
Annunziata knew her. It was the old woman who
dressed so queerly and ran about the streets of
Brinoë in all weathers.

She talked rapidly and with excitement while
Sister Annunziata listened. The gaunt nun had a
curious air of humility as if she wanted desperately
to please, not only Sister Maria Maddelena but
even the janitress.

"I will come," she said. "If she is dying we must
fetch a priest. Is she a believer? In the true
faith?"

"I do not know," said the janitress. "She goes
often to the church, mostly to San Giovanni. She is
devout and religious."

"I will come," repeated Sister Annunziata in her
deep masculine voice. She turned and disappeared
through the doorway, leaving the janitress to savor
her triumph over Sister Maria Maddelena. In a
moment she returned with a small bag. Without
another word the two women set out through the
dark, narrow streets. As they stepped through the
doorway the wind from Africa blew into their faces
like the wind out of an oven. They made haste, for
Sister Annunziata had another soul upon her conscience. She walked with the stride of a man, her
big feet and long legs covering in one step the distance covered by two steps of the stout short
janitress. The streets were empty and they passed
no one all the way to the gloomy archway that was
the entrance to the ruined Palazzo Gonfarini.

II

It was a quarter in which Sister Annunziata knew every door and every window, every cornice. She knew even the holes in the pavement, which had never been repaired in the twenty-nine years she had spent going from house to house where she was needed. She did not, like Sister Maria Maddelena, think in secret pride of these poor sleeping all about her as "they." To Sister Annunziata this was all of the world, its beginning and its end. She had lived in it so long, absorbed by its pain and sorrows, that she had long ago forgotten she had ever belonged in any other. She had forgotten too because this life had been happy and the other had never held any happiness.

She quite forgot that she was born Eugenia Beatrice d'Orobelli. Among the poor it was said that she belonged to a proud family, but long ago "they" too had forgotten, if they ever knew, what she had been in the world. She was simply Sister Annunziata whom "they" always asked for. Sometimes they called her, behind her back, The Ugly One, and sometimes The Mad One, but there was in both names a kind of affection of that simple quality which colors the feelings of the humble.

In twenty-nine years she had seen none of her family save Faustino, her only brother, and him she had seen only twice when he had come from Venterollo with family papers for her to sign. She knew that he had married an American woman and she knew that he had three sons, one of whom, the eldest, was an invalid and lived always with his

father at Venterollo. Faustino had troubled himself to write her these things, but from her sisters
and from her mother and father, who were long
since dead, she had heard nothing. When they put
her into a convent at sixteen they had forgotten her
as if she had never existed. Afterwards her mother
in speaking of her family spoke of "my son and five
daughters," as if Eugenia Beatrice had never existed
at all. As a little girl she had never been allowed to
see visitors who came to Venterollo. She was
always kept out of sight with the gardener's wife in
the little house by the river.

So as a child she had played alone most of the
time because she was years younger than her sisters
and because they were proud and showed her that
they did not want her about them. She had come to
make friends with the birds and the animals in the
park of Venterollo and to spend her days like a wild
thing under the ancient oaks and moss-grown decaying walls.

She was twelve years old when she understood
what it was that caused them all to treat her differently. She had been sitting quietly one day on a
little copse near the ruined pavilion watching a troop
of ants building a city, when she heard voices, which
she recognized as those of her mother and of her
aunt. They were devout women who went every
day to mass, and that day because it was hot they
had stopped on their way home to rest in the pavilion. Her mother was crying because there was
no money to marry off her five daughters. Two
were already grown and on their way to being old
maids. Her husband had only debts and would not

give up gambling and her son of twenty was wild
and always in trouble with women.   But worst of
all and hardest to bear was Eugenia Beatrice.   Why
had God sent her another daughter late in life?
And why had He sent her such a little monster who
was as ugly as if she had been the daughter of the
Devil himself?   Nobody would ever marry such
an ugly creature even with a dot of a million lira.
What chance would she have without a penny?
Why had she, a good woman, been punished thus?

There was nothing to be done with Eugenia
Beatrice, said her aunt, but to put her into a convent as soon as possible.   Even there a creature so
ugly was certain to frighten the other nuns.

That night Eugenia Beatrice did not return from
the park.   They searched for her, not too carefully,
for there was no one who really *wanted* to find her,
but at evening of the next day she was brought home
by a peasant living on the side of the mountain
fifteen miles away.   He had found her shivering
among the rocks when he went out with his goats in
the early morning.

III

As the two women passed through the great
arched doorway of the Palazzo Gonfarini, the janitress went ahead leading the way up the wide stone
stairway.   It was cool here, for the thick walls shut
out the hot wind that sang so perversely along the
ancient cornices.   At the second turning of the stairway, Signora Bardelli opened a door and they found
themselves in a long corridor with a row of cell-

like doors opening along one side.    It was lighted
by a single jet of flickering gas.    The whole space
had once been the great banqueting hall of the palace
but years before it had been filled in thus with parti-
tions and converted into a kind of rookery by the
grandfather of Father d'Astier, who now owned the
palace.    At the end of the corridor the janitress
turned and knocked and the two women stepped into
a small square room like a long box turned on end.
It was not more than ten by twelve feet in size, but
it was high, so high that in the dim glow of the night
light floating in a bowl of cheap blue pottery the ceiling would have been lost in shadow save for the
occasional glint struck by the light against the
ancient gilding of the painted beams.    As they
entered there arose a flutter and commotion from a
great number of tiny birds which rose from the end
of the bed where they had been perching and cir-
cled blindly about until one by one they settled on
the rows of cages hung against the grey wall.    In
one corner there was a narrow iron bed and on it
lay the dying woman, a coarse poor sheet drawn up
to her chin.

She was quite still and lay on her back with her
eyes closed.    It was a curious face, neither old nor
young, not beautiful and yet fascinating by the per-
fection of its modelling.    It was the first time anyone save Signora Bardelli had ever seen the face
without the hat and the thick veil.    Great masses
of red hair lay on the pillow.    In front it was cut
short in a long fringe that hid completely the forehead.

For a moment Sister Annunziata stood by the side

of the narrow bed looking down at Miss Annie
Spragg and then slowly, almost as if she was unconscious of the gesture, one of the gaunt ugly hands
touched the beautiful hair with a curious gesture
of reverence.

"She is not an old woman," said Sister Annunziata.

"She was like that when she came to me," said
the janitress. "She cannot be young. She has been
here for fifteen years. She has not changed much."

Then Sister Annunziata touched the brow, gently
pushing back a little the thick fringe of hair. Then
she listened to the breathing and while Signora Bardelli held the night light she bent over to look at the
pale, tired eyelids.

"She is dying," said Sister Annunziata. "You
had better go for Father Baldessare. I will stay
with her." She knew all the signs. For twenty-
five years she had sat at the side of the dying.

So the janitress went away again out into the hot
night and Sister Annunziata closed the great shutters against the heat of the African wind. When
she had done this she set about putting the room in
order, lifting the bedraggled tweed suit and the battered old picture hat and veil from the only chair in
the room. Then she sat by the side of the bed and
reaching beneath the sheet felt the wrist of Miss
Annie Spragg and knelt beside the bed to pray. It
was not to God that she prayed or to the Virgin, but
to Saint Francis of the Birds. He was her saint.
He was more than that. He was to Sister Annunziata the only God who had ever existed. She
prayed for a long time, commending to his care the

soul of the dying woman. The souls of all the
dying she commended to the care of Saint Francis.
He was *her* saint whom she adored since she was a
little girl.

At last she arose and opening the little bag she
brought with her took out a powder which she dis-
solved in water and swallowed. Sister Annunziata
was ill herself. Lately she had reached the age
when her body was sometimes racked with pain and
her mind seemed vague and confused and clouded.
Twice lately she had had visions in which she saw
Saint Francis far off in the midst of a bright field
filled with little daisies and primroses. He appeared to be beckoning to her but he came no nearer.
He was the simple Saint Francis of Giotto's picture
that hung in her room years ago at Venterollo.
Lately she prayed at times to him for some miraculous sign of his approbation. She prayed that Saint
Francis would show her a sign of his love. . . .

After bending once more over the sick woman she
seated herself by the bed and took out of her bag a
little worn leather-bound copy of *The Little Flowers
of Saint Francis* and began to read. Once she had
known it all by heart but lately with her trouble she
seemed unable to remember the verses in their
proper order. She was forced to hold the book
close to her face in the dim light because her eyes
were weak and swollen.

As she sat reading the little birds, who had been
watching her with bright eyes from the tops of the
cages, appeared to lose their fear and flew down in
small confused groups of two and three to perch
once more on the foot of the iron bed.

IV

On the day that Eugenia Beatrice was sixteen her
aunt took her dressed all in black to enter the convent. They kissed each other good-by coldly, since
the aunt had no affection for her and the child had
long ago ceased to look for any affection from the
world. The door closed and the great ugly girl
found herself among the sisters, shrinking and
frightened as she had always been in the presence of
strangers. They stared at her as intently as if
they believed there could be no creature so ugly in
all the world.

From that day on her life was given over to pleas-
ing others in the vague half-formed hope that out
of her service there would grow some reward of
commendation or affection. She scrubbed the floors
and swept the vast hallway and took upon herself
the meanest tasks, and sometimes there would be a
reward, a word of praise from one of the nuns or
even the Mother Superior herself. She knelt for
long hours on the cold stone floor praying to Saint
Francis who had love for all living things and so
might love her as well, even if God had made her so
ugly that she frightened people. For in the great
awkward body there was a soul so hungry for love
that it would have given itself over to torture and
slavery for the sake of anyone who had for her a
kind word. But her ugliness was so great that the
other sisters, almost without knowing it, thought of
her as something grotesque and strange and different
from themselves.

For three years she lived thus and at last when

she went out into the city to care for the sick and the poor she began for the first time to find her place in the world and to forget her childhood. Among the wretched she went about with that same humble manner of supplication, seeking to please them in return for kindliness. She entered their squalid houses as a creature unworthy of serving them. She sat at the bedside of old men dying of loathsome diseases and young mothers who died bearing their first children. She sat by young and handsome men cut off in the midst of life and risked her life by the side of children ill with smallpox and scarlet fever. She ate what the poor ate and slept as they slept, asking nothing of them in return but a word of kindness. And even the young men who loved only youth and the joy of being alive and the feeling of the hot blood in their veins came in the end to find a strange kind of beauty in the presence of sister Annunziata. It was an unearthly beauty that seemed less concerned with the ugly body and face of Sister Annunziata than with all that surrounded her. With her by their side even the young found death quiet and peaceful. They loved the gentleness of the huge misshapen hands. A kind of light seemed to flow from the ugly face.

And she knew sometimes that they called her The Ugly One and The Mad One and she smiled to herself and was glad because they would not have called her such names if there had not been affection in their hearts. In a way her body came to exist no longer save as an instrument to serve her spirit. She came, unlike other women, to cherish it not as an instrument of love or of beauty but as something

that was useful to her.   When at forty-five it began
to fail her she prayed desperately to Saint Francis to
give her strength.   It was not death that she feared
but the thought that her body's failing her might
shut her off from all those who called her The Ugly
One and The Mad One.   Saint Francis could help
her, whom she loved with all her soul.

Sitting by the bed of Miss Annie Spragg she read,
holding the page close to her weak swollen eyes:

"When Saint Francis drew nigh unto Bevagna he
came unto a spot wherein a great multitude of birds
of divers species were gathered together.   When
the holy man of God perceived them he ran with all
speed unto the place and greeted them as if they had
shared in human understanding.   They on their
part all awaited him and turned toward him, those
that were perched on the bushes bending their heads
as he drew nigh them, and looking on him in un-
wonted wise while he came right among them, and
diligently exhorted them all to hear the word of
God, saying, 'My brothers the birds, much ought
ye to praise your Creator, who hath clothed you with
feathers and given you wings to fly, and hath made
over unto you the pure air, and careth for you without your taking thought for yourselves.'   While he
was speaking these and other like words, the little
birds—behaving themselves in wondrous wise—began to stretch their necks, to open their beaks, and
to look intently upon him.   He, with wondrous fer-
vor of spirit, passed in and out among them, touching them with his habit, nor did one of them move
from the spot until he had made the sign of the

cross over them and given them leave; then with the
blessing of the man of God, they all flew away together. All these things were witnessed by his com-
panions who stood awaiting him by the way. Returning unto them, the simple and holy man began
to blame himself for neglect in that he not afore then
preached unto the birds. . . ."

The little birds were quite still now and sat in a
row on the end of the bed, some with eyes closed,
some watching Sister Annnunziata with their bright
eyes.

## v

It was nearly dawn when she was aroused by the
sound of creaking boots in the corridor. It was
Father Baldessare. She knew the sound of his
boots. He was a humble simple priest who had
come many times to the homes of the poor in response to her summons. His boots always creaked.
The door opened and he came in, fat and short with
a red pimply face, followed by Signora Bardelli.
They were both hot and panting from the long walk
through the hot wind and the climb up the great
stone stairway. As they entered the room the birds
fluttered up again to their cages and the woman on
the bed opened her eyes a little way slowly and with
the greatest effort. For a moment they were darkened by a strange look of terror in them as if she
thought herself already dead and was awakening in
a dark world of black-robed nuns and priests. And
then she appeared to recognize Sister Annunziata

and the look of fear faded away. She could not speak. Her lips were frozen.

Sister Annunziata made a gesture dismissing the janitress and then turned to the fat little priest. "We had better make haste," she murmured. "I will stay and hold her up. She cannot raise her own body."

And so they made ready to offer Miss Annie Spragg the last service they could give her on this earth and when Father Baldessare, after much panting and sweating, was ready Sister Annunziata knelt beside the bed and lifted the dying woman, resting the thin helpless body against her own gaunt shoulder. They found then that her hands were covered by white cotton gloves and when Father Baldessare tried to remove them a kind of convulsion shook her and into her eyes there came a look so terrible that Sister Annunziata understood her plea and they left her hands covered.

The fat little priest began to read the lines and administer the Sacrament and once more the little birds, no longer fearful, fluttered down one by one to the iron rail at the foot of the bed and sat in a row. The look of fear left the eyes of the dying woman and slowly the eyelids drooped with weariness.

When at last Father Baldessare had finished, the eyes opened a little way and again a look of pleading came into them. Then slowly in a kind of agony Annie Spragg lifted her right arm a little way and made a faint vague gesture which only Sister Annunziata understood. Still supporting the dying woman the nun leaned down and took from the chair the

copy of *The Little Flowers of Saint Francis* and
from her bag she took the stub of a worn blue pencil. She put the pencil in Annie Spragg's hand and
opening the book held it for her to write. Slowly
and with pain the dying woman scrawled seven
words and when she had finished the pencil dropped
from her hands and the eyelids drooped again.
There was a faint sigh filled with weariness and Sister Annunziata commended her soul to the care of
Saint Francis of the Birds.

They laid her back upon the bed and Sister Annunziata opened the page where she had written.
At first she could make nothing of the scrawl and
peered at it for a long time with her swollen red
eyes. Then slowly she understood it. The old
woman had written,

   *Open the window. Let them be free.*

When Father Baldessare loosened the heavy
shutters the first faint color of dawn had begun to
rise behind the mountains and the rosy grey light
was filtering down among the ancient ghost-filled
houses that surrounded the Palazzo Gonfarini. As
he stood there for a moment looking out into the
hot empty street there was a faint rushing sound all
about him. It was the little birds flying past him,
chirping and twittering, into the rising dawn. The
air was filled with the sound of wings.

After Father Baldessare had gone again, Sister
Annunziata drew the sheet over the face of the dead
woman and closing the door gently behind her went
down the long corridor and the great stone stairway
to seek a bowl of hot coffee. She needed it in order
to keep her weary eyes open any longer and she

could not ask Signora Bardelli to fetch it, for Signora Bardelli was a busy woman and had been up most of the night. The hallway and the cortile were grey blue with morning light and already out of the cell-like doors there had begun to appear figures which Sister Annunziata knew well . . . the old man who washed the streets, the blind old woman who sold flowers in the arcades of the Piazza Vittorio Emanuele, Galeazzo the lame stone cutter. They greeted her knowing that her presence in the Palazzo Gonfarini meant that there was suffering and death within its walls.  She understood what it was they wanted to know.  It was the stranger, she told them, who lived at the far end of the corridor. They crossed themselves and wished good health to Sister Annunziata and peace to the soul of the dead woman.

In a little while she returned bringing with her candles and a great kettle of hot water and when she had entered the room again she set about placing it in order.  She went through the drawers of the cheap pine table and the pockets of the grey tweed suit but she found nothing.  There were no papers and not even a lira in money.  The dead woman appeared to have no possessions but the clothes she wore and the little birds.

Then Sister Annunziata went to the iron bed and lifted the sheet and for a long time she stood looking down at Miss Annie Spragg.  The lines of pain had gone out of the dead face, leaving it transparent and smooth and peaceful against the masses of splendid tangled hair.  Again Sister Annunziata, who had a way of talking to herself, murmured,

"But she is not an old woman." And once more the great bony hand reached out with a gesture of reverence and envy to touch the beauty of the dead woman's hair.

As she set about her task with dim near-sighted eyes, she saw that the body of the dead woman was not old and that it was beautifully made and that in youth it had been superb. She saw that it was a body which perhaps had known the love which was shut out forever from the life of a nun. She had seen bodies many times that were young and splendid even in death when it was no longer wrong to look upon their nakedness, and each time it gave her a kind of twisting, sickening pain, so that in the end she had come to look away from them.

As she worked with averted eyes she tried to repeat the psalms she had learned as a child at Venterollo, but in her trouble and in the pain that racked her body and the clouds that obscured her thoughts she could not remember them. When she had nearly finished her task she discovered that she had not removed the white cotton gloves that covered the hands. She removed first one and then the other and then quite suddenly she made the discovery. On the palm of each hand there was a red scar as if both hands had been pierced by nails. For a moment she stared in silence, leaning close in order to see, and then gently, with a gesture almost of terror, she pushed back the fringe of hair that covered the brow of the dead woman, and there on the brow she discovered other scars as if a crown of thorns had been pressed upon her head. There was a great livid scar in the side and the two feet had the marks of nails.

For a second a vicious pain racked her body and a blinding light dazzled her poor weak eyes and then without a sound she slipped to the floor unconscious. For she had seen the Stigmata. It was the sign of Saint Francis of the Birds.

When Signora Bardelli climbed the stone stairs an hour later she found that all the birds had flown from the room and that Sister Annunziata lay unconscious on the floor. And on the bed lay the naked body of the dead woman bearing in its flesh the scars of the Crucifixion. The room was quite light now and the brilliant morning sun streamed in at the open window.

For the only time in her life Signora Bardelli was frightened. She felt a sudden wild impulse to fall upon her knees and pray to the very saints she had mocked. She had a strange fear of being watched by something which she could neither see nor understand.

She seemed unable to revive the unconscious nun and when Father Baldessare returned creaking and sweating along the corridor he found her still kneeling beside the prostrate figure. He too saw the miraculous scars on the body of the dead woman and knelt humbly in prayer by the side of the bed.

When at last Sister Annunziata opened her eyes, she seemed for a long time unable to speak. They gave her sour wine to drink and at last she told them a strange and muddled story. She said that as she stood over the body a great and blinding light had appeared on the wall opposite the bed and that

in the midst of it stood Saint Francis in a tiny field
of buttercups and primroses, surrounded by all the
little birds that a little time before had fluttered
about the room.   From his body there streamed
great rays of light.   These appeared to come from
his hands and his feet, his side and his brow, where
there were wounds like those of Our Lord.   The
light streamed toward the body of the dead woman.
After that she could remember no more.

As she told the story a strange unearthly look of
happy madness came into her face, so that even the
hard Signora Bardelli felt a sudden awe.

Before noon the story of the miracle had traveled
through all the quarter and crowds came streaming
into the cortile, up the staircase and along the corridor.   Pushing and crying out hysterically, women
thrust themselves into the chamber of the dead
woman and there tore her clothes and the very chair
and table into bits as relics.   They bore off the cages
of the little birds, and the night light, and one
woman soaked her shawl in the water that was in
the bowl of cheap blue crockery.   In their hunger
for relics they snatched the bedraggled roses from
the old picture hat and ripped bits from the very
sheet that covered the body of Miss Spragg, until
only torn fragments remained to hide its nakedness.
It was the police who at last cleared them from the
house, pushing them rudely back into the street.
But the crowd would not go away.   It hung about
the great arched gateway of the Palazzo Gonfarini
and women knelt in the dust to pray beneath the
windows.

Through all the confusion and the vulgar turmoil

Sister Annunziata went about calmly, with that strange new light of happiness in her face. She was loved at last. Saint Francis had sent her the sign.

## CODA

### I

O N THE morning following Mr. Winnery's extraordinary attack of romanticism he awakened slowly and lay abed for a long time after the goitered Maria, maidservant of twenty years, had come in and flung open the shutters. He awakened conscious that he was feeling exceedingly well and freed of the usual torpor caused by the combination of a bad liver and the wretched climate of Brinoë. He was aware that the wind from Africa had died out altogether and that in its place there was a cool fresh breeze that changed the brilliant sun and blue sky from a nightmare into a delight. It was odd, he thought, how well he felt, considering that he had been up walking the streets on the night before until after midnight. It occurred to him that perhaps you could break habits without inviting calamities. Perhaps breaking habits made life more exciting. It was a thing he had never tried before—this exciting way of living.

And then his eye fell upon the telegram, and he suddenly felt even happier. He remembered that now he could leave Brinoë forever. He would not have to be buried in the Protestant cemetery, among all the people who had bored him for twenty years. He would not have to rest through all eternity beside someone like old Mrs. Whitehead. He could now travel everywhere and anywhere, always seeking with the bright hope of an incurable romantic some spot that would be as paradisiacal as it was reported to be by poets and old ladies and tourist circulars. Aunt Bessie was dead, God bless her.

He rose, and before doing the exercises which kept his waist measure within moderation, and his liver in action, he went to the window and looked out. Below him in the little square the usual things were going on. There were bony horses and cab drivers in varnished leather hats, three English ladies in tweeds and picture hats, armed with umbrellas, Baedekers and cameras. An elderly American couple reading out of a book about the tower of the church opposite. They read a paragraph and then regarded the tower again, as if uncertain which things had been regarded by Mr. Ruskin as beautiful and which things had not. A brown-robed monk came down from the high monastery of Monte Salvatore. A herd of goats with the shepherd in a black smock playing a tune on a strange pipe held in the hollow of his hand. A Ford automobile with nine Italians. Though it was early morning they were dressed in full evening clothes, clearly bound for a wedding or a christening. A woman leaned out of a window and screamed at the goatherd. He halted the flock, put away the pipe and set himself industriously to milking one of the she-goats.

It was a delightful place, after all, Brinoë. Perhaps it wasn't as bad as he had thought. Now that he was rich he could keep a larger apartment and have a villa somewhere in the hills. Suddenly it

occurred to him that it must be later than he thought
and regarding the tower opposite he discovered
that it was already ten o'clock.   It couldn't be as
late as that.   The clock was Italian and therefore
probably an hour or two wrong.   It was never cor-
rect with the sun, and to Italians such things didn't
matter.   But his own watch showed him that the
clock was not fast (which he knew would be unusual
in Brinoë), but slow by half an hour.   It was half
past ten.   Maria had not called him and for the
first time in twenty years he had overslept.   For a
moment he experienced a wild desire to summon
Maria and abuse her, but something about the
square, the sky and the sight of the wedding party in
the Ford made him soften.   He decided to do nothing about Maria's dereliction.   It was odd, indeed,
how well he felt, and how young and spry.

Then he saw coming round the tower of the
church the tall awkward figure of a nun, walking in
great haste, her full black skirt swinging with her
masculine stride.   "It is the crazy one," he thought,
"Sister Annunziata."   As she crossed the little
square toward his house, he saw that she was smiling
and talking to herself in the most animated fashion
as she walked.   She turned and disappeared
through the archway by the old Palace of the
Podestas.

The sight of her brought to mind Miss Annie
Spragg.   Well, it was an interesting case and he
would have to go further into it.   If he continued
in his present health and spirits he would be able
to complete "Miracles and Other Natural Phenomena" within a year or two.   He must see Mrs.

Weatherby again and go further into the history of
Miss Spragg at a time when they would not be interrupted by the presence of such frivolous and worldly
people as Father d'Astier and the d'Orobelli woman.

At that moment he saw the black and red motor
swing from under the archway and cross the square.
In it were the Princess d'Orobelli and a man whom
he did not know, a dark handsome man who was
not Father d'Astier.   "Ah," thought Mr. Winnery,
with a sudden warm feeling of being a worldly devil,
"that is why she is in Brinoë at this time of year.
That is it . . . a lover.  A rendezvous."  It made
him feel almost a gay dog.

It made him also think, "If she is not too old for
love, neither am I.   A man lasts much longer than
a woman."   And that in turn made him think of
Miss Fosdick and reflect again that now he was rich
he could do anything he pleased.  With money you
could buy anything.  Perhaps he might rescue
Miss Fosdick from the dragon's den and marry her.
Now that he was rich he would have to upset a good
many habits and upsetting habits it seemed did not
bring disaster.  On the contrary, he never felt better. . . . Dear me, it was an odd world.

He decided that he would hire the fiacre once
more and drive out to the Villa Leonardo before
making up his mind entirely about Miss Fosdick.
It was a pleasant day and the drive would be refreshing.  He could wring more information from
Mrs. Weatherby, if he could prevent her long
enough from talking about herself.  And perhaps
he could have a word alone with Miss Fosdick.  He might ask permission to call upon her.

Yes, he would need a wife now that he was rich.
But he must be cautious.   At fifty-three one had no
time to indulge in mistakes.

He tried to pretend to himself that he was being
merely practical and not at all sentimental, but at
the same time he experienced again that pleasant
tickling sensation of satisfaction over his interest in
her.   It was no more than the shadow of desire.   It
flattered him that there was a certain . . . well,
grossness . . . in the feeling.   He had a most
stimulating awareness of adventure.

The door opened and fat Maria came in, looking,
decided Mr. Winnery, as if she had swallowed a
canary.   That, thought Winnery, is because she has
been guilty of a dereliction of duty and expects a
scolding.

"Buon giorno," he said brightly.   "Buon giorno."

Maria looked somewhat astonished.   Feeling a
little encouraged to gossip, she asked if Signor Winnery had heard the latest about Signorina Spragg.
Miss Annie Spragg was being buried today and the
burial was causing the local church authorities a
great deal of trouble and uncertainty.   The question
was a purely technical one.   No one could decide
whether the miraculous scars should be officially
recognized as a miracle and the body of Miss Annie
Spragg considered as that of a potential saint or
whether she ought to be treated simply with the conventional respect due a devout follower of the
Church.   There was even a party among the more
bigoted older priests which held that there was not
even any proof that she was a Roman Catholic and
that it was not proper to defile consecrated ground

with the body of a heretic.   And there was always
that ancient decree of Pope Sixtus IV issued against
Saint Catherine of Siena, Sixtus IV holding that
the miracle of the Stigmata was the exclusive monopoly of Saint Francis and that it was a censurable
offense to report it of anyone else.   The whole
thing threatened to grow into a scandal.   Miss
Annie Spragg had no money, so Sister Annunziata
was paying for the funeral.   Did Mr. Winnery know
who Sister Annunziata really was?   Well, it turned
out that she was born the Princess d'Orobelli, and
she was put into a convent because her family saw
no chance of ever marrying off so ugly a woman.

Maria paused for breath and then went on.   Had
Signor Winnery heard about Father Baldessare, that
little fat priest attached to San Giovanni?   Yes, the
one who had witnessed the miracle and found Sister Annunziata lying senseless after she had been
visited by Saint Francis.   Well, Father Baldessare
had left the Church and was going from town to
town, on foot, to preach in the market places.   He
was going to purify Christianity, she said, and begin
all over again.   That was a silly idea.   How could
there be any Christianity without the Church?
Wasn't the Church Christianity?

"He has always been a little cracked," she said,
"and now he seems gone out of his mind."

She had heard all this at the market.   "Ah,"
thought Winnery, who had quite forgotten that he
was still clad only in an Italian night shirt, embroidered in red cotton, "no wonder she was late."

Maria walked to the window on the opposite side
of the room and stood looking down into the market.

"Look," she said, pointing down. "There he is now."

Winnery crossed over to the window. In one corner of the market by the fountain of dolphins and serpents there was a crowd of cooks and chambermaids and cab drivers. On the edge stood the three English ladies with the Baedekers, umbrellas and cameras. One had placed her hand behind her ear in order to hear more distinctly. They surrounded a fat short figure clad in a brightly checked suit of the kind affected in London by bookmakers. In one hand the figure held an umbrella. The other hand was being used in emphatic but ineffective gestures. The crowd stood staring up at him, amused and astonished, but aware that it was being treated to an entertainment which cost nothing. The speaker's voice was weak and shrill so that it did not carry above the tumult of excited bargaining that was in progress on all sides. After a time the cooks began to drift away one by one to buy their leeks and spinach and potatoes. It was Father Baldessare, turned to plain Fulco Baldessare, leader of the new reformation.

Winnery, watching the spectacle, had a swift fleeting vision of humanity struggling to extricate itself from some colossal muddle. Then he returned to his breakfast, which he ate with a hearty appetite.

## II

From the moment of Miss Fosdick's hysterical flight into the great world life began to annoy Mrs. Weatherby. For twenty years she had managed to

subdue its annoyances because dear Gertrude had
seen to every tiresome detail—the packing, ordering
the food, shipping trunks, buying tickets, giving or-
ders timidly to servants—in short, doing all the
things which might have broken in upon the spiritual
quiet of the Great Religious Experimenter. It had
become a system so thorough and so monotonous
that Mrs. Weatherby had quite forgotten the grey existence of such troublesome details. Now that her
slave was gone, her life collapsed about her ears in
a confusion of petty annoyances.

Margharita wanted to know what Giovanni
should bring from the market. The men who were
building a cesspool found that the cement was of
the wrong kind. Should Giovanni buy a new tire
for the Ford? Lulu, the elder Pomeranian, spit up
her breakfast. There was no more sunflower seed
for Anubis. It was as if Mrs. Weatherby's star
had slipped into some profoundly disastrous con-
junction. She remembered with terror that her
horoscope foretold disaster and disappointments
during the six months beginning with August.

And she was forced to face and solve all these
calamities while suffering the greatest anguish of
mind. Had she not been betrayed by the one creature on whom for twenty years she had lavished the
wealth of affection and kindness of a mother? For
twenty years she had been harboring an ingrate,
nay, a viper, at her bosom. She kept saying this
over and over again to herself while she squabbled
with Margharita and dosed Lulu with castor oil.
And all those cruel things which Gertrude had said
the night before. She must have been thinking

them in secret for years while she lived on the bounty
of her doting Aunt Henrietta.   And to go away
without a word, not even telling her Aunt Henrietta
she had gone.

"But she will return," she kept telling herself.
"She will return in good time, perhaps today, perhaps tomorrow.   What is there for her to do but to
return?"

And when she returned she would be more con-
trollable than before.   After her ingratitude and
treachery she would seek to do penance.   Perhaps
it would be better in the end.   If there was a divine
law, people suffered for such behavior.

"I must not think evil thoughts," she told herself, "because evil thoughts make us old and tired
and bring on the twilight."

No, she would be sweet and forgiving when
Gertrude returned; sweet and forgiving, she repeated to herself, but firm as well.   She must not
give in too easily.

Suddenly it occurred to her that her misfortune
might have to do with the strange statue found in
the cesspool.   From the very beginning she had
disliked it as an obscene and disturbing thing, and
now since Miss Fosdick was gone and there was no
other object at hand on which to vent her ill temper
she began to hate the statue.   There was no doubt
that such an image aroused the lower nature.   It
was perhaps the sight of it that had caused Gertrude
to behave in so idiotic a fashion with the Duke of
Fonterrabia.   Perhaps it was the statue that had
driven her to run off like a madwoman.   She might,
she thought, give the statue to a museum, or, what

was better still, she might bury it again, even deeper
than it had been before.   Yes, that was it.   She
would have the workmen bury it once more, and then
Gertrude would return and Lulu would recover and
all these troubles would disappear.   Perhaps it was
silly to think such things, but you could never tell
about superstitions.   Sometimes they were quite
right.   She would not have the thing about leaning
against the ilex, watching everything that passed in
the garden.

Presently she began to worry again about the
Annie Spragg affair.   Isolated there on the side of
the mountain she could not discover what was happening, nor (what would have been the most valuable of all knowledge) the attitude the Church was
taking toward the miracle.   She was aware that she
must discover this before she spoke again to Father
d'Astier.   If the Church looked upon Annie Spragg
as an imposter then she must wash her hands of
Annie Spragg and support the Church by telling all
the dark things she knew about Annie Spragg.   If
the Church chose to regard the affair in the light
of a miracle then she must espouse the cause of Miss
Annie Spragg and appear as her friend.   It was all
perplexing enough without having the ungrateful
Gertrude disappear just when she was most needed.

At noon she ate nothing but retired to her room
for a siesta.   In her agitation she had not closed an
eye all night.   More than that, Gertrude had not
been there to will away the currents of evil directed
against her by her enemies.   Lying awake and alone
in the house she had kept hearing ominous noises in
the garden and in the rooms below.

It was four o'clock when she awakened at last and went down into the garden to attend to the business of reburying the hateful statue. When she saw it again, the halo of evil surrounding it struck her even more forcibly. It was only after the reflection of the wakeful night that she realized its full significance. Why, she saw now that portions of the statue had been stained, perhaps nineteen centuries earlier, in an obscene fashion.

In bad Italian and with the aid of much pantomime, she finally conveyed to the workmen her idea. When at last they understood her they exploded in a wild burst of protest. She was unable to understand any of it, though she understood well enough that they were in a tremendous state of excitement. They all screamed at her at once. In the very midst of the uproar Pietro, the old goatherd, who lived on the hillside below the villa, suddenly appeared bearing two melons and a branch laden with green olives. He was an immensely old man, dirty and unkempt, with a scraggly grey beard and pointed ears that stuck through apertures in the matted long grey hair. He walked with a limp sidewise like a crab. At sight of her he removed his battered hat and gave her a series of grovelling bows.

At first she thought he had brought the melons and olive branch as a gift for herself and touched by the picturesqueness of Italian customs, she quickly assumed the gracious manner of a chatelaine and came forward to receive the offering. But Pietro made it certain that they were not for her. As if he thought that she meant to take them from him by force, he cunningly shifted them behind his back

and made a flowery speech, of which she understood
not a word.   Then his true purpose was revealed.
He went past her and laid them at the very feet of
the horrid statue.   At the same moment, one of the
workmen, the bronze-chested Giovanni whose phy-
sique had caught the wandering eye of the Princess
d'Orobelli, said something to him, and he in his turn
began to gibber at the now completely distracted
seeress.   It appeared that the arrival of Pietro gave
them fresh courage.   She saw that they intended to
prevent her by force from carrying out her plan of
doing away with the obscene thing.   She was the
tenant of this property.   She intended to do with it
as she pleased.   Her fleshy nostrils began to distend in an ominous way.   Italians, so volatile by
nature, could not imagine the force of a granddaughter of Transcendentalists moved to anger by a
long series of torments.   And unlike Miss Fosdick,
they had never witnessed the full fury of one of her
tantrums.

But at the crucial moment there appeared from
the opposite end of the garden a whole procession of
goats which had faithfully followed Pietro up the
stony hill.   At the very end of the procession,
emerging from the tunnel of greenery, appeared Mr.
Winnery, nattily dressed for courting in a checked
suit, a new pearl grey hat and lemon yellow gloves.

III

Mr. Winnery, entering into the cool dark garden,
was overcome, as he had been once before, by the certainty that he had lost his mind.   He was aware

that as the last of a long procession of goats he had made an undignified entrance, but his resentment at this died almost at once before the spectacle of the Great Religious Experimenter surrounded by gibbering Italians who seemed bent upon doing her some bodily violence. Fearful that Miss Fosdick had perhaps already been done away with he hurried forward through the midst of the flock of goats, driving them out of his path with blows of his malacca stick (just purchased on the strength of Aunt Bessie's legacy).

At sight of a male foreigner, even so harmless a male foreigner as Mr. Winnery, the workmen grew silent, and Pietro retired into concealment behind them. Mrs. Weatherby, with a new face composed almost instantaneously, floated forward and greeted him, explaining at the same time that she was having difficulties with the workmen. There was perhaps some confusion owing to their inability to understand each other. Perhaps Mr. Winnery would act as interpreter.

He addressed the workmen and received in reply a perfect torrent of explanation. They all spoke at once and into their soft voices they threw whole gamuts of seduction. It would perhaps never have finished but in the midst of it he turned to Mrs. Weatherby—"They are saying that you must not bury the statue again. It is an ancient god of fertility and if you bury it they say the crops will be blighted and the she-goats barren and the eggs unfertile. They say you will bring calamity on the neighborhood. It *is* an ancient god of fertility. Priapus, offspring of Dionysus and Aphrodite, or, if you prefer the Asiatic version, of Sabazius and Astarte. They are quite right, though how they know such a thing is beyond me. You will find. . . ."

He would have, like the Italians, gone on for some time explaining the legend of Priapus, but Mrs. Weatherby interrupted. The nostrils had begun again to distend and quiver. She seemed about to snort fire.

"It is my garden," she said quite firmly. "I shall do with it as I like."

"Why not," suggested Mr. Winnery tactfully, "give the thing to a museum?"

"No, I understand about these things. Haven't I devoted my life to studies of the more psychic religions? It is an evil omen and ought to be buried again. I am certain of it. Ever since it was found I have been having misfortunes."

Winnery shrugged his shoulders. He failed to see quite how the seeress could with intellectual honesty support her own superstition and reject the much more ancient one supported by Pietro and his party. That, he supposed, was the common attitude of superstitious and religious people. But he simply turned to the workmen. He told them that the signora wanted the thing buried and that if they chose not to obey her, she would find other workmen. Deciding that they could risk a blight in the future more easily than the loss of a job in the present, they turned back sullenly, but not silently, and began to dig. Pietro made as if to launch a final protest and then fell silent. The goats had by now gathered in a circle about the scene of the conflict,

watching it with large round eyes. Mr. Winnery
had a fleeting impression that Pietro had winked
at him, but he could not be certain, and he could
not as a guest of Mrs. Weatherby endanger her
prestige by acknowledging the wink.

"Now that we have settled it," said Mrs. Weatherby more calmly, "you must have some tea."

As they started toward the villa Mr. Winnery
turned again to regard the statue in disgrace. It
was a remarkably fine thing, he thought, and a pity
to bury it again. Still, with this eccentric woman,
arguments would arrive nowhere. She placed no
value upon anything in the world but her own ego.
It was a fine thing, the statue. At moments it
seemed almost to have a life of its own. Just now
in the heat of the afternoon it appeared lascivious
and amused as if it were saying, "You may bury me
and unbury me a thousand times but you can't be rid
of me. I shall be with you always."

It was a pity, thought Mr. Winnery. It seemed
to him that the statue had brought him luck. Everything had happened since Miss Annie Spragg had
died and the statue was dug up from the cesspool.

"Shoo!" cried Mrs. Weatherby, making threat-
ening gestures and pushing her way through the
goats. "Shoo! Shoo!"

IV

They had tea, the same bad tea out of rusty tins
that tasted as if it were made of hay, and dried di-
gestive biscuits very nearly as old, thought Mr.

Winnery, as the freshly buried statue. Mrs. Weatherby at once struck an attitude in the fake Renaissance chair and began to talk about herself. Anubis the parrot blinked at them and gave out a series of disgruntled croaks. Everything was exactly the same as before save that one of the Pomeranians, instead of yapping, lay with a pallid expression on a Veronese green pillow trimmed with gold, and that the view through the loggia was even more magnificent in the clear transparent air that had followed the dust-laden sirocco. He was aware that there was still no sign of Miss Fosdick nor any reference to her. He reminded himself that it was Miss Fosdick after all whom he had come to see. He did not care to hear any more of the history of Mrs. Weatherby.

Once, however, Mrs. Weatherby did turn aside from her principal subject, but only long enough to ask for the latest developments in the scandalous affair of Miss Annie Spragg. He passed on to her what he had heard that morning from Maria. It was information which only left her where she had been before. He had not, he told her when asked, seen Father d'Astier, although he had seen the Principessa d'Orobelli driving across the square with a stranger, a man, to be exact. This bit of simple information he translated with the slight but meaning inflection that had come to be a habit born of long association with the old ladies of Brinoë.

"A very interesting woman," said Mrs. Weatherby. "I have never before seen an aura so red."

"Ah, you understand auras," murmured Mr. Winnery in a helpless effort to fill in time until he gained the courage to ask where Miss Fosdick was hiding. He was not interested in auras except as nonsense. (It was absurd that a man of his age should be as shy as a schoolboy. Why could he not utter Miss Fosdick's name?)

"Yes, it is a profound and interesting subject."

"Have you noticed my own?" asked Mr. Winnery wildly.

"Oh, yes, I noticed it at once yesterday by its paleness. I had seldom seen so pale an aura. But it has changed today remarkably. It is much redder."

"And what does that signify?"

Mrs. Weatherby simpered. "I don't know that I ought to tell you, Mr. Winnery. Still, you are an intelligent man and will not misinterpret my interest in such things."

"Yes . . . no . . . of course not," murmured Mr. Winnery.

"Red," said Mrs. Weatherby, "indicates passions of the body. I think—" she hesitated for a moment and then plunged. "I think someone, something, some new—shall I say—interest?—has entered your life since yesterday."

"Oh," said Mr. Winnery, somewhat startled. But he was aware again that he was flattered by the change in his aura.

"Green is the color of the passions of the mind. That of course is much worse . . . depraved, one might say." She was peering at him through her glistening pince-nez with a mystical intensity that made him squirm on the hard chair. He saw with terror that she was scrutinizing his aura. "I am glad to see, Mr. Winnery, that there is no trace of green in your aura."

Mr. Winnery murmured his gratitude and said modestly he supposed that that was a thing you could not control and that therefore he ought to take no credit to himself. Secretly he was feeling disturbed for fear that her intensity might increase and throw her into a trance. What could he do with her if she suddenly went into a trance?

She did not. "That is what interested me about the statue," she continued. "It has an aura, Mr. Winnery, a positive, unmistakable aura, and it is a vile mixture of red and green. That is why I thought the thing better buried again at once."

"And what does such a mixture signify?"

"That, Mr. Winnery, I cannot bring myself to tell you. Will you have more tea?"

But Mr. Winnery had done his duty to the social amenities and did not feel called upon to drink a second cup of hay-water.

"But I don't understand, Mrs. Weatherby, how a statue, an inanimate thing, may have an aura. I thought auras were connected, so to speak, with what I suppose you would call the life fluid."

He found himself wondering if Miss Fosdick had been forced to undergo much of this sort of thing, and his sympathy for her deepened and broadened.

"It is an extraordinary case. Doubtless the aura is an accumulation of evil thought directed toward the statue during its worship some centuries ago."

(Mr. Winnery thought, "I must ask after Miss Fosdick and yet how dare I after she has discovered the appearance of red in my aura.") Aloud he

said, "I have never had the pleasure of knowing anyone who saw auras. It must be very disconcert-
ing—I mean, always to see not only your friends but
their auras as well." He was beginning to be
afraid of the woman.

"It is a privilege given to a few," replied Mrs.
Weatherby with a certain smugness.

He then asked her about Miss Annie Spragg.
He felt, he said, that Mrs. Weatherby had been
somewhat constrained yesterday by the presence of
Father d'Astier and the Principessa d'Orobelli.
With him, of course, it was different. With him
she might feel quite free, as with a man of science.

But it was clear that her lips were to remain
sealed. She would say nothing. Yet there remained with him the certainty that she knew far
more than she chose to tell. At last he rose and
made his adieux, filled suddenly with the terrible suspicion that the seeress believed he had come back to
the Villa Leonardo because he found her attractive.
A certain mincingness had entered her manner. She
bridled and held out her little finger as she raised the
teacup to her lips. Quite suddenly he was terrified
and filled with a sense of panic. What did this
extraordinary woman expect from him? For a moment he had the fantastic idea that the stone god
(which by now must be safely buried) was having its
revenge upon her.

She went with him to the door, snapping her
pince-nez back on the gold fleur-de-lis pin attached
to her ample bosom and thanking him for the call.
She urged him to come frequently. It was a lonely
place. They seldom saw many people but of course

it was impossible for her to live where the confusion of twentieth century civilization broke in upon her meditations. She would always arrange it so that they could talk without intrusion.

As they reached the garden Winnery saw that the work had been done. The statue was buried again and atop the grave-like mound of reddish earth Pietro had left the olive branch and the two melons as a propitiatory offering. The goats had disappeared.

Wildly he said, "I have not seen Miss Fosdick? I was hoping to say good-day to her."

"She is not here," said Mrs. Weatherby.

There was a pause in which Mr. Winnery found himself at a loss for conversation. At last he said, "I did not know she was going away?" (Why should I know?)

"Yes. She has gone on a holiday, the first, I must say, that she has had in twenty years. I urged her to do it. I felt that she had had quite enough of me. Dear Gertrude is always so devoted. She never wants to leave me for a moment."

This cast Mr. Winnery down. "She must indeed be devoted," he murmured. And then suddenly—"Good-by, Mrs. Weatherby, and thank you for the tea."

At the mouth of the tunnel he turned suddenly, seized by what he felt must be the beginning of madness. If Mrs. Weatherby happened to be looking at his aura she must suddenly see that it had turned flaming red. "When do you think she will return?" he asked.

"I don't know," said Mrs. Weatherby. "That

was left open. I told her to stay away as long as she liked. I don't imagine she'll be away long. She has been so devoted for twenty years. A thing like that gets to be a habit. Have you ever noticed, Mr. Winnery, that it is our habits and our friends which give permanence and solidity to life?"

"Quite right, Mrs. Weatherby, quite right."

By breaking habits he had gotten himself into this muddle. Breaking habits by driving in the hot afternoon with the African wind blowing. Breaking habits by going to bed long after midnight. Breaking the habit of regarding people as literary material rather than human creatures. He had made this long trip for nothing. He had not seen Miss Fosdick. He had not had a word with her. He did not even know where she was and he did not know when she would return. He had had a wretched tea and ruined his clothes. The checked suit, the new hat and yellow gloves reeked with the strong smell of goat. But Mrs. Weatherby had clearly been attracted by him. That he could not forget.

v

Obstacles and difficulties, says an old sentimental proverb, only serve to increase a passion, and the disappearance of Miss Fosdick only served to inflame Mr. Winnery. If Miss Fosdick had been at the Villa Leonardo she might have said or done something which would have upset so precise and finicky a man. There might have been a hole in her stocking or she might have blown her nose too loudly or, being surprised by the sudden call of Mr. Winnery, her hair might have been done sloppily. Since she was not there, none of these things happened and Mr. Winnery left disappointed (which is always good for love) and cherishing only the memory of her richly curving bosom, her nice eyes and her dove-like air. And since, despite himself, he really wanted to believe in the beauty and virtue of Miss Fosdick and really wanted to have his life disturbed and exciting now that his liver troubled him less, he went on believing in these things more and more passionately.

In the days that followed Mr. Winnery grew animated and slept very little, walking a great deal and calling upon Mr. Winnop, the curate, and the few old ladies who remained in Brinoë. He was even seized with a fit of ambition to recover some of that glory he had known a quarter of a century earlier as a literary prodigy and set to work to bring order from the confusion of notes, copyings and false starts which represented the existing state of "Miracles and Other Natural Phenomena." He discovered that love (for he conceded that love was the proper diagnosis of his strange transformation) and the creative instinct possessed an obscure and subtle interrelation.

After much wrangling among the local clergy, Miss Annie Spragg was buried at last in the little cemetery on the far slope of Monte Salvatore. The various parties reached a compromise and it was decided at length that she was to be buried in consecrated ground but without the special attentions which should have gone to a woman who was a potential saint. Nevertheless a large number of the

poorer and more ignorant devout made up a disorderly cortège which followed the coffin through
the dust all the way from Brinoë to Monte Salvatore.  There were in it old men and women, a great
many dirty children who looked upon the excursion
in the light of an outing, three men who were quite
drunk and sang, and even a woman pushing a per-
ambulator.  Immediately behind the coffin marched
Sister Annunziata, who had disobeyed her superiors
and joined the cortège.  She still had in her plain
face the light of a happiness that did not come of
this world.  At her side walked Fulco Baldessare,
clad in his checkered bookmaker's suit and protect-
ing himself from the brilliant sun with the black cotton umbrella.  It was all very gay and dishevelled, in
the best Italian tradition.

And when the excitement had died away a little
so that Mr. Winnery felt he might undertake his
investigation discreetly and without becoming involved, he set out to visit Signora Bardelli.  The
janitress, he felt, would be able to give him a
straightforward and realistic account of what had
happened, unmarred and distorted by the trimmings
with which more religious and emotional witnesses
were certain to decorate the strange case of Miss
Annie Spragg.

But Signora Bardelli had disappeared from the
Palazzo Gonfarini, and the new janitress, a gaunt,
witch-like and very dirty woman who had been
among those in the disorderly cortège, proved taci-
turn and ill-natured.  It was only after Mr. Winnery
had pressed into her hand a fraction of Aunt Bessie's

fortune that she told him what had happened and where the former janitress could be found.

Signora Bardelli, it appeared, had behaved scandalously. No sooner had the body of Miss Annie Spragg been removed from the Palazzo Gonfarini than the janitress began spreading a singular story. She expressed it as her belief that Miss Annie Spragg was not a holy woman at all but that she had been in alliance with the dark powers of fertility during her entire lifetime. Her relics, said Signora Bardelli, were efficacious in the case of barren women. Although she conceded a belief that any of the relics possessed a certain power, she was convinced that its very center was concentrated in the only piece of furniture left behind by the relic-snatchers—the bed upon which Miss Annie Spragg had died. The act of spending a night in this bed had, she declared, a miraculous effect. She fixed a price of forty lira for the privilege and before Father d'Astier, her employer, discovered the outrage she had already accumulated three customers. And then Father d'Astier had come to the palace in person and had thrown her into the street. But she had taken the miraculous bed with her and she was now living in a tiny house in the village of Monte Salvatore, where she had set it up once more and was doing a good business.

Fate, reflected Mr. Winnery, was always drawing him back to Monte Salvatore.

But before going he went to seek out the fat little Father Baldessare and the gaunt Sister Annunziata to gather from them their version of the miracle. The priest had disappeared completely, none knew

whither.   His former acquaintances only confirmed
the gossip of Maria—that he had gone out to bring
the world back to the simplicity of Jesus.   He had,
they believed, now gone completely mad, but since
in Italy people paid small attention to crazy people
there was nothing to be done about it.   At the convent Sister Maria Maddelena told him that Sister
Annunziata could see no one.   She had been ill for
a week and quite out of her head.   In her illness
she had gone about saying such astounding and scandalous things that they thought it better to keep her
in seclusion until the poor thing had recovered her
senses.

Mr. Winnery, somewhat cast down, hired a fiacre
and set out for Monte Salvatore.   He felt that in
all the confusion of the superstition and madness it
would be refreshing to talk with a woman of hard,
common sense like Signora Bardelli.

## VI

As Mr. Winnery made his entrance Signora Bardelli was just receiving forty lira from a pretty
young peasant woman who had spent the night on
the bed of Miss Annie Spragg.   The woman was
telling her story for the third time.   She had been
married seven years and although she had prayed
to all the saints of fertility there had been no
answer to her prayer.   Her husband was growing
impatient.   He already had a child outside of wed-
lock and he was fonder of this child than of his wife.
The woman wept a little and Signora Bardelli
assured her with all the authority and brightness of

a successful surgeon that from now on everything would be all right.

It was a small room in one of the bilious yellow houses of Monte Salvatore and it stood on the slope of the hill overlooking the lonely valley where the Villa Leonardo perched in its decaying and lonely splendor. In the evening the very shadow of the monastery fell across its doorstep. Unwilling to intrude upon the delicate transactions that were taking place, Mr. Winnery waited just outside the door.

He heard the former janitress giving the young woman earnest advice. Then he heard her selling for ten lira a mixture composed, she said, of amber, laurel and a powder made from the hill viper. This the young woman was to put into her husband's wine every night for seven nights following the next change of the moon. And she sold a charm containing a phial of powder (composition undescribed during the transaction) which she was to wear suspended between her two breasts. If nothing happened within three months Signora Bardelli advised returning to spend another night in the bed of Signorina Spragg. Some cases, she pointed out, were more difficult than others. It all sounded, thought Mr. Winnery, rather like the last consultation he had had with the expensive Doctor Gosse on the subject of his liver.

Then the peasant woman departed and Mr. Winnery brightly made his entrance. He planned to take Signora Bardelli directly into his confidence and so let her understand that he knew she was a shrewd and clever swindler.

His plan failed. The former janitress eyed him at once with suspicion, and even after he had explained his mission and the great work he had undertaken in driving superstition from the world, she warmed only a little. And that faint shade of warmth he divined only when he referred to the superstitions of the Church. She was, however, willing to discuss the case of Miss Annie Spragg and asked him to sit down, giving him to understand that the talk would be in the nature of a consultation and would, of course, call for a fee.

Mr. Winnery, dashed a bit by his reception, thought bitterly, "These free, generous Italians."

It was a square plain room in which dried herbs hung from the ceiling together with strings of garlic and red peppers. The walls, once painted white, were blackened by smoke. At one side there was a row of shelves with pots and jars of many sizes, colors, and descriptions, neatly arranged according to size, and in one corner there was a sort of throne like that in a restaurant. It had a till for receiving money. The whole room was all arranged efficiently, rather in the manner, thought Mr. Winnery, of the office of a specialist who charged five guineas a consultation. Certainly it was an organized business, quite as organized as the Church itself. The room was quite clean.

Mr. Winnery seated himself on a wooden bench opposite the doorway, and Signora Bardelli, taking off her spectacles, seated herself opposite him. It was not until he sat down that he noticed the magnificence of the view. The doorway gave out upon the lonely valley and far off, dimly seen through the haze of heat, he discerned the dark grove of trees which marked the Villa Leonardo.

## THE JANITRESS' TALE

### I

SHE did not know how Miss Annie Spragg had come to take lodgings in the Palazzo Gonfarini. The old maid was already installed when Signora Bardelli took over the post of janitress on the death of the old man who had preceded her as caretaker. Miss Annie Spragg was already established and a fixture she remained. She was not a troublesome tenant. She did not, like some of Signora Bardelli's lodgers, return home drunk or beat her children or stab indiscriminately the other lodgers. She seemed to have no wants and in all the years she lived there she had never made a complaint. She was very clean and seemed content with a room which contained only a bed, a chair and a washstand. She always paid her rent regularly until three weeks before her death, and then, of course, she could not pay it because her money had come to an end. Where this money had come from Signora Bardelli did not know. Miss Annie Spragg had never in all the years she had lived in the Palazzo Gonfarini received a letter. She had no friends and much of her time was spent in the churches, mainly at San Giovanni before the celebrated paintings of Saint John the Shepherd. She had learned to speak a little Italian but she was never really able to converse in that tongue.

In the third year after the janitress came to the Palazzo Gonfarini, Miss Annie Spragg came one day and asked her if she knew where there was a place she could go in the mountains to pass a month now and then. It must be very cheap, she said, because she had no money, and she would like it to be in some rather remote region where she would not be troubled by tourists. Signora Bardelli thought at once of her sister-in-law who lived in a village called Bestia, high in a remote part of the mountains. She sent word by a cousin (since neither the sister-in-law nor her husband could read) and received an answer that they would be glad of the money to be got by having the visitor. It was arranged to meet Miss Annie Spragg at Analo, which was the terminal of the railroad. Beyond Analo there were only mountain roads and donkey carts.

It was a wild country, said the janitress, which she had not seen since childhood. There were a few olive orchards and herds of goats and halfway down the mountains they were able to grow vines in the crevices of the volcanic rock. There were wolves which in winter became ferocious and sometimes attacked people in remote villages and farms. At Bestia there was no church and the inhabitants were forced to drive all the way to Analo to communicate with a priest. Therefore, they seldom saw priests except when someone died or was born. Sometimes children grew to manhood and womanhood and died without ever being received into the

church.   They had a kind of religion of their own
which was a mixture of Christianity and old legends,
half lost in the mists of time.   It was at Bestia that
Signora Bardelli had learned the science of herbs
and charms.   The people there knew about such
things and one old woman, long since dead, had
taught all she knew to the janitress.

(She had long sold herbs and charms to the poor,
the janitress said, but it was only since she had acquired the bed of Miss Annie Spragg and lost her
place as janitress that she had really set herself up
in a legitimate way.)

The family of the sister-in-law consisted of the
mother and father (a goatherd) and eleven children.   There was a room over the stable which
they gave to Miss Annie Spragg when she arrived
bearing a straw suitcase and an empty bird cage.
The entire family slept in one room.

From the beginning their strange lodger proved
a help to them.   She asked nothing and she paid
regularly.   She did not talk much and spent a great
deal of time on the mountain, setting out in the
morning with bread and cheese and a little wine, and
returning at sunset.   On her second visit she offered
timidly to watch Giusseppi's goats while they wandered along the mountainside.   These were willful
and troublesome goats which wandered off into
ravines and woods and caused Giusseppi much
anxiety, but with Miss Annie Spragg their character
appeared to undergo a change.   They became docile
and stayed near her while she was making water-
color sketches or knitting clothes for Giusseppi's
half-clad family or simply wandering about over the

mountainside gathering wild flowers and listening to the birds. She was a great help to Giusseppi because her taking charge of the goats freed another son to help him in the rude orchards and vineyards. People began to notice that she had a strange power over animals and to regard her with respect. It was only the wife (Signora Bardelli's sister-in-law) who did not like her. She thought there was something strange about the lodger and even spread the story that Miss Annie Spragg had the power of the evil eye.

Among the children of the sister-in-law there was one, a little girl of nine, who, her parents believed, was possessed of a devil. The old priest from Analo had tried to exorcise the demon and when he had failed they sought the aid of the old woman who was the herb doctor. She also tried and failed. The child's name was Peppina and she gave them a great deal of trouble. She was a pretty child with thick black hair and great black eyes and for days at a time she would be well behaved and docile. But she had seizures when she would run away and hide among the ravines of the mountainside. Sometimes they would not find her for days. Once she fell into a stream and was nearly drowned and on another time she set fire to the house in which they lived. She fell down at times in a fit and had strange visions.

Upon this child Miss Annie Spragg had the same effect as upon the goats. With the old maid Peppina remained docile and well behaved, but as soon as Miss Annie Spragg left Bestia the child began once more to cause them trouble and they had to beat her and try new ways of driving out the demon. When she was eleven she took to accompanying the old maid and the goats when they set out in the morning to feed on the mountainside.

For five years Miss Annie Spragg went each summer to occupy the room over the stable at Bestia and each time when she returned to the Palazzo Gonfarini she brought with her a cage filled with small birds, most of them being a kind of sparrow which frequented the mountains and because of its smallness was worth nothing as food to the peasants. When she left her room in the Palazzo Gonfarini in the spring Miss Annie Spragg opened the window and allowed them to escape. Signora Bardelli believed they were always the same birds. They spent the winter at the Palazzo Gonfarini and flew back in summer to rejoin Miss Annie Spragg at Bestia. Once she even brought back with her a box filled with field mice.

In Bestia they no longer thought her queer. She became a part of the place. They even came to date things by the arrival and the departure of the old maid, as if her coming marked the beginning of summer and her departure the arrival of the long Italian autumn.

She might have continued going summer after summer to Bestia, said Signora Bardelli, but a strange thing happened. One night at midnight her brother-in-law was awakened by the smell of smoke and discovered that the house was burning. At first he believed that it was the demon in Peppina who had set the fire a second time, but when he had awakened all his family he discovered that Peppina

was not there at all.    He discovered too that the
lodger's room above the stable was empty and that
in the stable the goats had disappeared.    When he
had put out the fire he set out to find the goats.

In the darkness he went up the mountainside calling out Peppina's name and uttering at intervals the
half-human, half-animal cry which he used in calling
the goats when they had strayed.    But there was no
answer.    He had wandered for hours over the rocks
and pastures when dawn at last began to slip in
through the valleys and crevasses and down the wild
rocky slopes, and he turned toward home.    Cold
blue mist veiled the hillside and clung to the groves
of ancient olive trees planted among the outcrop-
pings of grey tufa.    The poor man, not knowing
what to think, began to believe that Peppina's demon
had swept Peppina and their lodger and his goats
off into limbo.    As his bewilderment increased he
became certain that he would never see any of them
again.    He regretted the loss of Peppina, said the
ex-janitress, far less than he regretted the loss of
the goats, for she was only a source of trouble to her
parents and goats were valuable property.    He began to fret over what he would tell the police when
it was discovered that Miss Annie Spragg too had
been swallowed up.    He told himself that this was
what came of having to do with a strange foreign
woman, and that his wife was right in suspecting her
of being a witch.

In the midst of his reflections he heard suddenly
the faint far-off tinkle of the bell that the black he-
goat wore about his neck, and halting, he stood listening until he made certain that he was not

imagining the sound, and then to discover from what
direction the sound came. Looking down he saw
far below him, half hidden in mists so that it was
visible one moment and not the next, a little procession which had a strange likeness to a procession of
children on their way from a first communion. At
the head walked sedately the black he-goat who
wore the bell, and behind him came all the herd.
In the rear, like the parents who followed the children, walked Miss Annie Spragg and Peppina.
They seemed to be wearing wreaths on their heads
and Miss Annie Spragg was without the black veil
she always wore.

There was no way of descending directly to them
and the puzzled man was forced to go by the tor-
tuous narrow paths that led down among the rocks
and trees. When he reached the bottom of the
crevasse the procession had disappeared, but there
remained in the red earth the neat little prints of
goat's hoofs.

When he reached the farm once more it was quite
light but he found that all his family were still
asleep, and that beside the oven on her mattress of
straw Peppina was also sleeping soundly. In the
stable the goats were in their pen as they should
have been and when he entered they pushed forward
behind their leader, the black he-goat, to be led
out to feed. And in the room overhead Miss Annie
Spragg was asleep. On the floor beside her there
were a few bruised and withered laurel leaves.

Thinking that he too must be possessed of a
demon who had driven him out on the mountain in
the middle of the night for nothing, the poor man

returned and roused his wife, telling her all that he had seen. Because he was confused and could not believe his senses they examined the beams above the oven to make certain there had ever been a fire. There had been a fire. The beams were all charred. They went to awaken Peppina but she could not be awakened. They struck her and called her evil names but the girl only slept on quietly. The smaller children wakened and began to scream with fright, and in all the confusion the father lost his head and sat down and wept. But his wife did not take leave of her senses. She cried out that their lodger was a witch and that she had known it all along and now they would be free of her at last. She went to the stable and roused Miss Annie Spragg, who said nothing in reply to the woman's abuse but packed her shabby bag in silence. Then the old maid set out along the road to Analo carrying her bag, her cage of little birds and her box of water colors. The wife followed her for three miles along the road, hiding from time to time in the bushes and behind rocks to watch and make certain that she did not return and to see whether she might not vanish abruptly into thin air.

When the figure of the old maid had disappeared at last on the serpentine road leading down the mountain to the high valley of Analo, the woman returned to the lonely farm and taking beeswax and three red hairs and seven nail parings from a little box, she moulded the beeswax into the image of the thin old maid and embedded the nail parings and the three hairs deep in the wax, and sticking a pin through the place where the heart should have been,

she threw the whole thing into the oven. She had
been waiting all the while. The red hair was Miss
Annie Spragg's hair and the parings were the
parings of Miss Annie Spragg's nails.

When the image had gone up in a burst of flame,
Peppina stirred on her bed and wakened, but when
they talked to her she could remember nothing.
She had, she said, been asleep in her bed all the
night.

She was fifteen years old at the time, and developed like a woman of thirty.

But it was the end of Peppina, said Signora Bardelli. After that the demon claimed her for his
own. She had many respectable suitors, some of
whom were rich, but she would have none of them
and ran off in the end with a corporal of the Cara-
binieri, who had been sent into the mountains to run
to earth a notorious brigand. He was a gigantic
and ugly brute, more like an animal than a man.
He beat her cruelly and was stabbed to death at last
by a man he found in Peppina's bed when he came
home unexpectedly. After that Peppina disappeared. A young native of Analo returning from
South America said he had seen her there in a
brothel on the water front of Rio de Janeiro. She
was dancing naked in the midst of a circle of sailors,
white men and black men, yellow men and brown
men. But no one knew for certain that the woman
was Peppina.

## THE ROMANCE OF MR. WINNERY

### I

MR. WINNERY, listening to the tale, grew more and more bewildered. This woman whom he had expected to find sensible he saw was no different from all the others. He saw that she believed all that she was telling him and that he could never persuade her that it was all nonsense. She too was like all the others, the prey of superstition, the victim of ancient legends. It was simply another kind of superstition, different and more ancient and more deeply rooted than the superstitions which led Sister Annunziata to believe that she was chosen by Saint Francis as the elect of God. Sister Annunziata was more than half crazy, and they were right perhaps in shutting her up, but this shrewd hard peasant woman was clearly not mad. To Sister Annunziata Miss Annie Spragg was a white saint and to Signora Bardelli the old maid was a black saint.

He said to her, "But the Stigmata? How can a witch have received the miracle of the Stigmata?"

She looked at him mysteriously and replied, "That I do not know."

"It is all very strange."

"I do not know," observed Signora Bardelli, "unless it is the work of the Devil. Perhaps it is a joke played on the Church by something that is older than the Church, older even than Christianity. I have been told that things like that are the oldest things in the world."

She was stubborn and would not be shaken from her beliefs into the admission that her sister-in-law and her husband might have imagined such a story, or that there had really been none of the marks of the Stigmata on the body of Miss Annie Spragg. She had seen the scars with her own eyes.

A figure suddenly filled the doorway, throwing a blue shadow across the earthen floor. It was a tall, heavy woman, a peasant with a light shawl thrown over her head to keep off the sun. She spoke to Signora Bardelli. She had walked down from the mountains twenty-seven miles to sleep in the bed of Miss Annie Spragg. She had been married for thirteen years and had never had a child.

Mr. Winnery, with a sense of intruding a second time upon a delicate situation, rose and gave Signora Bardelli ten lira for the consultation. Then he bade her good-by, aware that she had disapproved of him as one who sought to meddle in things he could not understand. The tall heavy peasant woman sat wearily down on the chair he had left, and he walked out again into the blazing square where the battered fiacre and the bony horses stood waiting for him in the shadow of an enormous fig tree. For a moment the light blinded him. He felt weary and hot. And then he saw the deep cool valley of Monte Salvatore coming into form and on its side the distant black patch of cypresses that marked the Villa Leonardo.

A sense of the immense futility of everything swept over him and he thought, "Why should I trouble myself about these things? Let them believe what they like. That peasant woman is happier in the hope that a night on the Spragg woman's bed will give her the power of bringing more brats into an over-crowded world. She is happier than if she had stayed in her village without any hope. Life is short and I have wasted most of it. It is time that I began to bring my life to something."

Suddenly he wasn't interested in miracles and other natural phenomena. He wanted to see Miss Fosdick. The heat, the smell of the fig tree, the sight of the former janitress doing her best to make the world a fertile place made him feel languorous. He became the prey of his own imagination. He, a respectable man of fifty-three who had led a virginal existence, was becoming amorous.

He wakened the sleeping driver and said, "Go to the Villa Leonardo." And pointing with the malacca stick he had purchased to celebrate the passing of Aunt Bessie and the beginning of his courtship he added, "It is yonder. That patch of cypresses."

He would face Mrs. Weatherby again and tell her the truth—that he proposed to marry her companion, and that nothing could stop him, not even the famous twenty years of devotion.

II

As he drove up the long avenue between the rows of grotesque and ancient oaks he was stirred again by the villa's sense of loneliness and utter isolation. The windows were again tightly shuttered and this time there was no red and black motor standing before the door. The white flame of yucca set among swords had turned brown and dead and withered away. He got down—it had become a habit with him, as if he were an old friend of the household—and went through the dark tunnel of greenery. The garden had an unkempt look, for the dry heat of early autumn had detached the yellow leaves of the plane trees and left them dead and drifted in little piles along the colonnades of mottled trunks. The grave where the statue had been reburied had sunk now so that there was a little hollow instead of a mound. Then he discovered that the back of the villa presented the same appearance as the front. It was closed. Every door and shutter was fastened. They had gone away (he saw) and Miss Fosdick was perhaps lost forever.

With the malacca stick he pounded on the door. A kind of recklessness entered his soul. He called out the name of Miss Fosdick but no one answered. He was about to leave when he saw emerging from the decaying stables the abundant figure of Margharita. The girl came toward him and when she was near enough to speak she said that Signora Wetterbee had gone away, not only for this season but forever. She did not know where she had gone but she supposed she had gone back to her house in Brinoë. When he asked her why she had gone away the girl said that she had taken a dislike to the place. The villa itself had been sold over Signora Wetterbee's head. The truth, she added, was that she had been driven out.

It was all the doing of the statue, she said. It ought never to have been buried again. It was tak-

ing vengeance on Signora Wetterbee. No sooner
was it buried than strange things began to happen.
Signora Wetterbee had been unable to sleep and in
the middle of the night she had heard music and
sounds of wild gayeties in the garden. She, Margharita, had heard none of the sounds nor any of the
other servants, but Signora Wetterbee insisted there
were sounds and accused them of disturbing her rest,
although, said Margharita, they had all been sleeping soundly. It went on night after night and then
one morning Signora Wetterbee packed all her be-
longings and got into the Ford with her dogs and
the parrot Anubis without even saying good-by, and
Giovanni drove her back to Brinoë. Signora Wetterbee, she said, was a strange woman and imagined
things. It was her belief that perhaps Signora
Wetterbee was a witch. She had seen her standing
on her head on the terrace in the moonlight clad only
in a pair of man's trousers. Surely such goings-on
could be indulged in only by a witch. What did the
Signor think?

Mr. Winnery, who by now had begun to think
that he was losing his reason, said that perhaps
she was a witch or perhaps she was only doing the
exercises that were part of a certain religious cult.
Who, he asked, had bought the villa?

It was the Principessa d'Orobelli. Margharita
had heard that she had bought it suddenly without
even asking the price and that she meant to retire to
it and spend the rest of her life there. She had not
even come to see the place. She had heard that the
Principessa planned to install bathrooms. That,
thought Margharita, would be exciting. She had

never seen a bathroom.    Was it true that the Principessa was an American lady?

And then quite suddenly Margharita said, "Signora Wetterbee went away three days ago but Signorina Fosdeek returned this morning."

"Where?" cried Mr. Winnery.    "Where is she?"

Margharita said she did not know it was Signorina Fosdeek he wanted to see.   She thought it
was Signora Wetterbee.   She even (and here she
became arch) thought that perhaps there was a romance with Signora Wetterbee.   Signorina Fosdeek
had arrived on foot carrying her bag.

"On foot?" exclaimed Mr. Winnery.    "In this
heat?"

"Si, si.    And she ran away on foot."

"Ran away?" repeated Mr. Winnery.

"She ran away.   Signora Wetterbee did not
know she was going."

A great light burst on Mr. Winnery.   He wasted
no more time talking with Margharita.   Leaving
her astonished in the midst of a long recital, he went
to the villa and this time without knocking he pushed
open the door.   There was a rustle of dried leaves
in the hallway and a rat scurried off into the
shadows.   He did not like rats.   The sight of
them made his hair rise up on end.   But he pushed
bravely on, calling out, "Miss Fosdick!  Miss Fosdick!" again and again.   But there was no answer.
The name simply echoed through the empty house.
Perhaps, he thought wildly, she has killed herself
and I shall find the body.   He went from room to
room.   All were closed and the only light filtered in
dimly from the cracks in the shutters.   The big

salon overlooking the valley was empty and the bare dining room and the small room under the stairway. He started up the stairs and was half way to the top when he heard below him a slight scuffling sound, among the dead leaves. Turning he saw Miss Fosdick. She had come out of the salon and was trying to escape before he discovered her.

"Miss Fosdick," he called out. "I've been searching for you."

She halted and stood against the wall without looking at him. She had in her hand the worn handbag. The black dress was covered with dust to the knees and her hat had slipped a little over one ear. She was flushed and trembling and her brown hair was all in disarray.

He came down the stairs toward her. "I've been looking for you," he said. "I've been twice before to call at the villa. Mrs. Weatherby told me you had gone off on a holiday." He tried to put her at her ease by behaving as if there was nothing in the least strange in finding her thus. "I really wanted to see you again."

She began suddenly to cry. "I don't want to see you. I don't want to see anyone. I only want to die. I'm useless and no good to anyone. I'm better out of the way. I ought to kill myself but I can't even do that properly."

He *had* arrived in time. She *had* been thinking of suicide.

Without quite knowing what he was doing he slipped an arm gently about her shoulders. She did not protest or draw away from him.

"You're not useless, Miss Fosdick," he said gently. "None of God's creatures are useless. Come, let's sit down somewhere and talk. I've been looking for you for days."

She seemed too tired either to protest or speak and he led her gently into the big salon. He did not think of his own feelings, for in the excitement he had forgotten to be literary. Miss Fosdick seemed plumper and prettier than he had ever imagined, and in her distress far more charming.

The furniture had been stacked into one corner. He selected one of the uncomfortable chairs and bade her sit in it. She obeyed him meekly as a rabbit. Then he opened the shutters and in a blaze of golden light the whole length of the glorious valley opened up before them. Drawing up another uncomfortable chair he seated himself and said, "Tell me now. Perhaps I can help you." But she seemed unable to do anything but sob. "Margharita," he said, "told me you had run away. She told me the whole story."

Then the flood gates burst and the whole torrent poured forth. She told him the long story of her twenty years' devotion to Mrs. Weatherby and how in the end when she could stand it no longer she had run away. And she had come back because her money had given out and at the pension they would keep her no longer unless she paid in advance. She had tried to get work as a companion. She had even advertised in the papers but there had only been three replies. One was from a clergyman's widow who required that she know how to crochet and do tatting. Another was from an elderly spinster who wanted to be read to in Italian, and the third was from a retired army officer with an invalid wife who required a woman who was young and pretty and who had been trained as a nurse.

"And I," said Miss Fosdick, "can do none of these things. So I came back. . . . I came back to Aunt Henrietta and now she has gone. I don't know what I'm to do. I haven't any more money and I don't know how to do anything but be a companion to Aunt Henrietta. I ought to die."

Mr. Winnery, feeling very masculine and mediæval, told her that they must first of all be practical. She must go back to Brinoë in the fiacre with him. He would lend her money until they worked out her problem. He told her about Aunt Bessie's death and how he was now a rich man. He had a feeling for her, he said, from the very beginning. He had known all along that she was unhappy with the seeress.

But Miss Fosdick suddenly grew respectable and unfeminine. "No," she said, "I couldn't do that. I couldn't accept any money from a gentleman I barely know. A lady can't do such things."

For a moment Mr. Winnery was irritated, and then he remembered that of course she was in trouble and he must be gentle with her. He tried to make her understand that it was purely a business matter and that she could pay him back. But beneath his arguments Miss Fosdick only grew more and more respectable. He might have been a lecherous old man planning the ruin of a young virgin. He wanted to say, "Well, if you don't borrow money from me what on earth are you going to do?" He would have

said it if he had not thought her so charming with
her plump face flushed and her eyes damp with tears.
And then he thought of a solution.

"You can pay me back by going to work for me."

"But how can I work for you? There is nothing
I can do."

Nevertheless at this shadow of hope she grew
more quiet and took a handkerchief from her handbag and began to dry her eyes.

Mr. Winnery explained to her all about Miracles
and other Natural Phenomena and the state of
confusion in which the vast amount of notes, copyings and references continually found themselves.
It would be her task to keep them in order, tied into
little bundles and ticketed. It was not a difficult
task, he pointed out, nor one that required training.
All it needed was a clear head.

"But I haven't a clear head," echoed Miss Fosdick. "I always muddle everything."

"Well, well. In any case we must make a try.
It will be a help to me and will provide money for
you."

While he was speaking Mr. Winnery made a remarkable discovery. It was this—that during the
period Miss Fosdick had apparently been drying her
tears her flushed face had grown perceptibly paler.
For a moment he thought with alarm that perhaps
she meant to faint. And then suddenly he understood the phenomenon. Undoubtedly there was a
powder puff concealed in the folds of the handkerchief. The discovery touched him. As a means
of powdering the nose it was a fashion so much
more refined than that used by women like, well,

like the d'Orobelli, who simply extracted an apparatus from her bag and sent boldly the powder flying in all directions.

Again he touched Miss Fosdick's hand. "There
now," he said, "you're feeling better, aren't you?
There's no need of ever going back to Mrs. Weatherby. Never again."

Miss Fosdick admitted almost grudgingly that
there did seem to be hope.

"And now we can start back to Brinoë. I have a
fiacre outside. I will pay you a week's wages in
advance and you can go back to the pension."

Miss Fosdick thought perhaps she had better take
less than that. She doubted whether she would last
a week. But Mr. Winnery reassured her. "Mrs.
Weatherby," he said, "always preaches self-confi-
dence is the first of the virtues. Besides, I am
certain that you are just the secretary I've been
seeking. I'm sure," he added with meaning, "that
you'll last for months and for years."

They went through the empty hall where the
dead leaves still rustled in the draught from the
open door, and on the steps leading down into the
garden Mr. Winnery halted a moment to regard the
view.

"It is a beautiful place," he said. "It would be
a splendid place to live, only I hear the Princess
d'Orobelli has bought it for herself."


III


They drove back to Brinoë, where Mr. Winnery
escorted her to her pension, and the next morning at

ten she appeared for work. She lasted one week,
and then two and then three, tasting for the first
time the sweets of a woman's economic indepen-
dence. She muddled the mass of notes and papers
hopelessly so that Mr. Winnery was unable to find
anything he wanted, whereas before he had been
able to find at least a few things. But it did not
seem to annoy Mr. Winnery and at the beginning
of the fourth week he asked Miss Fosdick quite
suddenly to marry him and quite suddenly she
accepted.

It was agreed that they were to go to Iowa on
their honeymoon because Mr. Winnery had a desire to see America and Mrs. Winnery wanted to
revisit Winnebago Falls. Not the least of her
motives was a desire to exhibit her rich and distinguished husband. As a kind of second thought
Mr. Winnery said that it would give him an opportunity to go into the very beginnings of the strange
case of Miss Annie Spragg.


IV


A week before Mr. Winnery paid Signora Bardelli the only visit he ever made her, the Principessa
gave in Venice the famous fête which each year
marked the peak of the season. It attained a new
measure of splendor and magnificence and attracted
the fashionable and the notorious from every part
of Europe. Millionaires, decayed royalty, gigoloes,
actresses, demi-mondaines; even two ministers of
state enjoying pompous holidays were present. It
went off in a blaze of triumph with Bengal lights and

three orchestras and a whole fleet of decorated gon-
dolas. Anna d'Orobelli and Oreste, Duke of Fonterrabia, appeared in the costumes of the Countess
Guiccioli and Lord Byron, and Father d'Astier was
seen moving about wearily and looking old and tired
in the robes of Mazarin, which suited him to perfec-
tion. It was the first ball in years which Mr. Winnery had not described at second hand in his correspondence to the *Ladies' Own World*.

And two days later when the curtains of Anna
d'Orobelli's bedchamber were pulled back to let the
morning sun stream in, there was a letter on the
lacquered tray beside her chocolate. It was the letter in the handwriting of the Duque de Fonterrabia
which she had been awaiting for nearly two years.
It was quite short and rather cold. It said simply
that he had been forced to undertake a voyage to the
Argentine and that he regretted not having had a
chance to bid his beloved Anna farewell. He would
write her and see her on his return. But she knew
well enough that it was the end. *Voyez, c'est elle la
vieille Princesse!*

For two days she was not seen and on the third
day she left Venice mysteriously and appeared with
equal mystery in Brinoë, where she quickly set about
restoring and preparing the Villa Leonardo. Because
it was lonely and because it was in a state of ruin, it
had been waiting for years a purchaser who saw its
virtues. With a kind of mad vitality she attacked
the refitting of the villa. Masons came and plumb-
ers and painters. To Margharita and the other
servants who lived on the place it all seemed a
strange proceeding for one who was simply prepar-

ing a spot where she might retire from the world.
Four bathrooms were installed and much furniture,
not furniture like that Mrs. Weatherby had strewn
about during her tenancy, but expensive and beautiful pieces that should have been in museums. The
old chapel was opened again and put in order for
religious ceremonies. There was such a confusion
as the old villa had not seen since the great days of
the Spanish Ambassador. And at last when the
Principessa came herself (dressed handsomely all in
black by Worth) to examine the progress of the
work she asked what had become of the statue they
found in the garden, and Margharita told her that
it had been buried again. The Principessa herself
superintended the reopening of the grave, but they
dug and dug without ever finding a trace of the
statue and at last Margharita confessed that she
knew all along it was not there. It had already been
dug up a second time and carted down the hillside
where it was set up in the barren rocky little garden
of Pietro the goatherd. The Principessa flew into
a wild rage and said that the statue was her own and
that she meant to have it. She herself went to
Pietro's hut to recover it.

And when the palace was finished Anna d'Orobelli
drove one day into Brinoë and sought out Father
d'Astier to show him the place she had prepared
for her retirement.

It was a warm day in April when the hillside
beyond Monte Salvatore was blue with violets and
wild hyacinths and the whole valley, that was by
nature so bleak and barren, had turned fresh and
green from the thin stream at the bottom to the wild

woods on its crest.    But in her black and red motor
the Princess drove so fast that it was impossible to
appreciate the beauties of the burgeoning country-
side.   They entered the villa by the main door and
went from room to room, from the great salon
with the anatomical paintings to the tiny room in the
top fitted as a cell, with a hard iron bed, a crucifix
and a wooden bench, where Anna d'Orobelli planned
to retire for days at a time in prayer.   They had
very few words to say to each other.   Father
d'Astier from time to time murmured banal com-
pliments upon her taste and the Princess showed the
rooms with indifference as if it were a duty, as if
she were saying all the while, "It is because of you
that I have come to this.   It is because of you that
I must end my life in barren loneliness here in this
solitary villa."   When he asked her why she had
troubled to put in so many bathrooms, she replied
that she thought God would not mind if sometimes
she had friends come to stop with her, and Father
d'Astier murmured that he supposed God would not
mind, though that was scarcely the Church's idea of
a religious retirement.

When they had finished the house, they went
down into the garden.   The colonnades of plane
trees were no longer yellow and brown as they had
been nine months earlier when they last walked together in the garden.   The whole place was covered by a canopy of fresh green leaves that in the
spring sunlight appeared luminous, giving off a pure
green light.   The roses that climbed over the
ancient stone balustrade above the valley were covered with white and yellow blossoms.

Once Anna d'Orobelli said, "This is a haunted garden. Margharita says at night they sometimes hear sounds of singing and dancing although the place is quite empty. It was the ghosts that drove away that preposterous Mrs. Weatherby. I don't mind that. I've never been afraid of ghosts."

They found themselves suddenly at the end of one of the colonnades before a niche let recently into the mouldering wall. It was a niche such as one finds in the gardens of Italy sheltering images of the Virgin, only the image was not that of the interceding Mary but of a figure more ancient. It was the statue that had been dug up out of the cesspool. On the slab of stone beneath it there was an inscription. Father d'Astier had need to read only the first line to know what it was.

*"Dans la damnation le feu est la moindre chose; le supplice propre au damné est le progrès infini dans le vice et dans le crime, l'âme s'endurcissant, se dépravant toujours, s'enfonçant nécessairement dans le mal de minute en progression géométrique pendant l'éternité."*

*Michelet.*

He turned away in silence and in silence they walked back to the villa and entering the motor, drove back again at a mad speed down the long hill through Monte Salvatore into Brinoë. They had talked a little but they had said nothing with words. It was the silence which spoke for them.

V

Father d'Astier never saw her again, and after that people said that he had suddenly grown old. The women whom he had once entertained by his wit and helped with his wordly advice and solaced by his spiritual comfort no longer found him either interesting or good company. He ceased to be amused by their vanities and even while they were talking to him his gaze would have a strange way of wandering off as if in search of something or some-one whom he would never find. At times he would pull himself up with a great effort and try again to be what he had once been, but in the end he was too weary. People who had once included him in din-ners and week-ends began to neglect him. He went about bravely as usual in search of converts, follow-ing the season from London to Venice, to Paris, to Vienna, but clearly there was no longer any heart in his journeys.

And so he came one night in July to be staying with the head of a great English Roman Catholic family. There had been people for dinner and after dinner, feeling a hunger to be alone, he withdrew into the great library where the old Duke kept his famous collection. There he left the other men and hid himself behind a great globe mounted in silver and mahogany to turn quietly, half-dreaming, the pages of an eighteenth century translation of Hor-ace. And presently when he had wearied of reading he allowed the book to slip into his lap and sat with his eyes closed. It was through the mists of sleep that he became aware of the voices.

Two men had seated themselves on the opposite side of the globe and were talking. One of them was English and the other spoke with an Italian accent. The Italian, he knew, was the cousin of Faustino d'Orobelli. He was a middle-aged man and rich with the profits of an automobile factory. The Englishman he thought must be Admiral Burnham, whom he had not seen in more than twenty years until tonight—not, he thought, since he had gone to Malta on Nina's yacht on the voyage that ended in meeting Anna.

The two men were gossipping. He heard the Italian say, "After all, my cousin Faustino was never much of a husband for a woman like that." And "She has kept remarkably young. She is quite extraordinary."

And then the Englishman answering. "I knew her when she was first married. I met her in Malta. Do you remember her?"

The voice of the Italian. "That was a long time ago. Even her second son, . . . the one who is quite all right . . . is a grown man. But I hear she has come to the same end as most of them."

There was a sound of the admiral stirring in his chair, as if he were sitting up with interest.

"She's found someone to console her," continued the Italian voice. . . . "A young Italian. He calls himself a duke, but there are so many dukes. He makes ends meet by gambling. . . ." There was a slight pause, and then, "By doing what he can. But he won't need to worry for some time. She's very rich. It was her money that saved Faustino's family. She's an odd woman. She has no sense of the value of money.   It's lucky she's always had so much.   She met the gigolo at Nina de Paulhac's."

The voice of the admiral sounded suddenly gruff and ill-tempered.   "I could never see why Nina has such people about."

"She has a list of them, for dances and week-ends. When a woman gets to be Nina's age, young men don't flock about for love."

There was a pause and Father d'Astier was aware that he must be very still lest they discover that he was sitting there, for he knew that two men will gossip and say things of a woman that they would not say if a third were present.   Honor to which he himself had sacrificed so much was, he thought, an artificial thing, like the clothes one put on before appearing in public.   He found himself praying that they would not speak of her again.   And then the voice of Faustino's cousin.

"They say that Oreste Fonterrabia went away on her account."

"Yes, she was always reluctant to give up love." A sigh.   "But a magnificent woman."

"We must remember what she *was*."

"I am glad to have news of her.   I haven't seen her in years."

And then the cracked voice of the childish old duke moving toward them.   "I think, gentlemen, that we will join the ladies."

When they had gone Father d'Astier replaced the volume of Horace, came out from his hiding place and fixing his mouth into a worldly smile went through the big door into the drawing-room where the daughter of Admiral Burnham who was the half-

sister of Victor d'Orobelli was playing Chopin
quietly in the far corner.   He noticed that she had
the same fine red hair and clear skin that Victor had.
She was young and very beautiful, and in his weariness and confusion it seemed to him for a moment
that she might have been his own daughter if he had
chosen differently.   He had only Fulco.

That night when he was alone again in his room
over the Georgian doorway that faced the park he
closed and locked his door and then sat down before
the fire they had made for him, because he sometimes had chills at night, even in July.   All through
the interminable evening he had been thinking in the
back of his mind, behind all the talk and chatter and
the music made by the Burnham girl, of Fulco, and
he made the astounding discovery that Fulco hadn't
any longer the power of irritating him.   He had
begun to think of Fulco as Poor Fulco in the way he
thought of Anna as Poor Anna.   That meant, he
knew, that he was really an old man and at the end
of things.   He saw that he alone was responsible
for Fulco's very existence and that he had in a way
always shirked that responsibility.   He saw poor
Fulco in his checked suit and umbrella wandering
from village to village in Italy, trying to "purify
Christianity," and trying to free it of all the centuries of tiresome accumulations and growths.   Fulco
who hadn't the power or the dignity or the presence
to convince anyone of anything.   Fulco attempting
a new Reformation. . . .

He turned away from the fire and began to un-
dress.   His hands trembled a little, like those of a
very old man.   They had never trembled before.

He was tired, but not too tired to make a resolution. He would go back to Italy tomorrow and go from town to town, searching out Fulco, and when he had found Fulco he would reason with him to return to the Church. He would even use his influence to help him and he would tell Fulco that he was his son and the only relative who remained in the world. Together they would perhaps work something out and when that was done he would retire into the monastery at Monte Salvatore and never come out again, not even in death. They could bury him in the end in the warm sunny garden above the valley. The old conflict in his ravaged soul seemed dead at last. The Church was his mother to whom he might return now that he had finished with life. The world had nothing better to offer. And he was tired of this world.

## VI

He left suddenly saying that he had been called back to Brinoë on business of the Church. It was in Bologna while his train was awaiting the train from Venice that he bought the newspaper and read the small paragraph at the bottom of the page. In Milan, said the paper, a man later identified as a renegade priest named Baldessare had been found on a street corner preaching Communism, and twelve vigilant and heroic young men in black shirts had pulled him down from the steps where he was speaking and beaten him and dosed him with castor oil. The offender had died the same night of his injuries. "It is by such vigilance and heroic conduct," read the last florid sentence of the brief account, "that our leader and our sacred Italy are preserved daily from the corruptions of those who would destroy both. It is hoped that the watchful young men will be properly rewarded for their service."

Father d'Astier closed his eyes and leaned back in the heat of the compartment. "Communism," he thought. "Poor Fulco had probably never heard of Communism." They had killed him for preaching what Christ taught.

In another day they would have made him a martyr and a saint.

That night when he arrived at Brinoë he went to the two bare small rooms and taking a few books from them he locked the door, and hiring a fiacre, drove up the long hill to Monte Salvatore. They were awaiting him for he had sent a telegram ahead from Bologna. Inside the monastery they told him that the Principessa d'Orobelli had not returned to the Villa Leonardo. She had leased it, they said, to some English people named Winnery who were recently married. For a moment Father d'Astier wondered whether it could be the pompous and common little man he had met on the day they found the statue in the garden, and then he told himself that a man like Mr. Winnery would scarcely be enjoying a honeymoon at his age. From the window of his room high up in the monastery above the house of Signora Bardelli, Father d'Astier could see the distant lights of the villa twinkling like stars in the darkness. He knew what he had known all along, that she would never return there.

He began by setting down the elements which appeared to him to be subject to a reasonable explanation. He wrote:

1. The Church appears to have been entirely right in quietly discrediting the so-called miracle. The scars on the body of Miss Annie Spragg appear neither to have been of miraculous origin nor to have appeared at the moment of her death, but clearly were the scars of wounds inflicted upon her at some time before the brutal murder of her brother at Winnebago Falls. It is on record that they were seen at the time of her examination in connection with the murder. The agency which inflicted the wounds will probably never be known, although it seems likely that they were inflicted by her brother, Reverend Uriah Spragg, a religious fanatic, as a punishment for some sin she had committed and in the hope of redeeming her soul. (See old Puritan law for the branding of women caught in adultery.)

2. The Church also appears to have been right in its quiet assumption that the visitation of Saint Francis to Sister Annunziata was not of a miraculous character but only an hallucination due to her period of life and to definite physical causes together with the discovery of what to her poor weak mind appeared to be evidence of the miraculous and authentic Stigmata.

3. On the surface there appears to be nothing which might indicate that Miss Annie Spragg was anything but an eccentric old maid of the

kind found frequently enough in small towns
and religious communities. It must be remembered that she was the daughter of Cyrus
Spragg, the Prophet, and the sister of Uriah
Spragg. The one was an over-sexed and lecherous old man and the other a religious fanatic.

4. The story of Bestia and the strange hap-
penings there with Peppina and the goats may
be explained, if they ever occurred at all, simply as the eccentricities of a half-mad old woman,
magnified and embellished by the imaginations
of superstitious and ignorant peasants and of a
woman (Signora Bardelli, the janitress) who
was, either sincerely or insincerely, a devotee of
the Black Arts. That Miss Annie Spragg was in
any way responsible for the subsequent behavior
of the girl Peppina seems unlikely. The character of the girl from childhood was clearly that of
an epileptic and a moral imbecile and of one destined from birth to end her career in a brothel.

5. The testimony of the nun Sister Annunziata and the priest Father Baldessare (later
killed in a riot in Milan where he was mistaken
by Fascists for a Communist) is highly unreli-
able owing to the unbalanced character of the
nun's mind and the general stupidity of the priest
who appears to have been the dupe of various
people throughout his life.

6. The brutal murder of Reverend Uriah
Spragg could have been committed by a passing
tramp or by one of his own flock in a fit of
hatred or religious insanity.

7. The apparently miraculous disappearance

of Cyrus Spragg, the Prophet, from the Temple at New Jerusalem lends itself to a much simpler solution than that put forth by his son Obadiah (that he was carried to heaven in a chariot of fire). It seems more likely that he was killed by the hot-blooded suitor of the pretty Maria Weatherby and that his body was buried secretly the same night by his two elder sons who then endeavored to carry out an imposture for the continued profit of themselves and their brothers and sisters. (In this they failed through a lack of the Prophet's vigor.) There is no evidence of an effort made to find and bring to justice the Kentuckian, Alonzo. Such a procedure would possibly have been embarrassing to the impostors by establishing the fact that the Prophet really *was* dead.

8. The behavior of Shamus Bosanky and the visions he had may be explained as due to epilepsy, of which he was clearly a victim. There is nothing unusual in his visions of Heaven, God, Saint John the Shepherd and the Angels, for he had heard of all these things from the priests and from old Mary Bosanky, who was of a strongly superstitious and religious temperament.

9. There is nothing unusual in Miss Annie Spragg's choice of Italy as a place of retreat after the death of her brother. Italy is filled with eccentric old ladies whose youth was starved for all the romantic and operatic background which Italy supplies with such extravagance.

Conclusion. All of these elements seem to

fall within the category of the natural and appear strange only as they are subject to the imaginations, the prejudices and the superstitions of the various witnesses involved.

On the other hand (wrote Mr. Winnery), there are certain elements which do not lend themselves to any reasonable solution. Among these are,

1. The statement of the undertaker of Winnebago Falls that the wounds on the body of Reverend Uriah Spragg were *like* those which might have been made by some pronged instrument such as the sharp horns of a goat. The skull had been pierced in three places by some sharp instrument. But it must be remembered that the black he-goat of Miss Annie Spragg was already dead at the time of the murder, having been killed that very morning by Uriah Spragg himself with a hatchet. Together with this element, there is also the fact that although the murder was committed on the open prairie in broad daylight with no shelter of any kind nearer than three miles and that although the body was still warm when found by Maria Hazlett, on one was seen and no trace of anyone was ever discovered near the spot. Nor was any weapon ever found.

2. The story told by Shamus Bosanky to Ed Hasselman and Maria Hazlett of the orgies which took place in the marsh at Meeker's Gulch. Shamus Bosanky had heard of God and the Angels and the Saints from the priests and

from his mother, but it seems impossible that he had ever heard of pagan gods either from the priests or from a mother who could neither read nor write. Therefore he could scarcely have imagined such a story, save by some obscure and scarcely believable trick of atavism. Nor does it seem possible that the story was invented by the woman Maria Hazlett, who, brought up in a poorhouse and scarcely able to read or write, had certainly never heard of Dionysus or Bacchus. The Hazlett woman, now nearly seventy years old, appears to be a simple countrywoman with an extraordinary attachment for the soil and for the drunken old man to whom she devoted her entire life.

3. The incident of Miss Annie Spragg's return at dawn from Meeker's Gulch accompanied by the black he-goat. This could be said to have been only the hallucination of the drunken milkman but for the discovery in the bedroom of Miss Annie Spragg of the chains and the crude handcuffs with which her brother chained her up at night.

4. The fact that from among all the saints Shamus Bosanky chose instinctively as his patron Saint John the Shepherd.

5. The most singular and astonishing fact of all, that Shamus Bosanky ran out into the storm to meet his death at the very moment when Miss Annie Spragg lay dying in the Palazzo Gonfarini on the other side of the world. Her own death occurred in the early morning of the fifteenth of August. At midnight of the four-

teenth Shamus Bosanky vanished into the storm
from the shanty by the railroad in Winnebago
Falls. It appears that he went directly to
Meeker's Gulch as to a rendezvous, for it was
here that he was found later by the Hazlett
woman, who alone seems to have known where
to look for him. Allowing for the difference in
time between Brinoë and Winnebago Falls, the
deaths must have occurred at almost the same
moment. (*Note.* This fact leads one to believe that if the elements of time and space were
always taken into consideration in such cases
there might emerge a whole and very strange
new world filled with undiscovered relation-
ships.)

*Note.* Many other minor and contributory
incidents have by the passage of time been lost
in an obscurity from which it is scarcely possible
to resurrect them for proper scientific examination. Among these may be noted the origins of
the Prophet, Cyrus Spragg, and the strange disappearance of Michael Bosanky, in the so-called
bottomless pond at Lakeville, Iowa.

## II

One other curious fact came to light some time
after Mr. Winnery had established himself at the
Villa Leonardo. He had been walking one morning
in the garden after breakfast turning over and over
in his mind the puzzling evidence he had just set
down on paper, when he found himself suddenly before the statue, reading with some dim portion of

his mind the inscription which began, *"Dans la damnation le feu est la moindre chose, etc., etc."* All at
once he was aware that the face of the statue possessed a similarity to the face of someone he had
known in life, and for a long time he stood there
studying the sensual and vigorous countenance, attempting to relate it to some face which hovered
elusively as a ghost in the back of his consciousness.
And then all at once he turned sharply about and
hastened back to his study where he took down from
a box a faded daguerreotype. Armed with this he
descended again to the garden and stood for a long
time comparing the face in the daguerreotype with
that of Priapus, God of Fertility.

When he returned at last to the villa, he took up
his note book and made in it the last entry he was
ever to make in the strange case of Miss Annie
Spragg.

> The strangest of all the facts (he wrote) is
> the likeness between the face of the statue found
> in the garden of the Villa Leonardo and the
> face in the daguerreotype portrait made of
> Cyrus Spragg on the day the Prophet retired
> into the temple at New Jerusalem, never to be
> seen again by any *man*. The daguerreotype
> (secured by the author after much difficulty from
> the daughter of one of the original Spraggites
> and therefore possibly a daughter of the Prophet
> himself) has faded with age, but not sufficiently
> to weaken the certainty that the face of Cyrus
> Spragg, the Prophet, and the face of the image
> of Priapus *are the same face*.

And then half-credulously, he added, "Perhaps the story told by the Prophet's son, Obadiah Spragg, was true. Perhaps Cyrus Spragg simply *disappeared*."

### III

He told Mrs. Winnery that the whole affair appeared hopelessly muddled and inexplicable, and that the solution was scarcely worth any further expenditure of his valuable time. Secretly he had a sense of it pointing toward something but what this was he could not say. He did not tell Mrs. Winnery that in attempting to solve one mystery he had simply confronted another and more terrifying one which neither scientists nor prophets nor saints had ever solved in all the centuries of the world's recorded existence. It made Mr. Winnery seem to himself small and insignificant and impertinent, and being a vain man, he did not care to have his wife share this discovery.

Out of all the muddle only one thing seemed to emerge clearly—that there was in the affair the evidence of some colossal struggle between all that was Christian and all that which Signora Bardelli described as "older than the church, older than Christianity itself" and that humanity was the battle ground upon which the two ancient elements waged their colossal and endless conflict. The Church of Rome, he thought (though he did not confide this even to Mrs. Winnery), was right just as it had been right in the question of Miss Annie Spragg's spurious miracle. It appeared to attempt a compromise.

He had discovered that a Primitive Methodist had been buried in consecrated ground by mistake but only he knew this for a certainty and he saw no reason to disturb the eternal rest of a poor eccentric old maid. Besides, such a thing did not seem to him to be a matter of any great importance. He bowed before the mystery and, feeling somewhat ashamed of himself for his impertinence, packed away in crates in the cellar of the Villa Leonardo, the vast accumulation of notes, copyings and false starts which represented Miracles and Other Natural Phenomena. This cellar he found, as he had supposed, to be of Etruscan construction.

But the next day he began with singular energy a new work. This time it was not a scientific undertaking but a historical romance teeming with local color. It was called Riccardo and Giuliana and the setting was Brinoë in the time of the Renaissance. The hero, Riccardo, was a man, fifty-three years old, who had spent his life in the service of the Dukes of Brinoë. The heroine, Giuliana, was a young girl of thirty-five who had been kept a prisoner since childhood in a lonely villa in the valley behind Monte Salvatore by an aunt who concealed a taste for sadism beneath a reputation for great piety. Among the subsidiary characters were Michelangelo, Leonardo, Machiavelli, Lucrezia Tornabuoni, Lorenzo the Magnificent, Cesare and Lucrezia Borgia, Botticelli, Fra Lippo Lippi (who supplied the comic relief) and a few others. In the end Riccardo rescued Giuliana and they were married amid celebrations in which the joyous and carefree natives of Brinoë and all the foreigners living there took part. He told Mrs. Winnery that he thought he had found at last the proper medium for the expression of his literary talents. During the last month or two of her pregnancy he read aloud to her chapter after chapter as they were completed.

She was confined six weeks earlier than they had expected. It was the month of October when the goatherd Pietro kept a perpetual heap of offerings before the statue in the garden and it was Sister Annunziata who brought him, pacing up and down in the ancient garden, before the statue, the news that he was the father of twin boys. They no longer kept Sister Annunziata shut up because her madness seemed of a harmless nature and madness was a thing never taken seriously in Italy. She simply believed that Miss Annie Spragg was an unappreciated saint and that Saint Francis was her guardian and companion day and night. In a vague gesture of gratitude toward the pagan gods of fertility, Mr. Winnery made a rich gift of money to Sister Annunziata's convent. It was used to restore abominably a series of famous frescoes by Gozzoli, which had faded almost into oblivion. So in the end Aunt Bessie's money came to embellish a nonconformist chapel in Bloomsbury and a Roman Catholic convent in Brinoë.

Mr. Winnery has completed his romance, for which he was granted the very rare honor of an interview with the Dictator and he has been made a

Knight of the Order of Saint Trevizius and a member of three societies of historical research having to do with Brinoë. Mrs. Winnery is about to have a third child and they are very happy in the Villa Leonardo and are likely to remain its tenants for years to come, for the retirement of the Principessa d'Orobelli grows each year more and more remote in its possibilities. The statue in the garden has never troubled them as it troubled others because they are by nature a pair of innocents.

Often as they drive happily into Brinoë, with the nurse and the twins on the seat opposite them, they pass the house of Signora Bardelli, lying close against the wall of the monastery, where Father d'Astier sought refuge. The retired janitress does a splendid business with the bed of Miss Annie Spragg and has grown quite rich. There has even been talk of offering her a medal for her efforts in behalf of the apparently new but really ancient movement toward greater fertility of Italy. Mr. and Mrs. Winnery bow to greet her pleasantly, for Mr. Winnery came in the end to the conviction that any belief which brought comfort to the human race had its own place in the divine scheme of things.

Frequently the Winnerys drive to the Campo Santo of Monte Salvatore to carry flowers from the garden of the Villa Leonardo to the grave of Miss Annie Spragg. They have never forgotten that their meeting was due to her and they are grateful to her for so much happiness. They always find there other flowers and sometimes branches of green olives and even melons and fruit, for there remain scores and even hundreds among the poor and humble and superstitious who continue stubbornly to regard her as a saint.


Florence
October, 1926
Socoa, B. P., France
July, 1928


**THE END**

171C